PRAISE FOR KA

MW00988621

"Karen MacInerney writes with verve and vitality, and her Natalie Barnes is a Maine original. I'm ready to book a room at the Gray Whale Inn!"

—Susan Wittig Albert, bestselling author of *Nightshade* and other China Bayles Herbal Mysteries

"Deliciously clever plot. Juicy characters. Karen MacInerney has cooked up a winning recipe for murder. Don't miss this mystery!"

—Maggie Sefton, author of *Knit One, Kill Two*

"*Murder on the Rocks* has just what's needed for a cozy evening in front of the fire with a good mystery book—a plucky innkeeper who's come from off island and a determined developer who wants her land. Set on a rocky island off the coast of Maine, you can hear the foghorns, see the circling seagulls, smell the wild beach roses, taste the wicked blueberry coffee cake and the killer cranberry scones (the recipes follow the story), and feel the satisfying shivers when the first body appears."

—Cynthia Riggs, author of the Martha's Vineyard mystery series

"A savory blend of New England charm, delightfully eccentric characters, humor, and mouth-watering recipes . . . all served with a side of murder."

—Candy Calvert, author of *Dressed to Keel*

"You'll have the reading time of your life with talented author Karen MacInerney."

—ReaderToReader.com

"A swift-paced, fun romp."

—Charlaine Harris, *New York Times* bestselling author

"A laugh-out-loud, wacky and hysterical romp."

—Sue Ann Jaffarian, author of the Odelia Grey mysteries

Mother's Little Helper

ALSO BY KAREN MACINERNEY

Margie Peterson Mysteries

Dewberry Farm Mysteries

Gray Whale Inn Mysteries

Tales of an Urban Werewolf

Mother's Little Helper

Little

Helper

A Margie Peterson Mystery

Karen
MacInerney

THOMAS & MERCER

Text copyright © 2017 by Karen MacInerney
All rights reserved.

Published by Thomas & Mercer, Seattle

www.apub.com

Amazon, the Amazon logo, and Thomas & Mercer are trademarks of Amazon.com, Inc., or its affiliates.

ISBN-13: 9781477820094
ISBN-10: 1477820094

Cover design by Cyanotype Book Architects

Printed in the United States of America

Dedicated to all those who stay up with sick children and wake up before dawn and make lunches and drive people to appointments and help with homework and go to work (whether it be at home or in an office) and pay the bills and go to sleep exhausted and get up early the next day and do it all over again.

CHAPTER ONE

There were a lot of reasons I avoided talking about what I did for a living at Career Day at Austin Heights Elementary. Today's job—standing in the Zilker Botanical Gardens swatting mosquitoes and hoping to nab a streaker with a penchant for wearing nothing but a Magical Unicorn mask and a shamrock sock—was one of them.

After dropping my kids off at their respective schools, I'd walked into Peachtree Investigations' temporary digs at the Pretty Kitten Brazilian waxing salon on a Monday morning to find Willhelmina Bergdorfer in our plastic visitor's chair, wearing a leopard-print caftan and a hot-pink scarf. We hadn't seen each other since she helped me solve a case involving a dead transvestite several months back. The septuagenarian lit up when she saw me. "Margie!"

"Willie!" I gave her a big hug. "What are you doing here?"

"Well, first I want to see if my pot roast plan managed to save your marriage," she said.

"Uh, it turned out the problems were deeper than pot roast," I said. Since my husband had come to terms with his taste for men in dresses, there wasn't enough pot roast in the world to put things right, and our marriage was well on its way to dissolution. Which was a good thing, since he was currently in love with a former gay-reform-retreat leader named Frank.

"Such a shame," she said. "Still, there are lots of fish in the sea. How's Snookums?"

"I actually adopted him out to a friend," I said. My neighbor had fallen in love with Snookums, a cat I'd been pretending to pet sit. Since Snookums and my incontinent Siamese cat, Rufus, hadn't exactly gotten along, it was a huge relief. Besides, I could only imagine how he'd get along with our most recent acquisition—Twinkles the "teacup" pig. Twinkles was already well past the size of a Thanksgiving turkey (and growing), with the personality of a surly warthog. I'd be tempted to turn her into bacon, but my six-year-old daughter, Elsie, was in love with her.

"What brings you here?" I asked.

"I have a streaker problem," she said. "And of course, your name was the first one to come to mind."

I wasn't sure how to take that, but since Peachtree Investigations was low on cases at the moment, I just smiled. Besides, I liked Willhelmina—or Willie, as she liked to be called.

"There's a streaker in your apartment building?" I asked. "How does he deal with waiting for the elevator?"

"It's happening at my garden club, actually," she said. "Between you and me, I think it's kind of exciting, but our president ended up in the heart hospital last week after the streaker paid us a visit, and the board decided it was time to do something about it."

"Aren't the police looking into it?"

"We called, but they wouldn't take the case. The thing is," she told me, "he's not totally naked."

"What do you mean?"

"Let me show you a picture," she said, pulling out her iPhone and producing a blurry shot of a very naked man—except for what looked like a white unicorn-head mask and a green-and-white sock that was the size of a tree trunk—pressed up against a plate glass window.

"Dear Lord," I breathed, staring at the man's sock-clad appendage. "That thing is enormous."

"I know!" she said. "It's a wonder that sock stays on. I think he must attach it with dental floss or something." She zoomed in on the picture. The shamrocks were bulging.

"What do you want me to do?" I asked.

"Why, find out who he is, of course!" she said. "I figure you can lurk in the bushes during our next garden club meeting and then jump out and surprise him. We're scheduled to meet tomorrow morning, so you'll have the perfect opportunity."

Which is how I found myself crouching in a bush in the Zilker Botanical Gardens, swatting mosquitoes and watching for men in unicorn masks, while inside the building a matriarch with a bouffant straight out of 1965 talked about spider mite infestations.

It was a topic I would have been interested in hearing more about—before I had kids and a job, I'd liked to garden, too—but I was too busy glancing at my watch and wishing I'd brought a bottle of Off! to pay much attention to the pest-control regimen she was outlining in her PowerPoint presentation. I had just slapped my nineteenth mosquito when my phone burbled "It's a Small World." It was my boss, Peaches.

"How's the job going?" she asked.

"Nothing yet," I told her in a whisper. "I'm outside sitting in a bush."

"Let me know if you need backup. By the way, I put up a Match.com profile for you. I've already got fifteen hits."

"What?" I yelped. "What did you write about me?"

"Let's see. 'Voluptuous thirtysomething redhead seeks companion for all kinds of adventures. Must like animals and children. Interests include football, skydiving, and lacy lingerie.'"

She was zero for three on interests. And while I did have red hair, I leaned more toward "pleasantly plump" than "voluptuous." "Skydiving?" I asked. "Lacy lingerie?"

"We'll buy some before your first date," Peaches told me. "Nobody's gonna go for a worn-out sports bra like you had on at the Sweet Shop." I shuddered at the memory of my brief and unfortunate foray down the catwalk at a strip club not long ago. "Anyway, there's a good prospect . . . His name is Trey, and he's actually kind of cute. How about Wednesday night?"

I was about to answer when there was a rustle in the bush across from me.

Peaches kept talking. "I've got a push-up bra you can borrow. I'd feel funny about lending you a thong, though . . ."

I shoved the phone in my purse while Peaches was still going on about underwear, and crouched down lower in the bush. Inside, the helmet-haired presenter was just pointing to a picture of a mottled tomato leaf when a man in a unicorn mask exploded out of the shrubbery and plastered his almost-naked self against the glass.

The ladies in the garden room turned in unison, their faces registering an assortment of expressions ranging from horror to what appeared to be rather prurient interest. Willie's eyes twinkled as she looked in my direction and gave me the thumbs up.

What else could I do? I jumped out of the bushes and took a swipe at the unicorn mask.

Three things happened at once.

An elderly woman in a yellow miniskirt popped up from behind a tree about ten feet away, brandishing a cane and yelling, "Stop swinging that banana around!" The Shamrock Streaker reared back, slamming into me so that my hands closed on air instead of the rubber mask. And as he pulled back, my purse buckle caught on the string holding the sock in place.

We were linked together for a long, tension-filled moment; then the string snapped and the sock sagged. The streaker grabbed it just in time and he sprinted away, running with both hands clutching his crotch, butt cheeks flapping, the unicorn mask askew on his head.

"What are you waiting for?" the woman in the yellow skirt demanded. "Go after him!"

I hesitated a moment, transfixed by the flapping buttocks, and then decided she was right. It's hard to run fast when you're clutching your crotch, and I might never get a better chance.

"Go!" the woman yelled again, and I heeded her advice, sprinting after the streaker, who was well on his way to the parking lot by now.

He was off to a good start, but his posture—and lack of shoes—was holding him back. I wasn't exactly a fitness enthusiast, but I was gaining on him. I was about twenty feet away when my toe connected with a tire stop, and I went sprawling across the pavement.

The streaker glanced back, hands still clutching his sock, and then, as I clambered to my feet, he squirted between two black SUVs and vanished into the trees.

I sighed and inspected the damage. My knees and forearms looked a little bit like ground beef, only with bits of asphalt embedded in them. My purse had skittered across the parking lot, emptying its contents as it slid.

And Peaches was still talking at me from underneath my minivan. "What should I tell Trey? Tomorrow night sound good?"

CHAPTER TWO

Y ou'd think the day couldn't help but get better from there, but
you'd be wrong.

The afternoon wasn't so bad. I picked up Elsie and Nick, fed them
a few cookies, and even managed to get the cat box clean. But things
went downhill after sunset.

Since my daughter, Elsie, was starting out in first grade at Austin
Heights Elementary School, my friend, Becky Hale, had invited me to
a get-together with a lot of the PTA moms. Evidently the liquor had
been flowing for some time before I arrived. What Becky had failed to
mention was that it was a Passion Party—kind of a pyramid-scheme
party where the goods for sale were a little racier than Tupperware or
Mary Kay.

When I walked in, a woman who had clearly spent a lot of quality
time with the mojito pitcher was sprawled on the couch, adjusting the
speed of a vibrator called King Kong while detailing her intimate rela-
tions with her husband.

Becky sure wasn't wrong about the "getting to know you" part. In
fact, I could stand to know a good bit less, I decided as I took the mojito
Becky offered me and nodded through a brief round of introductions.

"I sold my back door for a cruise to the Bahamas," the woman on the couch—Janelle Kingsley—announced as she flicked the switch on King Kong so that it sounded less like a dishwasher and more like an air compressor.

"You mean you—man," Pansy Parker said, looking at the behemoth in Janelle's hands with something like admiration. She was the PTA president, a highlighted blonde with bright-blue eyes and a trim figure that suggested long hours in a Pilates studio and a restrained ice cream habit. Or no ice cream habit at all. "Put some sandpaper on that thing and you could refinish the floors."

"Talk about multitasking," tittered a woman Becky had introduced as Frances Pfeffer. She wore her hair back in a tight ponytail and was dressed in a flowered romper that looked like an oversized onesie. She was testing out the Passion Potion by licking it off a peach slice. Becky was sipping her drink and inspecting an appliance called the Cabana Boy while Phyllis, the PTA secretary, looked on with something of a severe expression. She appeared to be drinking ice water. I, on the other hand, had retreated to a chair in the corner and was wondering how many mojitos it would take to keep me from dying of embarrassment.

"He wants a threesome now," Janelle continued as she fondled King Kong. "I'm thinking I might get a trip to Europe out of it. Should I?"

I didn't quite know what to answer. I glanced at Mr. Reliable. At least personal appliances didn't date drag queens on the side, I thought.

"I sometimes wonder if my husband is completely faithful," confessed another mom, Sarah Soggs, who had drunk even more mojitos than Janelle and was sitting with a tangle of edible underwear in her lap. She looked at me. "How did you know your husband was seeing another man?"

I glanced at Becky, who was turning pink and suddenly seemed very interested in the Cabana Boy. Clearly she'd shared more than she told me.

"Well . . . It's complicated," I said, deciding that Becky and I were going to have a chat later on.

"You're separated now, aren't you?" Phyllis asked bluntly.

"Yes," I said as all eyes—except Becky's—swiveled to me. "But we're trying to keep it quiet. For the kids' sake," I added with a strained smile. I shot Becky another look, but she had moved from the Cabana Boy to something that looked like nipple clamps, and was studiously avoiding my gaze.

"Oh," Janelle said, looking up from King Kong with unfocused eyes. "Our lips are totally sealed. Right, ladies?"

They murmured assent, but it wasn't what I'd call convincing. I grimaced at Becky, annoyed. Not exactly how I'd wanted to start off with the mothers of my daughter's new classmates. Elsie had recently moved from Holy Oaks Catholic School to Austin Heights Elementary, in part to help her on the social front. She had enough challenges already; for the last several months, my first-grade daughter had taken to wearing a rhinestone dog collar and insisting on being called Fifi. She didn't need kids teasing her about her parents, too.

"Margie's a private investigator," Becky said, still avoiding my eyes. "Maybe you should hire her."

Everyone's eyes widened, King Kong and Janelle's back door temporarily forgotten.

"Is that how you found out your husband was seeing a guy?" Frances asked.

"At least he's cute," Janelle announced. "I know because my husband goes to the gym with him." She untangled one hand from the thong underwear she had picked up and took another sip of her mojito. "He's completely buff," she said.

"Her husband, or his boyfriend?" Frances asked.

"Both. You should see their biceps. And such cute little butts . . ."

"Might be a threesome in your future, eh, Margie?"

I couldn't think of anything less appealing, other than perhaps lying down on a bed of fire ants while listening to the soundtrack to *High School Musical*, but I smiled politely. "I'm afraid I'd be a bit of a third wheel," I said, then turned to Sarah. "Anyway, yes, I'm a private investigator. I'd be happy to look into it for you, if you want." Besides, I needed the business. Single motherhood wasn't cheap.

"How exciting," said Janelle. "I think you should hire her," she told Sarah. "It's better to know, I always think. I mean, you never know what kind of diseases you might get if he really is sleeping with someone else."

"I'll think about it," Sarah said. "By the way," she said to me, "I know we haven't known each other very long, but after talking with Becky . . . well, we all chipped in and got you a kind of welcome present."

"You did?" I asked. "Why?"

"In light of everything going on with you and your husband, you know . . ."

Janelle procured a shoebox-size box wrapped in silver paper. "Go ahead," she said, ignoring what appeared to be anxious looks from a few of the other moms.

"Janelle," Frances began. "Are you sure . . ."

"Oh, stop worrying so much. Go ahead, Margie. Open it!"

I eyed the package warily. "Thank you," I said, and slipped off the bow. I took off the lid a moment later. Nestled in a mound of pink tissue paper was the biggest vibrator I had ever seen. And that included King Kong.

"It's called Mr. Big," Janelle said. "It lights up and everything!"

"Thanks," I said, putting the lid back on the box and feeling my face burn.

"That'll keep you warm at night," Frances said with a grin.

"Speaking of hot men," Janelle said, "I started training with Tristan Prescott."

Pansy looked up sharply, and the room suddenly seemed tense. "Did you?"

"He certainly is motivating," Janelle said with leering smile. "I think I'd let him have my back door for free!"

"Janelle!" Phyllis's hand leaped to her throat. "That's totally inappropriate!"

"Oh, it's just us girls," she said. "Don't get your panties in a wad. But he's got the cutest butt. Plus, I've lost ten pounds since I started using his LifeBoost."

"Me too!" Frances said. "I'm down five in the past week! My daughter's getting started on it, too. He says it's all natural . . ."

"I'd like to give him a whirl," Janelle said. Frances's face turned tight, and Phyllis continued to look affronted. Janelle plowed on, oblivious. "He looks like there's a lot under the hood, if you know what I mean."

I shoved Mr. Big into the diaper bag that passed as my purse and excused myself to the kitchen, where I refilled my mojito glass and leaned against the wall. What had I let Becky talk me into? I couldn't believe she'd told everyone my husband was seeing a drag queen—and then chipped in to give me a vibrator. To be honest, though, I was more worried about the PI disclosure; I'd been trying to keep my professional life separate from Elsie's school life. On the other hand, I thought as I took a sip, maybe it would bring in some business.

I had just added a little more mojito to my glass when Pansy walked into the kitchen. "Do you have a moment to talk?" she asked in a quiet voice. Behind her, a burst of raucous laughter rang out; they must have opened up the Bed, Bondage, and Beyond set.

"Sure," I said.

"Let's go out on the back porch," she suggested, touching my sleeve with a manicured hand. I followed her out the french doors at the end of the kitchen, still clutching my glass.

"What's up?" I asked once she'd closed the door behind us.

"I have a case for you," she said. "But you have to swear not to tell anyone I've hired you."

"What is it?" I asked.

She glanced over her shoulder. "The PTA is missing a lot of money," she said. "I'm afraid if I don't find out what happened to it, they'll blame me. I can't afford to let anything like that happen . . . The whole reason I got involved is to help my daughter." She took a sip from her wineglass. "She's got Asperger's syndrome," she explained. "The social stuff is really hard for her. I got involved in the school to make sure she gets all the support she needs—and so that if anything happens that shouldn't, I'll be the first to hear about it."

"I didn't know that," I said, thinking of Elsie's dog fixation.

Before I could ask how she'd had her daughter diagnosed, Pansy moved on. "At any rate, if you join the PTA, that will give you a good reason to hang out and check out the accounts."

"Who's the treasurer?"

"Janelle," she said. "As you can imagine, she's not exactly the person I would have picked to be in charge of the money."

"I can imagine," I said. Mojitos and money weren't a good mix—and I suspected Janelle spent a lot of time digging in the liquor cabinet.

"Maybe I can pitch you as an assistant?" she said. "Do you have any financial background?"

"I pay the bills," I said, "but that's about it."

"I'll just tell her you want to get involved, and that you've volunteered to help out with ticket sales for the carnival."

"Okay," I said, feeling a bit of misgiving. "Have you talked to her about it?"

"No," she said. "If she's embezzling, I don't want her to know I'm looking into it. I'm downloading copies of the account statements; I'll get them to you this week."

"Assuming I take the job," I said. "I'll have to talk it over with my boss."

"Please?" she said. "I need someone on the inside. Whatever your rates are, I'll double them. I don't want to jeopardize my position at the school—or Isabella's."

"I'll see what I can do," I said, and thought of Elsie again. "How did you know something was going on with Isabella, by the way?"

"She doesn't make eye contact," she said. "She's very literal—and she was obsessed with car engines for eighteen months. Wanted an engine block in her room. She can tell you everything you ever wanted to know about carburetors—and then some."

At least Elsie wasn't obsessed with engines, I thought. On the other hand, the eye contact and the literal thing did seem a bit familiar. "Did she have a hard time making friends?"

She nodded. "She has a hard time with social nuance," she said. "And strange situations really throw her off. She likes routine."

"How about foods?" I asked.

"White foods only," she said, and my heart sank. "If you're wondering if one of your kids is having issues, I'll give you the name of the doctor we see. He'll be able to help you."

"Is it expensive?" I asked.

She grimaced. "It's not cheap, I'll tell you that. And insurance only covers the evaluation . . . Any therapy is extra."

"Terrific," I said.

"At any rate, I'll let the girls know you're joining the PTA team," she said. "Do you have a card?"

"It's in my purse," I said, glancing back at the house.

"I'll just input your number into my phone," she said, pulling an iPhone out of her jeans pocket.

As she finished tapping my number in, Phyllis appeared at the door, looking pale and owlish. "Oh, there you are," she said, her eyes darting back and forth from Pansy to me.

"I was just talking to Margie about some of the PTA opportunities," Pansy said smoothly. "She's volunteered to manage ticket sales for the carnival. And she's going to organize the supply closet!"

"I told you I'd take care of that for you," Phyllis protested.

Supply closet? Nobody said anything about supply closets.

"You've got enough on your plate already," Pansy said, patting her on the shoulder. "I'm sure she'll be a great help." Before Phyllis could respond, Pansy said, "Let's get back inside before Janelle eats all the Passion Potion."

I followed them into the house, thinking I'd ended up with more than I bargained for—and I didn't just mean Mr. Big. Carnival tickets and PTA embezzlement. What had I gotten myself into?

And, more worrisome . . . was Elsie's dog issue more than a phase?

• • •

It was almost nine by the time I got home, Mr. Big shoved deep down in the old diaper bag I hadn't gotten around to replacing. Janelle had tripped over my purse three times on the way to refill her drink, and twice I'd had to jam the contents—including Mr. Big—back into it.

I wasn't surprised to see my soon-to-be-ex-husband's BMW in the driveway when I pulled into the garage. My husband was a frequent visitor; although the kids were staying with me in the house, we'd kept things flexible. When I walked into the kitchen, Blake and my mother were having tea at the kitchen table; since my husband had come out of the closet, he and my mother had gotten very chummy.

"How did it go?" my mother asked. Since Blake moved out, my mother had been staying with me to help out.

"Fine," I said, not wanting to discuss the Passion Party in front of my almost-ex. "How are things here?"

"Both kids are asleep," she said. "You have Elsie's fry phone, right? I told her you'd tuck it in next to her."

"I do," I said. The McDonald's fry phone, which had been available for approximately five minutes one February a few years ago, was Elsie's irreplaceable yet frequently misplaced attachment object. I'd put it in my purse for safekeeping when I dropped her off at school that morning.

"You're here late," I said, addressing Blake, who was dapper as always in crisp slacks and a white button-down shirt.

"I wanted to talk to you about signing Elsie up for soccer," he said. "I know she's having a tough time making friends. Maybe team sports will help."

I shrugged. "It's worth a try," I said. "I talked with Pansy—the PTA president—tonight; did you know her daughter has Asperger's?"

"What does that have to do with soccer?" he asked.

I opened the fridge and got out a can of fizzy water. "Nothing," I said. "I was just wondering if maybe Elsie . . . well, if the dog thing is more than just a phase. I'm not saying she has Asperger's, but there are a few similarities between Isabella and Elsie."

Blake blinked at me. "You think Elsie might have Asperger's?"

"I don't think anything, but it wouldn't hurt to talk to someone," I said. "It might be worth looking into, at least so we can rule it out."

"I still think if you cut the processed foods out—" my mother started, then stopped when I shot her a look.

"She's in a new school," Blake said. "She's just shy. It takes some time to come out of her shell."

"You could be right," I said. "But the all-white foods, the dog thing, the need for routine . . ." I took a sip of my fizzy water. "And she has a hard time making eye contact."

"She's just shy," Blake repeated. He reminded me of his mother, Prudence, when confronted with her son's interest in other men. She was still convinced it was just a phase.

"I'll think about it," Blake said, getting up from the table. "In the meantime, are you okay with signing her up for soccer?"

"It can't hurt," I said. "But I'm going to ask Pansy more about how to get her checked out."

"Let's talk before you go making any appointments," he said.

"Of course," I said. "At least she likes school now."

"That's something," he said, but his eyes drifted to the sofa cushion our daughter called her dog bed, and I could tell I'd rattled him.

"It's probably nothing," I said, half trying to convince myself.

"We'll talk this week," he said.

"Fine," I said, and walked back to kiss the kids good night. I fished in my purse for Elsie's fry phone.

The problem was, it wasn't in my purse.

I went through my bag three times, but it wasn't there.

"What's wrong?" Blake asked as I returned to the kitchen, dumped my purse out on the table, and pawed through the contents.

"The phone must have fallen out of my purse at Frances's house," I said. "One of the women tripped over it a few times; it must have slid under the couch or something. I'll text her. Maybe she can bring it to school tomorrow."

"You didn't say much about the party. Was it fun?" my mother asked.

"It was . . . interesting," I said, and excused myself to check on Elsie, deciding I'd rather face her wrath at the missing fry phone than discuss Mr. Big and edible underwear with my mother and my husband.

Besides, maybe she'd be asleep, I told myself as I stepped into her room. Elsie was breathing deeply, and I tiptoed over to kiss her on the forehead. The moment my lips touched her skin, her eyes popped open.

"Hi, Mommy. Do you have my fry phone?"

• • •

The next morning went as smoothly as it possibly could, considering I had once again lost Elsie's fry phone. Frances hadn't returned my text, but I promised my daughter I'd drive over to pick it up as soon as I could. I successfully refused a bid to take Twinkles to school in compensation, and the rest of the morning was blissfully uneventful.

I went to Peachtree Investigations and waited for the phone to ring, left a message for Pansy checking on her and asking about doctors, stopped by Frances's house—no one was there, unfortunately—and headed home a little bit early. My mother was out buying seaweed snacks or meditating, so I was actually going to have the house to myself for an hour before it was time to pick up the kids.

Unfortunately, when I opened the back door, the house looked like it had been ransacked by dwarves. Twinkles had escaped again. I found her in the pantry, where she had liberally distributed a can of cinnamon and was rooting through a bag of potato chips, and carried her protesting porcine body to the laundry room and reset the gate. She spent the next several minutes squealing indignantly while ramming her snout against the barrier.

"It's only for a little bit," I told her, tossing her a little bit of her favorite treat—hot dog, which I'd only gotten past my mother, whom I privately thought of as the food police, on the pretext of feeding it to the pig. (It was beef, not pork. I checked.) "Elsie will be home soon," I promised. She gulped down the hot dog and glared at me, then snuffed and trotted to the back of the laundry room, where she redoubled her efforts to dig her way through the ceramic tile. As soon as I left her alone, I knew, she'd be ramming the gate again.

I retreated to my bedroom, feeling worn out, closed the door so I wouldn't hear the grunting, and tossed my shoes onto the largely empty closet floor. Since my husband had moved out, I'd realized that most of the clothes in our house had actually belonged to Blake. Certainly all the nice ones. Maybe I'd have to treat myself to a shopping trip, I thought, then discarded the idea. I didn't have money to spend on clothes right now; I was using most of my disposable income on contraband cheese sticks and Pop-Tarts to make sure the kids ate something.

I'd just climbed between the covers for a quick nap when my cell phone rang. I didn't recognize the number.

"Hello?" I asked.

"Margie, is that you?" The voice sounded breathy.

"Speaking," I said. "Who's this?"

"It's Pansy," she said. "I need your help."

"I know," I said. "We talked about it last night."

"No. I mean I need your help *now*," she said. "Can you come to my house?"

"Can't we talk about this tomorrow?"

"No, no, no—I need you to come here now. It's an emergency."

"Did you bounce a check?"

"No! Look, I'll explain when you get here. The key is taped to the bottom of the table on the front porch." She gave me the address.

"You want me to let myself in?" I asked, confused.

"Please, Margie. I'm begging you."

I glanced at the clock; it was already 1:40, and I needed to pick up my four-year-old son, Nick, in just over an hour. The last thing I wanted to do was drive over and visit with Pansy, but I could always nap later. Besides, it wouldn't hurt to make an ally of the president of the PTA.

"I'll be there in a few," I said, jotting the address down on the back of an overdue library book slip.

CHAPTER THREE

I don't know what I was expecting. But walking in on the scantily dressed PTA president tied up to a Nautilus machine, with a man who was not her husband sprawled naked in the middle of her home gym, was not what I'd envisioned.

"Oh, Margie. Thank God you're here," Pansy said, her blonde hair dangling to the floor. Her face was bright purple—I wasn't sure if it was embarrassment or the result of being hung upside down. Her hands were taped to the handles of the machine. Her feet were trussed up as if she were a Christmas goose. And all she had on was a black bra and a pair of crotchless panties.

"What happened?" I asked, and then focused on the naked man lying motionless on the floor a few feet away. "Oh my God. Is he okay?" I asked reflexively, even though obviously he was anything but. "How did you manage to call me?"

"I dialed with my tongue," she said, nodding toward the iPhone just beneath her dangling blonde hair. "I wiggled around until the phone fell onto the floor, and then . . . Well, I couldn't use my hands, could I?"

"You kept your phone in your bra?"

"In case my husband called," she explained.

"Who is this?"

"Tristan. My personal trainer."

Ah, yes . . . the talk of the PTA. "What happened?" I asked again as I crouched over the trainer and tried to locate a pulse on his limp wrist. He was very fit, and it was easy to pick out every muscle on his buff body—because he was stark naked.

"I don't know," she said. "He'd just picked up Mr. Big and was about to turn it on, and then . . ." She swallowed. "He turned purple and fell over."

"You didn't call 911?"

She gave me a look.

"I see your point," I said, still searching for a pulse. No breathing, either—or at least not that I could see. Granted, I wasn't a trained medical professional. I had, however, learned CPR when the kids were born. "How long has he been like this?"

"I don't know. Twenty minutes?"

A little late to start CPR, I thought, but I should try anyway. I rolled him over, and he flopped over to the side of the Nautilus. "Wow," I said, somewhat shocked. "He's enormous."

"He works part time as an underwear model," Pansy said, as if that explained it. "Can you at least untie me before you start mouth to mouth?"

I took thirty seconds to let her down from the Nautilus machine, then began pumping the trainer's chest as she rubbed her wrists. After fifteen pumps, I positioned his head and put my mouth on his. His tongue was swollen and kind of protruding out of his mouth. I didn't want to think about what he had been doing with it before I got here.

"Poor Tristan," Pansy said, her eyes filling with tears as she stood over us. "Such a waste."

After fifteen minutes of CPR, I gave up. "It's not working," I said, sitting back, and Pansy gave out something between a hiccup and a sob.

"I can't believe he's dead," she said, wiping at her mascara-streaked eyes. "He was so young!"

I glanced over at the clock. "School's almost out. You might want to get changed," I pointed out.

"Oh," she said. "Right. I need to get myself together." She snuffled, then took a deep breath.

She had just turned to go to the bedroom when we heard the sound of the garage door going up.

"Shit," we said in unison.

"My husband must be home early," she said, eyes wide.

"What do we do?" I asked.

"We'll put him in the guest bathroom," she said. "I'll take his legs if you grab his arms," she said, tossing the sex toys in the corner and throwing a yoga mat over them. "Where did you park?"

"On the street," I said.

"Good," she said. "We'll get him in the tub, and you can sneak out when it's safe."

"What?"

"It's the best plan I have. Quick, let's get him out of here. Grab his legs," she said in a voice of authority that explained how she'd managed to rise to the top of the PTA.

Together we hauled Tristan down the hall and into the bathroom and heaved him into the bathtub, which was strewn with children's toys.

"You should probably get in the bathtub, too," she said. "Just in case."

As I clambered into the tub, Pansy pulled the shower curtain closed behind me, turned off the light, and slammed the door. She was gone, leaving me alone with two rubber ducks and a dead underwear model.

Not for the first time, I found myself reconsidering my choice of profession.

• • •

I'd been crouching in the bathtub between the dead trainer's legs for fifteen minutes before I realized I wasn't going to get out of Pansy's house in time to pick up my kids. I remembered now that my mom was at a Rolfing session that afternoon, so I texted Becky to see if she could pick up the kids.

I can't today, she texted back. *Kids staying at aftercare. Sorry . . .*

Tx anyway, I replied. I dialed my mom, who didn't believe in texting, and tried not to think about what Pansy and her husband were doing in another part of the house; by now I could hear something that sounded like rhythmic moaning in the distance. I could see how Pansy stayed so fit; she certainly got her exercise in.

"Mom?" I whispered when she picked up.

"Hi, honey," she said, then, "Why are you talking so quietly?" There was something like a scream from somewhere outside the bathroom. "And what is that noise?"

"You wouldn't believe it if I told you," I whispered as the moaning intensified. I climbed out of the tub and sat on top of the toilet lid, figuring I was safe for at least a few minutes.

"Where are you?"

"On a job," I said. And I was definitely planning on charging Pansy for my services. "Hey, I know you've got Rolfing, but could you pick up the kids?"

"I'm sorry, darling, but I've got a date with Karma right afterward. Can Becky get them?"

"No, I already checked," I said.

"How about Blake?"

"I'll call him."

"Love you, sweetheart!" she said. "Oh—Peaches called, and she put a profile up on Match.com for you."

"I heard."

"She e-mailed you the password. I checked it out . . . I didn't know you were into belly dancing!"

"What?" I barked. The moaning stopped. "Shit," I said, and clambered back into the bathtub, trying not to step on Tristan as I pulled the curtain shut behind me.

"Are you okay?"

"Gotta run," I said, and hung up, hoping Pansy's husband hadn't heard me. After a few moments, the moaning began again, and I let myself relax. I had just sat back down on the toilet seat when my phone rang. I slid my finger across the "Slide to Answer" button, but nothing happened, and "It's a Small World" kept burbling out of the phone. Ever since my iPhone had been swallowed by a pig, it had been acting temperamental. I stabbed at the "Silent" button twice, but nothing happened. I shoved the phone between my thighs and squeezed, but it was still audible.

A man's voice sounded from the hallway. "It's coming from here," he said.

"I don't hear anything," Pansy said, sounding almost frantic. I had opened the lid of the toilet and was about to drop my phone in when the song stopped. I clambered into the bathtub and pulled the shower curtain closed just as the doorknob turned.

A moment later, the light flicked on.

"I'm sure I heard something," said the low voice of a man.

"Honey, you're imagining things. Can't we go back to the bedroom?" Pansy pleaded.

"Just one moment," he said. I heard the sound of drawers opening and closing, and held my breath.

"I'm not done with you yet," she said in a low, seductive voice. "Come here, big boy. Look what Mama's got for you."

I didn't want to know what Mama had for him, but I would have given just about anything to get him out of that bathroom. Fortunately, whatever Pansy was offering was at least enticing enough to get him into the hallway. The lights flicked off and the happy couple retreated, leaving the door open so that I could hear all the grunting. Wonderful.

The thumping had recommenced and I had finally let my breath out when "It's a Small World" sang out again, lighting up both my phone and half the bathroom.

It was my soon-to-be-ex-husband.

I pitched my phone out of the bathtub and said a small prayer to the patron saint of unlucky private investigators, whoever that might be. I decided I should probably find out.

• • •

"I told you there was a phone somewhere!" Pansy's husband—at least I presumed it was Pansy's husband—said as the bathroom lights flicked back on. I shrank back into my end of the bathtub and attempted to come up with a reasonable explanation for hiding in the Parkers' guest bathtub with Pansy's dead, naked personal trainer. So far, I was coming up blank.

"Oh," Pansy said with a tinkly laugh. "Maggie Peterson came over for a chat." It was Margie, not Maggie, but I decided this wasn't the moment to point that out. "She must have left her phone behind." It had stopped ringing, finally.

"That wasn't here five minutes ago," he said.

"Nonsense," she told him. "You were distracted."

"That outfit's hot," he said, "but I still think I would have noticed a pink phone in the middle of the bathroom floor."

As if on cue, the phone rang again.

"It's Blake Peterson calling," she said.

"I heard that name. Isn't he the lawyer who fell in love with a drag queen and then dumped his wife for his gay-reform-group leader?"

I resisted the urge to jump out of the shower and strangle the man with Pansy's Pottery Barn shower curtain.

"Uh . . . I don't think that's the whole story, but the phone is definitely Maggie's," Pansy said.

"What was she doing here?"

"She's a private investigator," Pansy said. "I thought I might ask her to, uh, look into, uh, the missing funds from the PTA account."

"What?"

"I didn't mention it to you? We're missing several thousand dollars."

"Several thousand dollars?"

"We think it may be Janelle using it on mani-pedis," she said. "Plus, she likes those wraps. Anyway, I thought Maggie might be able to prove it; I just want that woman off the committee. Would you believe she wanted to replace the cake walk with a facial contouring station at the school carnival? Anyway, I'll make sure she gets it back tomorrow. In the meantime," she said, her voice switching from snarky to sultry, "where were we?"

Right in the middle of the room that I was stuck in, I thought as the sound of heavy breathing resumed.

Crap. I was in the Parkers' guest bathroom with a corpse, my kids were due to be picked up in fifteen minutes, the PTA president was getting it on not three feet away from me, and now I'd lost my phone, too.

In short, it was a typical Wednesday.

CHAPTER FOUR

"Where have you been?" Blake asked when I straggled into the kitchen, my quads still cramping from an hour of squatting in a bathtub. Blake had left a message, thankfully. "Your mom called and said you needed a hand; I tried to call, but you didn't answer, so I left work early to pick up the kids."

"I saw your call, but I couldn't answer; my phone is acting up." And had been in the possession of Pansy Parker's husband at the time. "Thank you so much for picking them up. I got stuck with a client." Stuck indeed. Pansy had finally managed to get her husband into the master bedroom shower and had come back and hurried me out through the garage.

"Here's your phone," she'd said, jamming my iPhone into my hand and hugging her tiny satin robe around herself. "Will you come back later?"

"Why?"

"I can't leave him in my shower!" she said. "What happens if the kids need to take a bath?"

"I'd recommend the master bathroom. You might want to retrieve their ducks, though." I glanced back inside the house. "Why don't you just call the police and tell them you got home and found him there?"

"He's naked!" she said. "And how am I going to explain how he got there?"

"He's your personal trainer. You could say he fell in the shower," I suggested.

"No," she said. "Too many questions. We've got to get him out of here."

I'd had more experience moving dead bodies than I cared to, and absolutely zero desire to repeat the experience. "Pansy, it's really better just to call—"

"Hurry. Mark is almost done with his shower. Now, go! Come back at six thirty tonight, okay? I asked him to take Isabella to her therapy appointment."

"I've got a date at seven thirty . . ." Peaches had texted me a confirmation.

"I'll pay you double. Heck . . . triple."

I paused. Triple pay would go a long way toward covering the electric bill.

"And I'll pay double for the investigation job for the PTA," she said.

"You weren't making that part up?"

"You don't know the half of it," she said. "See you at six thirty."

"But . . ."

"Go before he gets out. We'll talk later," she said, and shut the door on me.

Now, in my kitchen, as I grabbed a bag of contraband chicken nuggets out of the back of the freezer—I'd hidden it behind a package of frozen kale so my mother wouldn't toss it—and rifled through the cabinets for a clean cookie sheet, Blake was sitting at the kitchen table helping Elsie with her math homework. It was strange; now that the big secret in our marriage was out on the table, things between Blake and me had actually improved—and he was a lot more involved in the kids' lives than he'd ever been when we were together. Although we still hadn't figured out how to let the kids know Dad now had a boyfriend.

"Are you settling in at the apartment?" I asked when Elsie finished up her homework and headed into the backyard to throw a ball to herself. She was now eating food from a plate on the table instead of the floor, and had limited her barking and growling to after-school hours, but she still enjoyed a good game of fetch.

Small steps, I told myself as she fastened her pink rhinestone dog collar around her neck and loped across the backyard after a tennis ball.

"It's okay," Blake said. "Frank hasn't moved his wardrobe over yet, though." I wheeled around to look at my not-yet-ex-husband. He hadn't mentioned that he and his boyfriend were moving in together. "I think we may need a bigger place," he continued. "Feathers take up a lot of room, and he's got kind of a fetish for them."

More than I wanted to know, but it was too late now. "I didn't know you were moving in together," I said. "Are you sure it's not too early?" After all, they'd only known each other for a few months. Never mind the fact that Blake and I weren't even divorced. We'd told the children we were taking a break from each other, but we hadn't broken the big news, and Elsie was doing so much better since we'd moved her to Austin Heights Elementary that the last thing I wanted to do was tell her that her family was breaking up permanently. "What are you going to do when the kids come over?"

"We talked about it; he'll stay with a friend," Blake said, waving my concerns away. "I know it seems early, but his lease was up, and Austin rents are so expensive it seemed like the most cost-effective solution," he said. "How are things with you?" he asked as I dumped the frozen nuggets onto a slightly too-small cookie sheet and tried not to think about my husband kissing another man. "Are you dating yet?"

"Peaches set me up on a date—it's tonight—but it's weird. We're not even divorced," I said tartly. "And we've only been separated for a couple of months."

Of course, the recentness of our separation hadn't stopped Blake from pursuing his romantic interests. Then again, neither had our being married. I was trying not to be bitter, but it was hard. Now, thanks to Blake's no-longer-repressed desire for men with tweezed eyebrows and shaved chests, I was a single mom—and thanks to the addition of Blake's rent to our monthly expenditures, a single mom with a serious lack of cash in the bank account.

Blake sighed and swept back his well-coiffed hair. "I hate to think of you alone."

"I've got my mom," I replied, thinking how odd it was to have your soon-to-be-ex-husband encouraging you to play the field. Whereas I was looking more ragged than ever in shorts that were threatening to dissolve in the wash and a navy T-shirt with enough bleach stains it could be mistaken for a star chart, he was looking better than ever. My always-dapper husband was wearing crisp khakis and a blue-and-white paisley shirt, and it looked like he'd colored the few gray strands on his head. "I've never seen that shirt before," I told him. "It looks good on you."

"Thanks," he said. "Frank picked it out for me. Where is your mom, anyway?" he asked.

"She's got a date," I said as I grabbed a bag of desiccated grapes from the back of the fridge and tossed them in a bowl of water in the hope of plumping them up a bit. If worse came to worst, I could always call them extra-juicy raisins. Not that Elsie would touch them with a ten-foot pole, anyway.

"See? There's someone in Austin for everyone," he said. "Maybe you and Becky could put together a Match.com profile."

"Apparently Peaches put one together for me already," I said. "According to her, I like skydiving." I chose to omit the bit about lacy lingerie. God knew what else she had cooked up to put in my profile, I thought as I picked a few of the more wizened grapes out of the bowl. I peeled a brown banana and sliced it up. Elsie might not eat grapes, but at least she'd eat a banana. "Actually, I'm glad you're here. Would you mind hanging out until my mom gets back tonight? I need to head out in about a half hour. I have some . . . business I need to take care of."

"A big case?" he asked.

"Sort of." Big being about six feet two and two hundred pounds of dead weight. Literally.

"I'd be happy to," he said. "Frank has a gig tonight, so I'm on my own."

"A gig?"

"He's been doing a lot of work at parties lately," he said.

"I didn't know he was working parties. Is he a caterer, or a party planner?" I hadn't asked a whole lot about Frank, I realized. I hadn't really wanted to know.

"Actually," Blake said, "he's a performer."

"Really? Like a dancer?"

"Umm . . . no. He's, uh, working as a Madonna impersonator," Blake said, turning slightly pink. My husband was becoming more comfortable with his *out* status, but certain things still embarrassed him. "He's actually quite convincing. He's got the cheekbones for it."

And the figure, I thought ruefully, looking down at my less-than-svelte physique. My recent diet regimen of Cadbury Dairy Milk bars and pint-size containers of Blue Bell Chocolate Chip Cookie Dough ice cream—generally eaten in the garage or car, out of sight of my mother—hadn't done much to get me into my prepregnancy clothes. Despite the fact that my youngest was now four years old, I still thought of my little extra roll as baby fat. I was thinking it might be time to make a shrine to my single-digit-size clothes—either that, or take a truckload to Goodwill.

"How are things going with your parents?" I asked.

"They're still in shock, I think," he said. "It's going to take some time."

"Are you at least talking to them?"

"Not exactly," he said with a grimace. "I'm hoping they'll come around before Christmas."

"It was a bit of a surprise," I pointed out. He'd broken the news to them over dinner at a restaurant and introduced them to Frank on the spot. I'd never known my father-in-law could turn mauve.

"I don't mean to push you into the dating scene," Blake said, returning to the previous subject. "Take all the time you need. Oh—I signed Elsie up for soccer, by the way."

"Thanks for doing that."

"First practice is tomorrow at six. Can you take her? It's at the Austin Heights Elementary field."

"Sure," I said.

There was a grunting noise, followed by the sound of a large animal ramming into a metal gate. "What are you going to do about Twinkles, by the way?" Blake asked, looking over at the laundry room, where Elsie's rapidly expanding potbellied pig was pressing her pink snout against a baby gate. I'd rescued Twinkles's pregnant mother, Bubba Sue, from a pignapper a few months back; as a thank-you gift, Bubba Sue's owner had gifted my daughter the piglet of her choice.

Lucky me.

"What's your apartment complex's position on pigs?" I asked.

He gave me a wan smile that answered my question. "Besides," he said. "I'm at work all day. Who would take care of her?"

I worked, too, but I didn't feel like arguing, so I didn't bring it up. "Elsie's pretty attached to that pig," I said. "She's barking a lot less since we got her."

"How are things going at school?" he asked.

"Okay, I think," I told him as I adjusted the temperature on the oven. "At least no one is tying her to a tree at Austin Heights." Holy Oaks Catholic School had not—to say the very least—been a welcoming environment.

"Are you still thinking of getting her tested?"

"I'm going to look into it," I said.

"My mother thinks it's just a phase."

"I hope she's right."

Both of us turned to look at Elsie, who was crawling across the backyard on her hands and knees with a tennis ball clamped between her teeth. I reached for an apple to peel—apples without skin were white, and therefore on the Elsie-approved list—and sighed.

Parenting hadn't exactly been what I'd envisioned. Then again, I thought, glancing over at Blake, neither had marriage.

CHAPTER FIVE

When I showed up at her house at 6:35, full of misgivings and wondering if I should drop private investigating and take up hosting Passion Parties instead, Pansy was waiting at the front door.

"You look . . . done up," she said, eyeing my green dress and teased hair.

"I have a date," I reminded her.

"You move on fast," she said. "We're good. I locked the bathroom door—told him the cat had an accident and I hadn't had a chance to clean it up—and he's taking Isabella to her appointment. I just hope the neighbors don't see us carting Tristan out to the curb."

"Is that what you plan to do with him?" I asked.

"I was hoping you'd have a better idea, to be honest. Can you fit him in the back of your van?"

"I have a standing rule: no dead bodies in my vehicles," I said. Sadly, this was the second time this year I'd had to invoke that rule.

"We'll put him in mine, then," she said. "I have a Suburban. Let's go."

"I'll help you get him into your car," I said. "But after that, I'm out."

"How am I going to get him out of the back, then?" she asked.

"Roll him?" I suggested. "Seriously. I shouldn't even be here." Triple pay or no triple pay, I had a very bad feeling about this undertaking.

"It's not like someone murdered him," she said. "He dropped dead of a heart attack."

"How do you know it was a heart attack?" I asked.

"Well, what else could it be? Let's just get him out of my bathroom before Isabella comes home and walks in on him, okay? I don't want to scar her for life." She turned and walked into the house; after a moment of hesitation, I followed, wondering what had become of my common sense.

"It's for Isabella," she told me, sensing my hesitation. She knew my weakness.

Tristan was right where we'd left him, only—I discovered as I tried to bend his right arm—a lot stiffer. "His arm is stuck under the soap holder," I said.

"Maybe if I move his legs, his arm will come loose," she suggested, grabbing one leg and attempting to shift him. After the third try, we managed to dislodge him. She stood back and stared at his very fit, very dead body. "Such a waste." I might have been mistaken, but I thought I detected a tear in her eye.

"How long had you been seeing each other?" I asked.

"Only a month," she said. "He was helping me plank once, and put his hand on my back, and well . . ." She shrugged and swiped at her eyes. "It just kind of went from there. I can't believe he had a heart attack, though. He was so young and fit." Her eyes drifted to his nether regions.

That was what was bothering me. A portly middle-aged man dying of a heart attack I could see . . . but Tristan didn't look to be a day over twenty-nine and was anything but chunky. And then there was the whole tongue thing. "Let's just get this over with," I said. "I'll get his arms if you grab his legs."

"Don't you think we should put some clothes on him?" she asked.

"Let's get him out of the tub first."

Together we maneuvered him out of the bathtub without getting too tangled in the shower curtain, but we ran into another issue at the door.

"Can you bend his arm down?" she asked.

"I'm trying," I said. "I don't want to break it. Can you shift him sideways?"

"This is like moving a sofa," she said as she heaved him to the right. Her hand slipped, and he hit the tile floor with a thump. We both froze, holding our breath, but nothing in the house stirred. Certainly not Tristan.

"Let's try again," she said, grabbing him by the ankles. This time we had more luck, and together we maneuvered him down the hallway to the garage. Pansy retrieved a bag with his clothes and we attempted to dress him. We managed the shorts, but with his arms frozen the way they were, the shirt wasn't happening. "That'll have to do," she said, stepping back to look at our handiwork. "Let's put him down for a moment so I can open the back of the Suburban and put a tarp in."

"A tarp?"

"I just got the car cleaned. I don't want to mess up the carpet," she said. A few minutes later we were shutting the tailgate of the Suburban, Tristan safely ensconced in the back. Well, as safe as a dead person could be, anyway.

"Don't speed," I advised her.

"Don't worry," she said. "I'll use the tire iron to lever him out. But you can't breathe a word of this to anyone, okay? If I got a divorce, it would kill Isabella." She bit her lip. "Oops . . . Sorry about that."

"It's fine," I said, although her words made my heart ache. *Your divorce is not your fault, Margie,* I told myself. And the kids still had two loving parents. I was sure they'd be fine. Mostly sure, anyway.

At least I hoped they'd be fine.

"I'm getting out of here," I said. "Don't tell me what you plan to do with him; I don't want to know."

"I thought I'd drop him by his apartment," she said. "Or maybe his gym."

"What are you going to do, leave him in the parking lot?" I raised my hand. "No. Like I said, I don't want to know."

"Thanks for your help," she said, glancing at the back of the Suburban. "I think I can take it from here. We'll talk about the embezzling case soon, okay?"

"Got it."

"You'll be at the PTA meeting, right?"

"I'll be there," I said, edging toward the door.

"And you might want to donate a few hours of consultation to the Austin Heights auction, by the way. It'll be good advertising."

Could we maybe talk about this another time? I thought, but just said, "See you at school tomorrow?"

"You bet," she said. "And I won't forget this."

Unfortunately, neither would I.

CHAPTER SIX

I walked into Hula Hut with something that could generously be called trepidation. I'd borrowed some of Becky's clothes and attempted to replicate the makeover magic she'd done for me in the past, but the result wasn't quite what I'd hoped for. My hair was about three inches taller than normal, my lips felt like they'd been shellacked, and I barely recognized myself in a mirror.

The person who most resembled the picture Peaches had texted me was sitting by the bar, wearing a neon-green Dri-Fit shirt and a pair of running shorts that exposed legs that reminded me of furry toothpicks. Unfortunately, the fur didn't extend to his head, which, aside from a curly fringe around the sides, looked like a monk's tonsure and appeared to have been recently buffed and glossed. Either he'd been wearing a toupee in his profile picture, or the picture had been taken about fifteen years ago.

As I wobbled toward the bar in a pair of borrowed wedge sandals, wishing I hadn't let Becky talk me into wearing a short dress, he raised a glass of virulently green juice to his lips, then turned to scan the room. When his gaze fell on me, his eyes narrowed appraisingly.

"Margie?" he asked.

"Yes," I said. "You must be Trey."

He nodded and gestured toward the bar stool next to his. "Pull up a chair."

As I levered myself onto the bar stool, he took another swig of the revolting-looking green liquid. "Want one?" he asked.

"What is it?"

"Spirulina-wheatgrass juice with a shot of vodka. I bring my own juice with me, and they mix it up. It's low carb," he said, his eyes running up and down my figure. "They make it special for me because I'm a regular. Have you given low carb a try?"

"Ah, no."

"It's hard to get used to, but your clothes will fit so much better."

I was speechless. Not that it mattered; he just kept going.

"Your photo looks like it was taken a few years ago," he said. "Let me guess: pre-baby?"

"Actually, it was taken last week," I said.

He looked doubtful.

"How about you?" I asked.

"Oh, it was just a snapshot from last month," he told me.

Either he was lying, or he was a big fan of Photoshop. We weren't off to a rip-roaring start, and I was trying to decide whether to manufacture an emergency call from home, but I figured maybe a little liquor might help. After a moment's hesitation, I flagged down the bartender. I'd been out of the dating pool for a long time; a little bit of practice wouldn't hurt.

"Really, though," Trey said. "Your photo was a very flattering pic. Your face looked a lot . . . well, less round."

"And you kind of looked like you had . . . well, a little more on top," I replied.

He held his hand over his head as if it were an infant I had threatened. "It's a little thin, but I still have a pretty full head of hair," he said.

I nodded. "It's probably just the lighting." The bartender rolled up as Trey rearranged the fringe above his ears; I thought I could spot a glint of amusement in the bartender's eyes. "A mojito, please," I requested.

"With agave, Splenda, or sugar syrup?" the bartender asked.

"I'm telling you, you really should try low carb," Trey suggested.

"With sugar syrup," I said firmly. My order placed, I turned back to my date. "So. How long have you been on the dating scene?"

"My divorce was finalized six months ago," he said. "She took me for everything I had. And would you believe she still kept my name?" He shook his head and took another sip of his drink. "Said it was for business purposes."

So it wasn't exactly amicable. "Do you have kids?"

"Two," he said. "One of them is a soccer star; she's the youngest kid on her team. The guy who runs the league told me she could be the next Mia Hamm; she's fast, and she's got a hell of a leg." He took another slurp of his drink. "We were just running wind sprints before I got here."

That explained the attire. "How old is she?"

"Six," he said.

"My daughter's six, too," I said.

"Brianna's just amazing," Trey went on, as if he hadn't heard me. "Her mom's pretty fit, but I think it comes from my side, really. I played soccer for UT before I blew out my ACL. I was up for the US team, but my knee got in the way."

"I'm sorry to hear that," I said.

"It's probably for the best. If I'd been on the team, I wouldn't have had time to get my MBA." As he spoke, his phone buzzed. He checked it, and without excusing himself, picked it up. "Hey, dude," he said as the bartender appeared with a large mojito.

"Thanks," I said to the twentysomething man sliding my drink across the bar.

"I tossed in an extra shot for free," the bartender murmured, tilting his head almost imperceptibly toward my loud companion. "I thought you might need it."

"You're awesome," I told him in a low voice, and sucked up about a quarter of the drink through the straw. By the time Trey got off the phone with his golf buddy—they were setting up tee times for Sunday—I'd finished about half my drink and was eyeing the exit.

"So," he said when he'd relinquished his phone, clapping his hands together and leaning toward me with a disconcertingly intense stare. "I'm a big believer in efficiency. Before we spend our resources, might as well find out if we're compatible. Cost-benefit analysis, you know?"

"Fine by me," I said, thinking the analysis was definitely not weighing in his favor.

"So far," he said, "you don't seem too into healthy eating, and I'm guessing fitness isn't a big thing for you."

"I eat a variety of things," I said. Primarily ice cream and chocolate, but he didn't need to know that. "And I spend a lot of time in motion. How about you? You're into your kid's soccer, I can tell, and apparently healthy eating. What else?"

"What else is there to life?" he asked. A young woman in a low-cut tank top and short shorts sat down at a table to our left, and Trey's eyes wandered in her direction for a few moments before coming back, seemingly reluctantly, to me. "I'm a money manager," he told me, puffing himself up a bit. "I take care of some of the biggest names in town."

"That must have made your wife—ex-wife—very happy."

He squinted at me. "Was that a joke? Are you saying she married me for my money?"

"I'm saying she must have been happy with the divorce settlement," I clarified, thinking it probably made her happy in more ways than one.

"Humph," he said, not sounding convinced. "Anyway, how about you?"

"What about me?" I asked, not feeling particularly interested in divulging any details about my life to Trey. Not that he seemed at all interested. I was about to sketch out the basics when he held up a hand.

"On second thought, don't tell me," Trey said. "I'm pretty good at reading people. Let's see. You squeezed out a couple of kids, spent all your time paying attention to them, and your marriage fell apart."

"Not exactly," I said.

He drained the rest of his drink. "Well, to be honest, I don't think we're much of a fit. I really like women who are into fitness and healthy eating . . . six-pack abs, you know?" He glanced down at my one-pack midriff. "Besides, I have an instinct for these things, and I believe in thin slicing. Cost-benefit analysis, you know?"

I could not believe this man was such a jerk. I could feel the blood rush to my face, but I somehow managed to keep my cool. I leaned forward and looked into his eyes. "You know, Trey, I was just thinking that you might want to get some hair transplants—and maybe some calf transplants, too. I've seen more-muscular legs on a newborn fawn." His mouth worked, but no words came out. I took a sip of my drink and added, "A personality transplant would be even better, but I don't think they've developed those yet."

"I knew you were a bitch," he spat. "I'm glad I didn't pay for your dinner." He fumbled for his wallet.

"Do you need me to close your tab?" the bartender asked politely.

"I'll pay for my own drink," I said, and even though I couldn't afford it, I fished out a ten-dollar bill and slid it to the bartender. "It's been, uh . . . interesting . . . getting to know you," I told Trey, "but I think I'm going to have to pass on dinner."

"Good," he said, curling his lip. He glared at me for a moment, then grabbed the dregs of his green drink and stalked over to the table with the young woman. His head was still beet red, but he put on a smarmy smile and slid onto the stool across from her.

Behind me, the bartender said, "I'm sorry you had to deal with that. He's a real jerk."

"Does he come here a lot?"

"This is his favorite place for first dates. Most of them don't handle him as well as you did."

"Thanks," I said as I watched Trey attempt to put the moves on the young woman in the tank top. "He doesn't waste time, does he?"

"Thing is, his wife was a looker. I have no idea what she saw in him."

"Love is blind," I said. As I took another sip of my mojito, I heard a familiar voice at the other end of the bar. I looked up; it was Becky's brother, Michael, looking handsome in jeans and a button-down shirt. "Michael!" I called.

He turned, surprised, and his face lit up in a smile. "Margie? Long time no see," he said, crossing the distance between us. "You look terrific. What are you doing here?"

For some reason, I felt awkward telling him I was on a date, but I did anyway. "Peaches put a Match.com profile up for me and set me up with someone."

"How'd it go?"

I glanced over toward where Trey was moving in on the tank-top-clad twenty-year-old. Something about it reminded me of one of those nature specials where a crocodile sneaks up behind its prey. "I think I'd rather stay single," I said. "How about you?"

"I'm, ah, meeting someone here, actually."

"Can I get you a drink?" the bartender asked.

"A Shiner Bock, please," he said, and turned back to me.

He'd been my crush in high school, and he still made my heart go pitter-patter. Becky had told me he was interested in me once, and he'd asked me out a few months ago, but I'd been hoping to get a few dates under my belt first to see if I still remembered how to talk to straight men. I found myself glad I'd worn a dress.

"I'm so sorry about you and Blake," he told me. "How are you and the kids holding up?"

"I've been better," I said truthfully. "I think the kids are okay, though, all things considered."

"If there's anything I can do . . ." There was a warmth in his eyes that made me melt inside.

"I appreciate it," I said, trying to play it cool, but thinking another dinner invitation would be a nice start. "How are things with you?"

Before he could answer, a tall, willowy woman came up behind him and touched his shoulder. "Michael?"

He turned and smiled. "Salima! I was just about to tell Margie about you."

"Good things, I hope?" She returned his smile, exposing a line of white teeth. She was irritatingly pretty.

"Of course," I said, and proffered a hand. "Margie Peterson. I'm good friends with Michael's sister."

"Salima Garcia," she said. "Nice to meet you."

At that moment, Michael's pager buzzed. "Perfect timing!" Salima said. "Our table is ready. So nice to meet you, Margie."

"Likewise," I said.

"It's good to see you," Michael said. "Let's catch up sometime."

"That would be great," I said, watching as Salima snaked an arm around Michael's waist and the two of them walked to the front of the restaurant. Michael glanced over his shoulder at me, looking . . . embarrassed? Regretful? Or was I projecting?

I sucked down my mojito. I'd been on the dating scene for approximately twenty-three minutes, and it was already a disaster.

CHAPTER SEVEN

The lights were still on, but Blake was asleep on the couch, our Siamese cat curled up next to his right leg, when I got home a half hour later. Rufus blinked at me, then tucked his head back in and purred contentedly; he had missed Blake, apparently. I tiptoed into the living room and studied my husband, whose sprawled body reminded me of the way Nick distributed himself across his entire bed. I recognized Elsie's dark-winged eyebrows and Nick's curved lower lip on the peaceful face of my husband, and felt a deep pang of loss for the years we had shared—and the family I had tried so hard to give my children.

Feeling deflated, I turned away from my husband and walked to the kids' rooms. Like his father, Nick was on his back, breathing deeply; I kissed his sweaty forehead and then went to check on Elsie, who had fallen asleep with her tennis ball on one side and Twinkles, who was snoring lightly, sprawled out on the other. I reached out and smoothed a lock of dark hair away from her peach-fuzz cheek. They looked so content I didn't have the heart to relocate the pig to the laundry room.

My mother wasn't home yet—*her date must be going swimmingly,* I thought—when I retired to what had once been Blake's and my bedroom and inspected myself in the mirror above the dresser. I looked tired and wan, my reddish hair pulled back into a clip, my Spanx holding in about 30 percent of me under Becky's dress. Not too bad for a late-thirties single mom, I thought, trying to pump myself up. What was the dating scene like these days, anyway? Would anyone want to go out with a slightly plump, frazzled mother of two small children?

I had just turned away from the mirror when my phone rang. I looked down at the number: it was Pansy. I considered turning it off and ignoring it until morning, but I knew I'd worry about it all night, so I picked it up.

"Margie? It's Pansy. I went to IronAbs Gym, but a cop tried to stop me after I dumped Tristan in the parking lot."

"You dumped him in the parking lot?"

"He was too heavy for me to move on my own," she said. "What else was I supposed to do? Anyway, I guess the cop thought I was speeding or something. He chased me halfway down Bee Caves Road before I managed to lose him."

"You didn't stop?"

"I panicked," she said. "But I made it home okay."

"But they probably have your license plate number," I pointed out.

"You think?" There was a ringing sound.

"Is that your home phone?"

"No . . ." There was a pause, and then a lively string of invectives.

"What?"

"Tristan left his phone here," she said. "What do I do?"

"I'll be right there," I said, and grabbed my car keys again.

● ● ●

When I arrived at Pansy's house, she was sitting across the room from the phone, looking at it as if it were a dead rat.

"What do I do with it?" she asked.

"Well, we have to get rid of it, obviously," I said.

"Can't they trace it to my house?"

"I don't know," I said, although I was pretty sure they could. I thought of Tristan's purple face and swollen tongue. "Did he eat or drink anything while he was here?"

She nodded. "He forgot lunch. He had a protein shake, then opened a LifeBoost," she told me. "I think it's still in the gym." Her face paled. "Oh my God. Are you thinking there might have been something in his drink?"

Tristan's phone lit up. I looked down; he'd gotten three texts from someone named Doctor K, asking something about numbers, and one from someone called Hot Mama.

"I don't know," I said. "Let's go open it; does it smell like the other drinks?"

We walked into her exercise room. She twisted off the lid and took a sniff. "It smells green, just like the rest of them."

"Do you have any other drinks in the fridge?"

She nodded, and went to retrieve them.

They all smelled the same.

"Did he bring it with him?"

"I think he got this out of the fridge; I just got them. Do you think there was something wrong with them?"

"I don't know," I said, wishing we hadn't moved the body. "Did he take any supplements or put anything into his drink?"

"Wait . . . He did take some supplements," she said. "He popped about six pills into his mouth when he got here, and made himself a protein shake. He's always taking things to build muscle."

"Do you still have the glass he drank the shake from?"

"I washed it. And I dropped off his bag with him, so there's no way to check on the supplements." She bit her lip. "I bet there's nothing in those drinks, but maybe I should throw them out all the same."

"Maybe it's just a bad batch . . . Have you had any?"

"No," she said. "I just bought them today. Thank God Isabella didn't drink one. That would have been just horrible . . ."

"We don't know if the drinks were the problem," I said. "It's just a possibility . . . Besides, he took pills. It could have been those, or a bad reaction or something."

"Maybe," she said.

"I was looking at his phone a few minutes ago," I said, changing the subject. "Do you know who Hot Mama or Doctor K is?"

She shook her head. "He didn't talk much about his business partners. I know Tristan was putting his LifeBoost drink company together with a bottling company and some Chinese-medicine guy, and he used his sales skills to pitch it. I know they got some funding recently, but he didn't say where it came from."

"If you remember anything, let me know."

"I will. Thank God you came and rescued me," she said. "I was going to have to make up something about a sexual assault or something."

The phone in my hand buzzed. Hot Mama again. *At our spot . . . missing you . . . where r u?*

"Apparently he had another date," I said. "Any ideas on what the pass code might be?"

She shook her head. "His birthday was June 3," she said. "Try zero six zero three."

It didn't work. We tried a few other options, but nothing worked.

"What do we do with it now?" she asked.

"I don't know," I said. "Turn it off, maybe, so that it can't be tracked? You could turn it in to the police, but that might not be the smartest idea. He probably had the appointment with you on his calendar."

"I keep wondering who Hot Mama is," she said. "I wish we could get into that phone."

Since Tristan was dead, it didn't really matter to me who Hot Mama was. "Turn it off and hide it for now; we'll figure out what to do with it later."

"Are you sure?"

"I don't know what else to do," I said. "Ideally you'd give it to the police, but there's probably stuff on it that might mess with your marriage." Besides, if his death wasn't from natural causes, the last thing Pansy needed was a phone with an appointment on it indicating that Tristan was at her house when he died.

"You're right," she said. "You made me feel so much better. Like I said, send me a bill for triple your time, and please don't breathe a word of this to anyone!"

"My lips are sealed," I said.

"And I'll get you started with the PTA the day after tomorrow," she said. "We meet in the workroom right next to the teachers' lounge."

"Sure," I said. "Two o'clock?"

"It's a date," she said, looking positively giddy with relief.

Which made one of us.

• • •

I walked into the office at nine the next morning, cringing (as usual) at the moans and groans from the waxing rooms at the Pretty Kitten. Peaches was sitting at the desk, thumbing through a file. She wore purple lipstick that coordinated with her purple nail polish and sequined purple minidress.

"Hey," I said.

"Nice outfit."

I glanced down at my baggy denim shorts and Austin Heights Elementary T-shirt. "It's clean," I said. My standards had dropped perilously with the birth of each of my children. Now that I was a working single mother, they were so low I was afraid I might trip on them.

"How'd your date go?"

"Don't ask," I said.

"That good, eh?"

"It lasted twenty minutes. At least I didn't dump my drink on him."

"Well, you gotta kiss a few frogs," she said. "Any luck with the streaker?"

"I almost got him," I said, "but some lady in a yellow miniskirt popped up out of a bush and started yelling at him about bananas."

"From what I hear, he's pretty well endowed," Peaches said. "Did you at least get a shot?"

"No," I said. Even if I had, I'd probably have only gotten a shot of his butt cheeks disappearing into a bush. "There's another garden club meeting coming up, anyway. But I'm more worried about Elsie's fry phone."

"Oh no. Not again."

"I think I left it at one of the PTA moms' houses, but I can't get in touch with her."

"I'm sure it will be fine," Peaches said. "At least a pig didn't eat it this time."

"That's looking on the bright side," I conceded. "Speaking of the PTA, I got another job."

"I knew you were a go-getter. Who is it?"

"Someone at Austin Heights. The president of the PTA in fact."

"I had a feeling that place would be a jackpot," she said, rubbing her hands together. "What is it? Adultery? Or kidnapping?"

"Not exactly," I said. "Somebody's been embezzling from the PTA."

"Of course," she said, rolling her eyes. "White-collar crime."

"But that's not the only thing," I said.

"I knew it. Lay it on me," she said, eyes gleaming.

I glanced behind me to make sure the door was shut. "Anyone else here?"

"Just us chickens," she said. "Now, what's the scoop?"

"I helped move another dead body last night," I said.

She stared at me for a moment, then shook her head. "I hope it wasn't your date."

"No!"

"Good."

I told her about Pansy's frantic call—and the way she was dangling from the Nautilus machine when I let myself into her house.

"What kind of sex toys?" she asked.

"I think they were nipple clamps. There was a honking-big vibrator, too," I said. "It was enormous. And so was he. But that's not the point . . ."

"Not anymore, anyway, since he's a stiff. Hard to get a stiffy when you're dead."

"Anyway," I said, "he left his cell phone at her house. And we're thinking he might have been poisoned."

"Poisoned?" she asked. "Why do you think that?"

"His tongue was all swollen. He had a half-finished drink, but she threw it out before I could really look at it."

"Maybe he put some special vitamin in it," she suggested. "Lots of those fitness people do crazy stuff like that. Pig placenta, kangaroo penis . . . all kinds of weird shit."

"Maybe. Speaking of weird . . . things," I said, "what's up with the Match.com profile?"

"I figured someone had to do it," she said. "You've got another potential date, by the way."

I groaned. "You're kidding me, right? I haven't recovered from the last one."

"He seemed like a nice guy," she said. "His language was kind of prissy . . . makes me wonder if maybe he's got a bit of a stick up his butt. Even though Blake's got more than a stick—"

"Enough," I said, putting a hand up. "I don't want to think about it."

"Too soon?" she asked. I gave her a look. "Anyway," she said, wisely changing the subject, "Do you think someone offed your friend's personal trainer?"

"I guess the autopsy will show it. Unfortunately, the police tried to pull her over right near where she dumped the body, but she took off. And his phone was at her house."

"Let's hope nobody offed him, or your friend may be behind bars."

"I kind of thought that, too," I said.

"Anyway, we're supposed to go find Wanda for a meeting."

"Isn't she next door?" Wanda was the owner of the Pretty Kitten, the business we were subletting space from.

"She wants to hire us," she said. "We can't meet at the salon."

"I'm in," I told her. "As long as we're taking your car."

"Last time we took yours, it took me twenty minutes to unstick myself from the seat," she said.

"Vanilla milkshake," I said. "Elsie spilled one, and I can't get it all out of the upholstery."

"The Regal it is."

CHAPTER EIGHT

Aside from the six Boston cream donuts I managed to put down at Howdy Donuts and the assignment from Wanda—she wanted one of us to be a mystery shopper at one of her waxing salons to see if we could figure out why the store was suddenly unprofitable, but I'd talked her into a temporary receptionist role instead—the day was relatively uneventful. No frantic calls from Pansy, no terrible dates, and no family meltdowns . . . until it was time to leave for soccer practice.

"I'm not going without her." Elsie was standing in the doorway of her bedroom, wearing a white soccer practice shirt, cleats, and a pink dog collar. Twinkles was behind her, rooting through her pajama drawer—probably looking for illicit snacks.

"I don't think they allow pigs on the practice field, honey," I said in my most reasonable voice.

"If I can't have my fry phone, then I'm not going without Twinkles."

I glanced at my mother, looking for help.

"I'll tell you what," she said. "If you go to practice by yourself tonight, you and I can take Twinkles on a walk around the neighborhood when you get home."

"No," Elsie barked, and I could tell by the tension in her small body that the time of reason had come and gone. Right on cue, a low, menacing growl reverberated in her small chest. Things were about to get hairy.

"Let me check the field policy," I said with a sigh. I had hoped not to bring the pig with us—Elsie was already unusual enough with her sparkly collar and her penchant for yipping—but if Twinkles was going to soothe her, it might be worth it. Besides, the fry phone was still missing; I still hadn't heard from Frances. Most kids were attached to blankets and dogs. Elsie, on the other hand, had a Happy Meal toy and Twinkles the pig.

"Are you sure you want to set this precedent?" my mother asked as I walked into the next room and grabbed the computer.

"We're on the edge of a meltdown," I said. "Maybe if we take Twinkles the first night, Elsie will relax and we can leave the pig home next time."

The growling increased in volume, and my mother sighed. "I still think if we cut the gluten . . ."

"I know," I said. "You've told me that, and I'll think about it. But we just need to get through tonight."

"If you leash her up," my mother suggested, "Nick and I can keep an eye on her."

"Twinkles, or Elsie?"

My mother rolled her eyes. "The pig, Margie."

"I know, I know. But she's getting pretty big," I said doubtfully, looking at Twinkles. Like her mother, Bubba Sue, she was rapidly becoming a porker of some substance. "Are you sure you'll be able to manage?"

"If I raised you, I can handle a piglet," my mother said with a smile. I chose not to dwell on that comparison.

We headed back into the living room together. "We'll bring Twinkles," I told Elsie.

"Yay!" she said with a big smile.

"I'll help take care of her," Nick said solemnly.

"Thanks, sweetie," I said. Maybe the evening wouldn't be so bad after all.

"And I've got a curried squash casserole warming in the oven," my mother said, "so dinner's taken care of!"

Or maybe not.

• • •

The field outside Austin Heights Elementary School was filled with small girls in white shirts, and the bleachers were populated by the women I'd met at the Passion Party, including Pansy, Phyllis, and Janelle. Elsie immediately ran over to see Becky's daughter, Zoe; they hugged and trotted toward the gaggle of ponytailed girls. I breathed a sigh of relief; crisis averted.

"What is that?" Janelle said, stabbing a lacquered talon at Twinkles, who was sniffing the ground as if she expected to find truffles. Unfortunately, she had a better chance of finding cigarette butts and old gum.

"Twinkles," I said. "She's Elsie's pet."

Pansy blinked at me. "You have a pet pig?"

"She was a gift," I said. "It's a long story."

"She's so cute!" Becky said. "Everyone, I know you know Margie, but this is Margie's mother, Connie, and her son, Nick. He goes to preschool at Green Meadows; he'll be at Austin Heights in a year or two."

Greetings were exchanged, and I sat next to Becky on the bottom bleacher while my mother and Nick drifted down the sideline, following Twinkles's snout.

"Where's Frances?" I asked.

"She's been under the weather," Janelle said. "Probably mourning that personal trainer . . . Did you hear he died?"

Pansy's eyes leaped to mine. "What personal trainer?" I asked, as if I hadn't spent a good bit of quality time with him in a bathtub recently.

53

"The one I was talking about the other night, silly," Janelle said. "Such a waste. Honestly, I think Frances was kind of sweet on him."

Phyllis's lips had formed a thin line. "He wasn't that kind of trainer," she said.

"That's what you think," Janelle said. "I hear Frances had a lot of . . . intimate sessions with him."

"Where did you hear that?" Pansy barked.

"Word travels," Janelle said.

Phyllis flashed both women a venomous look. "I don't think this is an appropriate conversation for a children's soccer practice," she bit out.

Janelle sighed. "You're a party pooper, but you're probably right. I want to talk about the pig, anyway," she said, turning to me. "Can you house-train them?"

"That's what I'm told," I said, feeling very tired. "We're still working on it. She lives mostly in the laundry room; Elsie's very attached to her."

"But the cat hates her," Becky supplied, obviously relieved that the conversation had moved on.

"It's probably good for Elsie to have the company, with her father gone," Phyllis said in a sorrowful tone.

"She sees plenty of her dad," I said with a tight smile.

"So do a lot of other guys, I hear," Janelle said with a leering wink. She took a sip from an insulated mug, and I got a whiff of something that smelled suspiciously like Chardonnay. Her blowsy blonde hair was a tangled halo around her face. She appeared to have attempted to use contour makeup; the result reminded me of one of Picasso's later works. "A friend of mine saw him at Oilcan Harry's the other day; he was pretty popular, from what I hear."

My face burned. I glanced toward Nick, hoping he was far enough away that he couldn't hear.

Phyllis shook her head. "Your poor kids. I've heard divorce can really be damaging to children—with long-term effects. Are you sure there's no way you can patch things up?"

"Maybe if she grew a set," Janelle crowed, and took another sip of her Chardonnay.

"So," Becky said cheerfully, clearly trying to change the subject, "when's our first game?"

"Couple of weeks, I think," Janelle said, undaunted, then turned back to me. "How's Mr. Big treating you, by the way?"

"Can we please talk about something else?" Becky said.

"Sure," Janelle said, and swiveled to face Pansy. "I still can't believe Tristan died. Have you heard anything about it?"

Pansy paled. "Nothing yet," she said. "No wonder he didn't turn up for our appointment, though. I had to do the whole workout by myself."

"That's funny. I heard the police found his car right near your house," Janelle said.

Pansy and I stared at each other. His car. Why hadn't we thought of his car? It hadn't been parked in front of her house, but of course he had to have had his car with him! My palms began to sweat.

"What are you talking about?" Pansy said, tearing her eyes from me and trying to look normal.

"My neighbor's husband is on the police force. They said they found it this morning."

Pansy swallowed. "I had no idea," she said. "I don't even know what his car looks like."

"Sure your hubby didn't get jealous?" Janelle smirked.

"Look," Pansy said. "A man has died, and it's a tragedy. I'd appreciate it if we could keep the . . . the idle gossip to a minimum," she announced, smoothing her white tennis skirt and nodding toward the gaggle of girls. Elsie was no longer with Zoe, I noticed; Zoe had joined the rest of the girls, and Elsie was sniffing the goalposts.

"What's she doing?" Pansy asked from behind me. I could hear whispering among the other moms, but I ignored it.

"Oh, just hanging out," I said, praying she didn't decide to pee on the field. I glanced back at the other moms and faked a smile.

Pansy glanced at her watch. "Where's the head coach?"

"He's probably running wind sprints with his daughter," Janelle said, rolling her eyes. "I swear, he thinks she's going to join the national team next year. If he doesn't play my daughter this year, I'm going to complain to the league." She grimaced. "His ex-wife, Michaela, says he's an absolute jerk; he doesn't believe that their son has ADHD, and won't pay for any treatment."

"You're kidding me, right?" Pansy said, obviously grateful that Tristan was no longer the topic of conversation. "I helped out at the winter party last year; the kid was like a Ping-Pong ball. Mrs. Grayling said he can't stay in his seat for more than six seconds at a time."

"I'm surprised he passed the STAAR test," Phyllis said sourly. "I hear he had to take it three times."

"An active body doesn't mean you have a disorder," Chantal Morgenstern said, walking up to the bleachers.

She hadn't been at the Passion Party, but I'd seen her at school. She was a gaunt vegan who claimed to be gluten free, and I was terrified to introduce her to my mother. I glanced down the field to where she, Nick, and Twinkles were walking behind the goal.

"He probably just needs more structured activities," Chantal intoned.

"Besides," Phyllis said, "ADHD isn't a real diagnosis; it all comes down to parenting. Parenting and discipline. I mean, one of the kindergarten teachers suggested that River might have some focus problems. We just told him if he didn't come home with all As, we'd give his hamster away."

In kindergarten? I felt a twinge of apprehension. Maybe the switch from Holy Oaks wasn't going to be quite so seamless after all.

"Oh, there's the coach," Janelle said, stabbing a wobbly finger at a distant figure with a bag of soccer balls over his shoulder, looking like a middle-aged Santa Claus in cleats. He was striding down the far end of the field, a young girl trotting beside him, shiny ponytail swinging. "Michaela says he's going out with twenty-year-olds. Apparently he went on a Match.com date the other day, and the woman was ancient. Her photo must have been taken years ago."

"You can't trust those photos," Phyllis said.

"How do you know?" Janelle asked.

"My sister's divorced," she muttered.

"Oh no," I murmured as the man came closer. Dri-Fit shirt, head that gleamed in the evening sun, legs like toothpicks . . .

It was Trey.

I leaned over to Becky. "That's him," I whispered.

"Who?"

"The guy from the blind date," I said.

Her eyes widened. "No. Trey Volker?"

I grimaced. She snorted, trying to stifle a laugh.

"It's not funny. He kept lecturing me on my diet and my weight. The date did not end on a positive note."

"Oh, Margie." She reached out and squeezed my arm, still trying not to giggle. "What are you going to do?"

"Pretend it never happened," I said grimly. As I responded, there was a grunting noise; Twinkles was pulling my mother back to the bleachers. She must have scented snacks.

"This pig is getting awfully strong," my mother said, pushing her bangled bracelets up her arm. She sat down next to me and glanced over at Chantal. Uh-oh. "You taught that yoga class the other day, didn't you?"

"I did," Chantal preened.

"Your Happy Baby is amazing," she said. "I envy your flexibility."

"Practice," Chantal said. "I'm sure you'll get it."

"Twinkles!"

I looked down just as the pig tipped over Chantal's handwoven purse. Before I could grab her, she had snatched a bag of kale snacks and was taking off down the field, leaving a trail of green chips on the turf.

"Twinkles!" I shot up from the bleachers and raced after her, Nick in my wake.

Trey had just bellowed to the girls to line up. Elsie was still sniffing the goalposts; she hadn't seemed to hear him. As Twinkles began weaving in Elsie's general direction, the kale chips crinkling in her mouth, the coach spotted my daughter dawdling. "Hey, you!" he said. "It's time for practice."

Elsie ignored him and began circling the pole.

"Young lady!" he said. "I said it's practice time."

"Elsie," I pleaded as I tried to corral Twinkles.

My daughter sat down on the field, crossing her arms.

Trey, who by now had turned red again, marched over to her. "It's not playtime, young lady. It's time to huddle up."

Twinkles's little ears perked up, and she watched Trey advance on Elsie. She turned and began trotting toward him with what looked like a new sense of purpose. I, on the other hand, had a sense of foreboding.

Trey reached Elsie before Twinkles and I did. He towered over her, hands on his hips. "It's practice time," he barked. "If you want any game time at all, you had better get your butt over with rest of your team."

Elsie didn't answer.

"Come on, Elsie!" I called. I'd broken into a sprint now; so had Twinkles.

As I watched, Trey reached down to grab her arm. The movement seemed to trigger something in Twinkles; she switched from a trot to a gallop and let out a menacing grunt. Trey looked behind himself just in time to see fifty pounds of uncured bacon bearing down on him; then she launched herself upward and planted her snout firmly into his derriere.

He yelped in pain and surprise and stepped away from Elsie. Twinkles took the opportunity to place herself in the gap between Trey and Elsie, and lowered her head—I swear she actually pawed the ground.

"Jesus Christ," he said. "Whose demon pig is this? And what the hell is a pig doing on the field?"

"Sorry about that," I said as I huffed up to Twinkles and grabbed her collar.

His jaw dropped. "You. What are you doing here?"

"This is my daughter, Elsie," I said, by way of explanation. "And her pig. Twinkles."

"Twinkles?" His head swiveled between my daughter, me, and the pig, who was still eyeing him with a distinctly frosty air. "I was right. You're a fucking lunatic."

"Mommy." Elsie looked up at me. "The coach said the *f* word."

He didn't answer; he just stalked down the field toward the rest of the team.

The season was off to a terrific start.

CHAPTER NINE

"How did practice go?" Blake asked when we got home. He had swung by to drop off Elsie's leash, which she'd left at his apartment.

"It was interesting," my mother said, adjusting the crystals around her neck.

"The coach said the *f* word," Elsie announced.

"He what?"

"In his defense," my mother said, "Twinkles had just goosed him, so it wasn't unprovoked." Shooing the kids out of the kitchen, she asked, "Why don't you go and play?"

"Who is the coach, anyway?" Blake asked.

"A guy Margie had a date with," my mother informed him.

"Really," Blake said, giving me an appraising look.

"It was very brief," I said. "We didn't get along super well."

"Sounds like soccer is off to a great start," Blake said. "Are we sure this is the team for her?"

"Zoe and a lot of the first-grade girls are on the team," I said. "It's a social opportunity. I'm hoping it will help her make friends."

"Aren't there other teams?"

"I'll look," I said, "but I think maybe you should take her to practice tomorrow."

"Tomorrow?" Blake asked. "I thought it was a recreational team."

"He seems to take it very seriously," my mother said. "At least the other moms are entertaining. And the yoga instructor mom is lovely. She's going to help me with my Downward Dog on Monday."

"Terrific," I said, turning to Blake. "So can you take her to practice tomorrow?"

"I wish I could," he said, "but I have, uh, an appointment."

"That's right," my mother said. "It's that big female impersonator contest tomorrow night, isn't it?"

Blake turned purple.

"Uh, yes," he said.

"Isn't Frank going to be in that?" my mother asked. "I heard his Madonna impression makes him a top contender."

I turned to my husband. "Journey to Manhood must have been a smashing success."

"I think he took an alternate route, honey," my mother said.

"Great," I said. "What does he sing, 'Papa Don't Preach'?"

"Actually, 'Like a Virgin' is his specialty," Blake told me. "He's really good. He's going to audition in New York in a couple of weeks." He reached to adjust his collar and turned to my mother. "Connie, I meant to talk to you about that, actually. Do you think you could cover for me while I'm gone?"

"Anything for the kids," my mother said. I glared at her. She seemed to be just fine with Blake's new dating life. "Are you sure your mom isn't jealous?"

"Jealous?"

"Yes. I get the feeling she's not thrilled that I'm here. Something about her aura."

"I'm sure you're just imagining it," he said. "She's always liked you."

My mother didn't look convinced, but she didn't pursue it.

At that moment, my phone buzzed. I glanced at the screen; it was Pansy.

The cops just came by, she texted. *Call me.*

"I've got to go make a phone call," I said, adrenaline pumping through me—did the police know we'd moved the body? "I'm going to head back to the bedroom. If I'm not back before you go, I'll see you tomorrow."

"Not tomorrow," he reminded me.

"The impersonator show," my mother said.

"I'll take them next week, though, if it works with your schedule." My phone buzzed again. *Margie?*

"Fine," I said, and stalked down the hall to our former bedroom, wondering what I'd done in a former life to wind up in my current situation.

• • •

"Thanks so much for coming," Pansy said when I pulled up at her house twenty minutes later. I followed her through her enormous front hall to a cavernous kitchen that was the size of my entire house. "They just left," she said, sounding panicked. "It was the car that tipped them off. I think someone poisoned him, and I think they think it was me."

"Did they say anything about poison?"

"No," she said, grabbing a LifeBoost out of the fridge and offering one to me.

"These aren't the same ones, are they?" I asked.

"Of course not! But I'm a person of interest now, I think. They told me not to leave town."

"I'll pass on the drink, thanks. But at least they didn't arrest you," I said, trying to look on the bright side.

"Oh God. What would Isabella do?" she asked as she took the lid off the bottle and sat down at the kitchen island. I sat down next to her. "The whole school would be talking about it!"

"So let's figure out what happened," I said. "I'm guessing he didn't die of a heart attack, or they wouldn't have been here."

"But I can't think who might have killed him. He was such a nice man. So understanding and caring . . ."

I could hear the emotion in her voice. "Maybe someone was jealous," I suggested.

"Of what?"

"Of his relationship with you," I said, remembering the comments I'd heard from some of the other PTA moms. "Was he married?"

"I don't think so," she said. "He didn't wear a ring. He never really talked about himself; he always wanted to know more about me, and my life. We talked a ton about my husband . . . He's never here, and doesn't pay much attention to me when he is." Her face crumpled, and she looked very young. "Tristan used to tell me Mark didn't know what he was missing." She hiccupped. "I shouldn't be telling you all of this. It's just . . . I don't have anyone else to tell."

"I understand," I said. "I won't say anything to anyone."

"Everything is a mess. This . . . and we've got a big PTA meeting next week, and they're going to go over the finances, and I don't have any answers," she said. "If I lose the PTA post, they're going to elect someone like Phyllis, and it will be a total nightmare. The school needs me."

"I need the statements," I said. This was my second school embezzlement case so far; financials weren't exactly my forte, but if I had documents, Peaches and I might be able to figure something out.

"I made copies of them for you," she said, and pointed to a manila envelope on the kitchen table.

"Great," I said. "What about Tristan?"

"I don't know what to do," she said. "What should I do with his phone?"

"You still have it?"

"I . . . I couldn't get rid of it," she said. "I turned it off, though."

"Well, that's something," I said. I didn't think police could trace phones that weren't on. "Have you figured out how to get into it at all?"

"I didn't really try," she said.

"Maybe we should give it another shot," I said. "Just in case."

"In case what?"

"In case someone did kill him, and the police decide you look like an easy suspect."

"You don't think . . ."

"Who was the detective?"

"I think his name was Bunsen," she said, and my heart sank. Detective Bunsen and I had already tangled on two cases, and were not what I'd call fast friends.

"What?"

"Nothing," I said. No point in making her worry more.

• • •

We didn't have any luck with Tristan's phone, but Pansy was right; there were some pretty big checks written from the PTA account. Like five thousand dollars to a teacher supply store. And a few big withdrawals at ATM machines.

"So if I can't get copies of the checks, do you think the stores will have records?" I asked Peaches the next morning. I'd walked into the Pretty Kitten with two Starbucks coffees, grimacing at the sound of women in pain. There were days when I didn't care for my job—last night, for example—but I had to admit it was better than ripping pubic hair off other women. At least I was pretty sure it was.

Peaches put her stiletto-heeled feet on top of the desk and reached for her e-cig as the door swung closed behind me, muffling the sound of women groaning. "Did she give you access to the account?"

"I probably should have asked for that," I said.

"That would help," she said. "If you have access to the account, maybe the bank can help you track the withdrawals. Or you could go into the bank with the client."

"Good thinking," I told her. "The trainer's phone was in her living room, by the way. And the cops told her not to leave town; he was found dead at IronAbs Gym, but his car was parked by her house."

"She didn't notice it sitting in front of her house?"

"It was around the corner," I said.

"Ouch. How's she going to explain that?"

"She's just going to play dumb."

"Think the cops'll buy it?"

"She can be pretty persuasive," I told her.

"Any luck on the streaker?" she asked.

"Not yet," I said. "Their next meeting is this morning, though. I'm hoping it'll turn out better."

"He'll probably be expecting someone this time," she said. "You might want to just look like a dog walker or something."

"I don't have a dog."

"You have a pig, though," Peaches pointed out. "How's Twinkles doing, anyway?"

"Massive," I said.

"Comes by it honestly," Peaches said, reaching for another fried pork rind. "Bubba Sue wasn't exactly sylphlike. By the way, Wanda scheduled you to start as a temporary receptionist tomorrow." Thank God I'd managed to talk her down from the whole mystery shopper thing; from what I'd heard from the treatment rooms, I had no desire to experience a Brazilian wax personally.

"Tomorrow?" I asked. "But I'm on a case!"

"I know, but I've got to go to a dance-off with Jess, so I can't do it myself. Oh—I got your date set up for you, by the way."

"I've changed my mind," I said. The last thing I needed right now was another dating disaster; I had enough on my hands already.

"Too late," she said. "I already set it up. And I totally updated your profile."

"No."

"He's nice. And I didn't say anything about lingerie."

"And skydiving?"

"No skydiving at all. He seems like he'd be a fun night out, at least." She tapped on her keyboard and pulled up Match.com, then clicked on a profile of a good-looking man with high cheekbones and a head full of dark hair.

"Hmm. Wonder how old that photo is?" I asked.

"The hairstyle looks recent; I saw one the other day that looked like a mullet circa 1982. Anyway, get a load of this. 'Screenwriter and performance artist seeks easygoing, fun-loving woman who wants to write a new romantic story with me. Help me bring out my alter ego!'"

"Not too bad," I said. "Although screenwriters are a dime a dozen around here."

"At least he's not a gay lawyer," Peaches pointed out. "And if nothing else, it might be fun."

"It doesn't say a word about female impersonators, that's true." Then again, neither had Blake.

"Shall I say okay for tonight?"

"No," I said.

"Already cleared it with your mom and sent the e-mail," she said as she tapped away.

"Peaches!"

"I'll let you know what he says," she told me with a grin.

CHAPTER TEN

Twinkles and I pulled up at Zilker Park at ten thirty, about twenty minutes before the garden club meeting was supposed to start. I'd put her in the back of the van, which was not her preferred location, and my ears still hurt from the squealing.

"Relax," I said as I opened the back of the minivan and reached toward her collar. She gave me a nasty look and retreated.

"It'll be fun," I promised, but she didn't look convinced. "And it might involve hot dogs," I said, pulling the bag of cut-up, uncured, eight-dollars-a-pack hot dogs from my back pocket.

She gave the bag a sniff and then lunged for it.

"Walk first," I said, wrapping my arms around her and lifting her out of the back of the van. She immediately started nosing at my jeans, looking for hot dogs, as I attached the leash and closed the back of the van. "Come on," I wheedled, and started walking toward the path, holding out a piece of hot dog to persuade her. After a moment's hesitation, she lurched toward me, and by offering hot dog pieces at five-yard intervals, I managed to get her in the vicinity of the clubhouse.

I adjusted my hat and sunglasses—I was trying to go incognito—and slowed as I approached the building. I could see Willie, dressed in a turban and a Hawaiian-style maxi dress, sitting at a table with three other women, all of whom kept darting glances—some nervous, some rather hopeful—toward the plate glass window. Willie spotted me and waved. I gave her a quick nod and then shifted my focus to Twinkles, who was pulling on the leash and trying to yank me into a patch of poison ivy.

"Twinkles," I said sternly. "No."

But she wouldn't be dissuaded. Snuffling loudly, she continued to pull toward the patch of lush green foliage. "Twinkles, here's a hot dog. Look!" She dug in harder, then gave a sharp tug. I almost lost the leash.

I looked behind me and spotted a metal bench. "Come on," I said, trying to lure her with hot dog again. When she wouldn't move, I scooped her up and carried her across the trail to the bench. I couldn't help but notice that the women in the clubhouse had given up all pretense of meeting and were now staring openly. I got to the bench and tied the leash to the arm, then sat down and pulled a paperback book out of my purse. I'd suspected that our "walk" might not be particularly smooth, so I had put a book in my purse as Plan B.

As I opened the book—Sue Ann Jaffarian's *Too Big to Miss*—to the middle, pretending to read but really keeping an eye on the bushes on either side of the clubhouse, my phone buzzed. It was Frances.

We need to talk.

Great. Do you have the fry phone? Twinkles was pulling, but I did what the pig trainers on Google had suggested and ignored her. The idea was that not rewarding negative behavior with attention would help extinguish the behavior. I'd tried the same strategy with Elsie's dog fixation with poor results, but I was hoping pigs were more malleable than children.

Let's talk first, she replied—which sounded suspiciously like a ransom note. How was I going to tell Elsie her phone was being held hostage by a PTA mom?

The bench shifted a bit as Twinkles strained, but I just dug my feet in and texted back: *Do you have it?* There was a rustling sound now—it appeared to be coming from the poison ivy. Had she smelled a squirrel or a snake? I wondered. The bench moved again.

"Twinkles," I admonished. She tugged again, ignoring me, and the knot came loose. Before I could grab it, she hurtled across the path, directly into the poison ivy.

"Twinkles!" I yelled, shoving my phone in my pocket and racing after her. The last thing I needed was a runaway pig. She plunged further into the poison ivy. I hesitated, but the thought of Elsie's disappointed face when I told her I'd lost her pig in addition to her fry phone spurred me on, and I plunged in after her, already feeling itchy as the big leaves brushed against my bare arms.

I took two steps, and then something else barreled into me. My first thought was that it was Twinkles, but it was too tall—and Twinkles didn't have a horn.

It was the Shamrock Streaker in his Magical Unicorn mask.

"Shit!" we yelled at the same time, and cracked heads a moment later. He reached out unconsciously to clutch at me; I caught a whiff of Axe body spray and sausage.

So did Twinkles, apparently. As we tottered for a moment, Twinkles surged out of the undergrowth, teeth bared, and grabbed at the end of the shamrock sock. I looked down in horror. He appeared to have waxed—the slack skin was entirely hairless—and had a rainbow tattoo that extended from his left hip to the shamrock sock, as if what was underneath it were a pot of gold.

"Shit!" the streaker yelled again as the sock stretched, then popped off, affording both me and the ladies of the garden club a better view of the streaker than any of us—or at least I—wanted.

It wasn't a pot of gold.

He let go of me, reaching down to cover himself, and then took off, his unicorn horn listing to the right as he sprinted down the trail.

"Wait!" I called reflexively, not terribly surprised when he didn't do as I asked. I would have followed him, but I didn't want to lose

Twinkles, who was crashing off into the underbrush with her sock, leaving bits of the Hickory Farms sausage, which the streaker had evidently been packing, in her wake.

"Twinkles, stop!" I yelled. She didn't respond, either. I took off after her, and we sprinted past the plate glass window, which now had four women plastered against it.

• • •

Together, we emerged from the poison ivy onto the crushed-granite trail. She was surprisingly fast for such a large pig—and agile. She darted between pedestrians, narrowly skirted a triple-wide jogging stroller, and leaped over a tree root, with me gasping behind her. "Twinkles!" I yelled, ignoring the stares of fit passersby and wishing I'd spent a little more time at the gym. Or any time at the gym.

We'd gone about what felt like fifteen miles, but probably was only half a mile, before she paused and dropped her prize. I put on an extra burst of speed, seeing my opportunity . . . but as soon as I got within ten feet of her, she caught a glimpse of me from piggy eyes, grabbed the sock, and darted into a big stand of sticker burrs, the sock still trailing its broken dental floss.

The last I saw of her was her curly tail. She was gone.

• • •

"I lost Twinkles," I told Peaches as I headed for the house; already my skin felt like it was on fire, and my shorts were covered in burrs.

"Did you at least get the streaker?"

"No," I said as I turned out of Zilker Park, wondering how much of the poison ivy had transferred to the seat.

"What happened?"

"He was hiding in poison ivy and had stuffed his sock with a Hickory Farms sausage."

"Willie did say he filled that sock out well. And at least we now know to look for someone who's covered in a red rash."

"And a rainbow tattoo that ends at his groin. He waxed, too."

"Did he?"

"Either that or he was born hairless," I said.

"I'll ask Wanda if she's got any clients with rainbow tattoos," she said. "Not that it's much to go on. Austin's a big town."

"I'm heading home to take a bath in Caladryl lotion and make some 'Lost Pig' signs," I said.

"What are you going to tell Elsie?"

Oh God. First the fry phone, and now Twinkles. "I don't know. What do I tell her?"

"Tell her the truth. That Twinkles took off after a naked man wearing a unicorn mask, a sock, and a sausage," she said.

"Maybe I should get a job selling personal appliances after all," I said.

"What would be the fun of that?" she asked. "At least you'll be out on a date tonight," she reminded me.

I glanced at my swelling face in the rearview mirror. "Tonight?"

"Yeah. He wants to meet you at Ruth's Chris Steak House this evening."

"Terrific," I said. "If I keep swelling up, I'm going to look like the Elephant Woman."

"Think of it as a practice date. Besides, even if the date's a bust, at least you'll get a steak out of it," she said. "I told him you don't go Dutch."

"Thanks," I said.

"It's one of the few good things about being a woman in the South," she said. "Who said there's no such thing as a free dinner?"

"We'll see," I said. My experience was that you ended up paying the piper in the end. And it turned out I wasn't wrong.

CHAPTER ELEVEN

Despite thirty minutes in the shower with Ivarest and a wash-cloth, I was breaking out in welts by the time I got to Austin Heights Elementary that afternoon. Pansy and I had agreed to meet an hour before the meeting, and she recoiled when she saw me.

"What happened to you?" she asked as she led me back to the PTA closet. "Did you get one of those chemical peels?"

"The free kind," I told her. "I got dragged through poison ivy."

"Ouch." She winced. "Maybe it isn't the best day to get started?"

"I'm here. Besides, I need to talk to you about the bank account," I said in a low voice as we walked down the waxed tile corridor.

"What about it?"

"I assume you don't have receipts?"

"No one can find them," she said.

"If we go to the bank together, we can at least look at copies of the checks and withdrawals."

"Let's go tomorrow morning."

"Any more calls from the police?" I asked.

"Not yet. I'm thinking I might bring them donuts today . . . It always works for the teachers."

"I don't know if that's the best idea . . . They might think you were guilty, or something."

"I'll say I'm just showing appreciation. I might bring them some of those mini Bundt cakes next week. Well, here we go," she said as she fit a key into the lock and turned the knob. "You might want to stand back."

"What?" I asked, but too late. She opened the door, and a giant box of plastic balls came tumbling out, turning the second grade hallway into a Chuck E. Cheese's ball pit.

"Drat. Phyllis's been in here again." As she spoke, a bell rang; a moment later, children and two dismayed-looking teachers crowded into the hall. Another moment later, the air filled with flying balls.

"We don't throw things," admonished the younger of the two teachers, reaching down to grab the balls. "Now, let's put them all in the box that the nice lady is holding." The children all turned to me, and a few of them looked slightly scared.

"Is my face that bad?" I asked Pansy.

"It'll heal," she told me, reaching out to pat my hand, and then changing her mind.

"Put them in the box," the other teacher said, breaking the spell. Unfortunately, I had just righted the box and was standing behind it. A half second later, two dozen plastic balls came raining down on me, bouncing off and tumbling in all directions.

By the time the teachers had corralled the children and Pansy and I had corralled the balls, the welts on my skin made it look like I'd been flogged with stinging nettles.

"As you can see," Pansy said as we wedged the box of balls back into the closet, "it could use a little work. I'm so glad you've volunteered your organizational skills."

I gave her a weak smile. I hadn't volunteered anything—and if I had, organizational skills would have been last on the list. I couldn't even keep the cereal in the cereal cabinet, much less rein in the plastic-filled house of horrors that was the PTA closet.

"I think a few hours should have it all sorted out," she said, looking into the closet with a bemused smile, then turned to me. "But to be honest, you should probably go home and take some Benadryl, and maybe an oatmeal bath."

Together, we heaved our shoulders against the door until it closed. A crushed red plastic ball was still sticking out of the doorframe, looking a little like a deflated clown's nose, but I ignored it.

"You know," Pansy said as she locked the door and handed me the key, "I've got a bit of free time. Want to go to the bank now?"

"What about the Benadryl?"

"I'm sure the nurse has some," she said, trotting down the hall with me in her wake.

• • •

We got to the bank soon after that. My fingers had started to swell like sausages, and I was beginning to feel like an overripe tomato, but the nurse had assured me that the Benadryl would kick in soon. "I'm sure you'll be fine, but if you can't breathe, go to the ER," she'd said.

"That's encouraging. Thanks for the tip."

"Do you have an EpiPen?" she asked.

"The things they use for anaphylactic shock? No," I said.

"I'll give you the one I keep in the car," Pansy had told me.

"Are you sure I'll be okay?"

"Ninety percent," the nurse said. "Poison ivy's a pain in the patootie, isn't it?"

Twenty minutes later, I felt like my skin was splitting, but Pansy didn't seem worried.

"Can we help you?" the bank manager asked, giving me a bit of a concerned look. "Are you all right, ma'am?"

"Poison ivy," Pansy explained, and the manager recoiled slightly. "We'd like to add her to the PTA account," Pansy said.

"And we have a few questions, too," I added.

"Follow me," she said, and Pansy trotted after her to her cubicle, where we arranged ourselves across from her. "Driver's license, please?" she asked. I handed it over, and she looked back and forth from the picture to me.

"I promise it's her," Pansy said.

"Okay," the manager said.

As she pushed the forms across the desk to me, I said, "There have been a lot of withdrawals on the account recently. Is there any way to find out who made them?"

"Of course," she said. "I'll look and see which card it is." As I filled out the forms, she pulled up something on the computer. "Let's see. It looks like the card belongs to Pansy Parker."

"That's me," Pansy said. "But I haven't been making any withdrawals."

"All of them?" I asked the bank manager.

She ran through the list. "Yes," she said.

Pansy opened her purse and pulled out her wallet. "It's not here," she said, rifling through her cards.

"Did you lose it?" I asked.

"No," she said. "Someone must have taken it out of my purse."

"When did you last use it?"

"I never use it," she said. "I always come into the bank to make deposits."

"Let me see if I can get the video from the ATMs," the bank manager said.

"Here's my card," I said, pushing a Peachtree Investigations card across the desk to her.

She peered at it. "Is that a peach?"

"Theoretically. Anyway, please call me if you can get video."

"Can we freeze the account for now?" Pansy asked.

"It'll tip off the thief," I told her.

She sighed. "How long do you think it'll take to figure it out?"

"Only a couple of days, I hope," I said.

She sighed. "Fine. What's another couple thousand dollars, anyway?" she said gloomily. "At least if we catch whoever's doing it, we can get it all back."

Unless it was already spent, I thought but didn't say.

CHAPTER TWELVE

The PTA meeting was well attended, which was no surprise, since we'd all woken up to an article in the paper announcing that Austin Heights' favorite trainer had been found dead in a parking lot. Nothing like fresh gossip to boost attendance at a PTA meeting. Thankfully, the article said nothing about Pansy. Yet.

She interrupted the gossip with a call to order.

"Thanks for coming," she announced with a brittle smile. "I'd like to introduce Margie Peterson," she said. "Will you stand up, Margie? She's agreed to take over the PTA closet."

There were murmurs as I stood up and gave a little wave, and I heard the words *private investigator*. I sat down quickly after scanning the audience for Frances. She was in the back, wearing a pink tank top and shorts. I marked her position; I was not letting her get away without giving me Elsie's fry phone.

"Now," Pansy continued. "As you know, we've got a lot of important business to cover. Like baskets for the carnival."

"Don't put Josephine in charge of them again," Phyllis complained. "She used colored cellophane on them, so no one could see what was inside."

"Did you hear the new scoop on Tristan Prescott?" Janelle asked the woman next to her. Pansy's head whipped around.

"No," Pansy interjected, composing her face. "What about him?"

"It was in the paper this morning; they're thinking he was murdered," Janelle said.

Phyllis's hand moved to her throat. "Murdered?"

"They're doing an autopsy," she said. "They found him in the parking lot at the IronAbs Gym. I thought it was weird for someone so fit to have a heart attack or something," Janelle said. "Such a waste; he was so hot."

"Janelle! That's terrible!" a woman I didn't recognize said, but she looked more gleeful than horrified.

"You think it might have something to do with the fact that he was sleeping with half the moms in Austin Heights?" Janelle blurted. There was a collective intake of breath, and stunned silence. No one looked at Pansy, but three women cast sidelong glances at Frances, whose hand had leaped to her mouth and who was turning pale. "I'm kidding, ladies," Janelle said, apparently realizing she'd overstepped her bounds. "I'm sure it was an accident. Probably took too many supplements or something."

"I just saw him two days ago," somebody said.

"Ladies!" Pansy said. "A man has died. We need to think about his family."

"You're right," a short woman with brown hair said. "I wonder what happened?"

"Maybe someone got jealous," Janelle said.

"What?" Frances barked.

"You had a session with him this week, didn't you, Pansy?" Janelle asked. "Did he say anything?"

"What do you mean?" Pansy said, looking uncomfortable.

"About someone who might have wanted to kill him."

"I wouldn't be surprised if somebody's husband did him in," the brunette put in.

"What do you mean?" Phyllis asked sharply.

"I already told you. He was totally into MILFs," Janelle said.

"Ladies! We don't know anything about what happened to him yet," Pansy announced, as if she hadn't been trussed up to a Nautilus machine watching when Tristan met his maker and the police hadn't questioned her about her involvement with the dead man—something I didn't think they did for straight-heart-attack victims. "And this has nothing to do with the school carnival. Let's cut the gossip and get down to business, shall we?"

"But . . ."

"She's right," Chantal said. "This carnival isn't going to plan itself! Besides, we still need to talk about having a gluten-free, sugar-free option for the cake walk."

"I still think we should do the *Magic of Tidying Up* thing in the supply closet. You know, only keep the things that bring us joy?" someone suggested.

"There'd be nothing left," Janelle said, "unless you have a thing for pipe cleaners and googly eyes."

As we settled down to an in-depth discussion of themed carnival auction baskets and the merits of stevia and rice flour in baked goods, I found myself looking at Frances, who had been remarkably quiet. She was still pale and looked as if she were about to burst into tears at any moment. I was guessing Pansy wasn't the only one Tristan was seeing on the side.

If Tristan had been murdered—and I had a feeling he had been—there was no shortage of potential suspects. I was definitely going to have a chat with Frances—and decided it might be a good idea to invite Janelle out for drinks.

· · ·

As soon as the meeting was over, I made a beeline for Frances, who was heading for the door. "Frances!"

She turned, looking stricken.

"The fry phone," I said. "Do you have it?"

"You're a private investigator, right?" she asked. "I need to hire you."

"I'm already kind of full up at the moment," I said.

"I need to hire you to find some money for me. But I don't have money to pay you."

"I can't take pro bono cases," I said.

"It's not pro bono," she told me. "I've got your daughter's fry phone."

"What? You're kidding me," I said.

"I'm not." She glanced over her shoulder. "Meet me at the Starbucks by Randall's in an hour."

"But . . ."

She flashed me her phone; it was a picture of the fry phone sitting next to a gas barbecue. I felt my breath catch.

"Just do it," she said, and turned on her sparkly wedge heel.

I was still staring after Frances when Pansy collared me. "I thought it might be a good time to take another look at the supply closet," she said, steering me down a hallway away from the gaggle of gossiping women. "What's going on?" she asked in a low voice when we were out of earshot.

"Nothing," I said, still processing Frances's threat . . . and the image of the fry phone next to the grill.

"You look upset. Is something wrong?"

"No," I said, "but I have an appointment in an hour, so I have to run. Have you talked with the police any more?"

"Not yet," she said, looking pale under her professional-grade makeup, "but I have a feeling they'll be by again. Can you find out what happened to him?"

"I've done it before," I said.

"I'm hiring you for this case, too," she said.

"Fine," I said as we got to the closet. "Any idea who might have done him in?"

"No," she said. "The only thing I can think of is something to do with his business. It was doing really well."

"Do you know who gets his share of it?" I asked.

"He didn't say. It would be worth looking into, though. I still have his phone, by the way. I've been trying to figure out the pass code."

"Did you turn it on at your house?"

"I know it's risky," she said. "I was home alone last night, and I couldn't leave Isabella by herself, so I turned it on. I thought it just might be the clue we need. Anyway, just find out what happened, okay?" She eyed the closet door.

"I'm not so hot at organization, just so you know," I said.

"I'm sure you'll be able to do something with it," she told me as she unlocked the door and opened it, releasing two dozen plastic bouncy balls and a small avalanche of construction paper.

"Um . . . Wow," I said, impressed all over again by the chaos. "Who had closet duty last year?"

"Janelle," she said. "I wouldn't be surprised if there were a few Jack Daniel's bottles back in here somewhere, to be honest."

"What exactly do you want me to do with this?" I asked, surveying the piles of school supplies. It looked like someone had set a group of angry toddlers loose in a teacher supply store.

"Whatever you can," she said, bending down to retrieve a ball. Together, we gathered the balls and paper, wedged them back into the closet, and leaned against the door until we heard the latch click.

"You could suffocate in there," I said.

"It's pretty bad," she admitted.

We were just turning to go back to the PTA meeting room when I recognized a familiar voice.

It was Detective Bunsen.

"You? Again?" Bunsen peered at my swollen face. "What the hell happened to your face?"

"It's a long story," I said, blushing—not that anyone would notice, since my face was already the color of a clown nose. "What are you doing here?"

"I wanted to talk to her," he said, indicating Pansy, who had turned pale. "But now I'd like to talk to you, too. What are you two up to back here?"

"PTA business," Pansy said.

"We were just assessing the supply closet," I said.

"The supply closet?" Bunsen asked.

"It's a mess," Pansy said, brandishing the key. "Want to see?"

"Not really," he said. "But we would like to know why we were able to track Tristan Prescott's phone to your house."

Pansy blanched. "What?" she barked.

"We have a search warrant," he said. He showed her the document. "We'll be searching your house this afternoon."

"I don't understand," Pansy said, drawing herself up. "Why are you searching my house?"

"Let's see," he said. "A dead man's car was found around the corner from your house. You were spotted near the body and evaded officers." He stared at Pansy. "And now the deceased's phone is evidently located in your house."

She swallowed. "I need to call an attorney," she said.

"That sounds like it would be a good idea. But we've got a few questions to ask you first. And your pal, too," he said, glaring at me.

"Here?" Pansy asked. "If the other parents know you're here to talk to me, it could be bad for my credibility."

"We'll duck into a classroom," he said. "No one needs to know."

"How about the coffee place down the street?" I asked.

He ignored me, and as he ushered us both to an empty classroom, one of the kindergarten classes filed out into the hall, and we were fixed by twenty pairs of curious eyes.

"Terrific," Pansy groaned as we followed Bunsen into the room.

• • •

"Well, that wasn't too bad," Pansy said when we emerged thirty minutes later. I glanced at my watch; I had to leave within fifteen minutes to get to Starbucks.

"I'm impressed that you didn't answer any questions," I said.

"I couldn't. My attorney wasn't here yet." She twisted her hair. "What if they find Tristan's fingerprints in my house?" She blushed. "Oh my God. Or on the Passion Party toys in the bottom of my underwear drawer?"

"Well, he was your trainer," I reminded her. "All we can do is find out what happened. If worse comes to worst, I can testify that I found you . . . incapacitated."

"But it would be all over town, then," she said. "And my husband would divorce me."

"But you wouldn't be in jail," I pointed out.

"There's got to be another way. I think the business is where we should be looking," she said. "Follow the money, my husband always says."

"Speaking of husbands," I said, "is it possible yours knew what was going on with you and Tristan?"

Her eyes got big. "Are you thinking that Mark might be responsible?"

"It's possible," I said. "Jealous people do all kinds of things."

"But then I'd be married to a murderer! And Isabella . . ."

"It's just a possibility," I said. "Something to think about. Where was he that afternoon?"

"At work, of course," she said.

"Any way to know that for sure?"

"I guess I could look at his appointment schedule," she said. "But do you really think he might have killed Tristan?"

"I don't know." And I didn't. How could he have been sure he'd poison Tristan and not Pansy? Or did he care? And how had Tristan really died, anyway?

"That's horrible!" she said. "What if he decided to kill me, too?"

"Has he acted differently lately?" I asked.

She shook her head. "Same old same old. Normal boring life. He does his job, and I do mine."

For a moment, I found myself jealous—I missed that normal, boring life. But I put that aside.

Pansy smoothed her skirt. "I wish I knew how long they were going to be in the house. I can take Isabella for ice cream and then to the mall, but what do I tell Mark?"

"You never told me; does he know about you and Tristan?"

"Of course not!" she said.

"The rest of Austin Heights seems to," I said. "You might want to have a chat with him."

"But what if he's the murderer?"

"You've lived with him for years. What's a few more days?"

"I never should have agreed to sleep with that man," she said. "I'm such a sucker for a nice butt. It's terrible."

"Is this your first affair?" I asked, curious.

She gave me a sidelong glance. "Have you met my husband? I didn't marry him for his bedroom skills. We have . . . an arrangement."

"An arrangement?"

"It's not official or anything," she said, "but he provides the money, and I keep myself in good shape and take care of whatever Isabella needs," she said.

"Are you sure he doesn't know about your affair?"

"I don't think he does," she said.

"Does he have affairs?"

She blinked at me. "Why would he? He's married to me."

I didn't say anything, but I had to admire her self-confidence.

"What am I going to tell him about the cell phone?"

"Say you found it on the sidewalk and didn't know whose it was," I suggested. "Tell him you were going to take it to the school lost and found."

"That'd be a good thing to tell the police, too," she said.

"Talk to your attorney and call me later," I said. "I've got to run."

• • •

When I got to Starbucks, Frances was waiting for me, sipping a cup of coffee and looking nervous. I skipped the line and just sat down across from her.

"What do you want?" I asked.

"I've got a problem," she said.

"I gathered. You're missing money?"

She nodded.

"I invested in a business," she said.

"And?"

"It was secret," she said, her eyes darting around the room. "I was supposed to get my money back as soon as the big investors came in. But now . . ."

"Now what?"

She lowered her voice. "The person I gave the money to is dead."

"Oh no," I said. "Tristan?"

She burst into tears. "Yes," she said. "I was helping him get his LifeBoost business started, and he was going to pay me back with interest, and now . . . now he's dead!"

"Surely whoever takes over the business will pay you back?"

"That's the thing, though. It was supposed to be under the table, so I didn't get any documents . . . and now there's no record of it!"

"No checks?"

She shook her head. "Cash. I took it out of the bank account."

"And he didn't give you a receipt?"

She grimaced.

"How much?"

Her eyes filled with tears. "Twenty thousand."

I blinked. "Dollars?"

"That's why I can't pay you," she said. "I have to put that money back into the account before my husband sees the investment records. He has no idea."

"You didn't talk about it with him?"

"He didn't know about our . . . relationship."

"Oh," I said, understanding. "You were having an affair."

"Shhh!" she said. "Not so loud!"

"So you want me to get your money back," I said. "How am I supposed to do that?"

"I don't know," she said, then leaned back. "But I've got your daughter's fry phone. That should help get the creative juices flowing."

"You would do that to her? Would you do that to your own daughter?"

"Of course not to my own daughter," she said. "But I'm in a desperate situation. And desperate times call for desperate measures."

"If I agree to take the case, will you give me the fry phone?"

"No," she said.

"What if I waive the fee?"

"You're already waiving the fee."

For a woman who had forked over twenty grand to her personal trainer and not asked for a receipt, she was driving an awfully hard bargain.

"I want that phone."

"I want my twenty thousand dollars. And if you say a word to anyone, you can kiss that phone good-bye."

We were at an impasse.

"Okay," I said finally. "I'll do it." What choice did I have? "But you have to tell me what you know about Tristan."

"Why?"

"It may help," I said to her.

"Fine," she said. She raised her hands and spread them about six inches apart. "He was about yea long, with a little curve—"

"That's not what I mean."

"Oh. Sorry," she said, blushing. "He was pretty amazing, though." She looked forlorn for a moment. "Anyway, he was single. We'd been seeing each other for about six months; he got the idea for the company about a year ago, when a friend's bottling plant lost a big contract."

"How was he getting funding?"

"I think friends, mainly. He was courting a big investor, though . . . It just came through about a month ago. He kept saying he was going to pay me back with ten percent interest, and then this happened . . ."

"Who was the investor?"

"Steven Maxwell. He's one of the big venture capitalists in town."

"Why don't you go and talk to him?"

"Because he knows my husband," she said. "And my husband isn't supposed to know."

"I'm a little unclear," I said. "He's not supposed to know you gave money to Tristan for LifeBoost, but you want me to somehow get you your money back."

"That's right," she said.

"How do you propose I do that?"

She shrugged. "You're the professional. That's your job." Her phone buzzed and she looked down at it. "I've got to go pick up the kids. You've got until the end of next week."

"That's it?"

"That's when the next statement closes at Fidelity," she said. "The money needs to be back in the account by then." She finished her coffee, stood up, and smoothed down her pink tank top. "Nice talking to you. I'll touch base tomorrow."

Terrific, I thought as I watched her wobble out of the Starbucks. I sat for a minute digesting what had just happened. Then I threw out her empty cup and followed her out the door.

CHAPTER THIRTEEN

My mom took over kid-chauffeuring duties, and I spent the rest of the afternoon plastering Zilker Park with "Lost Pig" signs and checking my phone. Frances texted me two more photos of the fry phone: one dangling over a garbage disposal, and the other in a microwave oven. When I got back, Elsie was still inconsolable without her two attachment objects, and had curled up on her dog bed, refusing to do her homework and snapping at anyone who came near. I felt like the worst mother in the world.

"I'm so sorry to leave you," I told my mother, who was hanging crystals in the kitchen window as the kids sat down to what I'd generously call "dinner."

"Why? Peaches said this guy was handsome. And an artist, too. That would be a nice change after all your years with an attorney."

"Mom!" I said, nodding toward Elsie and Nick, who were looking at the brownish-green substance on their plates. As I watched, Nick threatened to flick some of it across the table at his sister. Elsie responded with a menacing growl and bared her teeth before climbing down from her chair and crawling back to the sofa cushion she called her dog bed. I made a mental note to pick up a loaf of Mrs Baird's white bread on the way home.

"Maybe the crystals will help," my mother said in a worried tone as my daughter curled up into a ball and started licking her own leg.

"The food change doesn't seem to be making much of a difference," I commented. Of course, Elsie hadn't actually eaten any of the vegan delicacies my mother had concocted—I'd been secretly feeding her cheese sticks, apple slices, and white bread to keep her from starving—but it didn't keep my mother from trying.

"Give it time," she said.

It had been six months, and although she was doing better in school now that we'd moved her out of Holy Oaks, she persisted in her Pekingese fixation. My mother-in-law, Prue, was convinced it was a response to my failing marriage with Blake, but I wasn't so sure. I hadn't seen much of Prue since Blake introduced his boyfriend during a family dinner a few months ago. I knew his father was holding out hope that Blake's fixation with cross-dressing men was a phase. The kids had met Frank but were still operating under the assumption he and Blake were just friends. Since Blake and Frank had moved in together, I didn't know how long that little fiction could last.

"Nick seems to be doing fine, at least," she said after Elsie's brother joined her in the living room. I retrieved their full plates from the kitchen table and attempted to chisel off the goo. I hoped she was right.

"What is this stuff, anyway?" I asked as I scraped the last of the mold-colored substance from Elsie's plate.

"It's called Soylent," she said.

"What is it, though?"

"It's the complete nutrition package," she said. "Full of prana, and completely anti-inflammatory. No artificial anything, but it tastes delicious."

"I can tell," I said dryly, wrinkling my nose at the cruciferous tang wafting up from the drain. Even if tonight's date was a total bust, I told myself, at least I'd be eating steak instead of reconstituted soy protein laced with cauliflower.

"Any word on Twinkles yet?" my mother asked in a low voice, glancing toward the living room. I'd told Elsie that Twinkles was visiting her mom, Bubba Sue.

"Nothing yet," I said. "But surely someone will call. I mean, how many pigs can there possibly be running around Austin?"

"I hope she doesn't end up on a spit."

"Thanks for the encouragement. At least I know a little more about the Shamrock Streaker," I said. I told her about the rainbow tattoo I'd seen on his wrinkled, hairless stomach.

"Was the tattoo saggy, or did it look kind of crisp?"

"It looked relatively recent, if that's what you're asking."

"Have you considered calling tattoo parlors and asking around?"

"Are you kidding me? That would take years; I think half the population of Austin is tattooed. Besides, I was too busy putting up 'Lost Pig' signs." And trying to figure out how to get Frances's money back. I hadn't heard anything from Pansy since the meeting today, but something told me that wouldn't last.

As I put Elsie's plate into the dishwasher, my mother peered at me. "You look pretty bad, Margie."

"I took some more Benadryl," I said. "Hopefully it will kick in soon."

"If not," she said, "you might want to ask your date to drive you to the emergency room."

"Is it that bad?"

"Let's just hope the Benadryl works. Don't worry about me tonight." She smiled. "A friend of mine is going to come and watch a movie with me once I've got the kids down."

"Thanks so much. Would you make sure Elsie does her spelling words?"

"Of course," she replied, assessing my swollen face again. "Are you sure you're going to be okay?" Despite the liberal application of a tube of cortisone cream and half a bottle of Mary Kay foundation, my eyes still looked like slits in a red balloon.

"It's too late to cancel. Besides, I want to get this over with."

"Well, have fun," she said in a doubtful tone. Elsie growled from her makeshift dog bed. I felt terrible leaving my mother to deal with the fallout of the last few days; I was going to have to treat her to lunch at her favorite macrobiotic restaurant soon.

Not for the first time, I cursed Frances Pfeffer . . . and prayed Twinkles was okay.

• • •

By the time I got to Ruth's Chris, my face looked like a skinned tomato, and the Benadryl made me feel like I was swimming through pudding. I skipped the valet parking and eased the Dodge Caravan in between a Lamborghini and a Smart car, then squeezed my feet into the stilettos Becky had lent me and trotted down the sidewalk toward the restaurant, hoping my Spanx wouldn't explode. The bar was empty when I walked in, and for a moment I couldn't decide if I was relieved or disappointed. I ordered the happy hour drink special before I remembered I was on Benadryl and retreated to an overstuffed chair by the lobster tank to keep an eye on the door.

Now, as I sat watching the lobsters in the tank climb over each other in hopes of finding a way out, I found myself wondering if I should have gone ahead and canceled the date. I had pulled up my phone and was about to text him to cancel when the front door opened and a handsome man with dark hair and chiseled cheekbones walked in. I took a reckless sip of my drink and smiled, feeling as if the movement might make my skin split open. He scanned the bar, and when his eyes came to rest on me, his eyebrows went up as he registered my appearance, a reaction that might have been shock and might have been surprise. I glanced at my hazy reflection in the lobster tank and took another sip of my drink, wishing I were anywhere but here. Even the lobster tank might be an improvement.

"Fabian?" I inquired as he began moving toward me with an expression that struck me as apprehensive. His left hand was stuffed into his jacket pocket, but he extended his right as he approached, looking wary. I think at that moment we might both have preferred to be in the lobster tank.

"Margie?" he said tentatively in a rich, baritone voice. "You look more . . ."

"Swollen?" I finished for him. "I had a run-in with the poison ivy thicket today. I was about to text to cancel when you showed up."

He smiled, looking relieved. I shook his hand; it was warm and reassuring. Maybe this dating thing wouldn't be so bad after all, I reflected, taking another swig of my drink.

"I'll let the hostess know we're here," he said. I stood up and followed him, tottering in my too-tall heels. The Spanx had begun dividing my midsection in two; it felt a little like being trapped in a circular vise.

"We have your table ready." The slim young hostess beamed at Fabian. Her mouth drooped as she turned to me and registered my blimplike countenance, and her tweezed eyebrows shot up toward her hairline.

"Poison ivy," I explained, feeling as if my face were turning redder, if that was possible.

We followed her through the cavernous dining room to an intimate table near the kitchen. "Your waitress will be right with you," she said in a hushed voice, as if she were an undertaker delivering bad news. She seated us, then shot me another furtive glance before gliding back toward the front of the restaurant.

"So," he said, "you're a private investigator. That must be very interesting."

"It can be," I replied, relaxing a little bit. "And you are a performance artist?"

"Yes," he said. "In fact, I'm preparing for an upcoming show."

"Really? When is it?"

"It debuts next month," he told me, flashing a white-toothed smile. His dark hair was shiny, and his eyes had cute little crow's-feet at the corners when he smiled. I could feel my heart go pitter-pat. I just hoped my balloonlike face wouldn't put him off.

"Is it a play?"

"It's more of a one-man show. Or two men actually." As he spoke, his left hand shot up from beneath the table.

It was covered with a white athletic sock.

CHAPTER FOURTEEN

S omeone had glued orange yarn hair, googly eyes, and two red pipe cleaners to it. "You bet it's a two-man show," Fabian said out of the corner of his mouth in a squeaky voice that reminded me of Elmo. As I watched in horror, the sock's mouth opened and closed, ending in a leering grin. "This guy here wants to take all the credit. We all know who's the real star of the show, though, don't we, Fabian?"

"He's a little full of himself," Fabian said in his normal voice, giving me a rueful grin.

"What happened to her face?" the sock puppet asked, closing its pipe cleaner mouth primly and inspecting me with plastic eyes. "She looks like an overstuffed sausage."

"Marshmallow, we talked about being rude." Fabian admonished the sock in a stern tone, then turned to me. "I'm sorry about that. I'm still working on manners with him."

I didn't know what to say, so I reached for my drink and finished it, looking wildly for the waiter and wondering if it was too late to jump into the lobster tank.

"So," I said, trying to sound casual. "Did you make your puppet yourself?"

Marshmallow's pipe cleaner lips curled, as if it had just eaten the lemon slice out of Fabian's water glass. "What did she call me?" the puppet—er, Fabian—squeaked.

Fabian's right hand reached out and began stroking Marshmallow's orange yarn hair.

"It's okay, buddy," he cooed to the puppet. "I'm sure she was only joking." He looked up at me, then put his fingers on the sides of Marshmallow's head. "Marshmallow is very sensitive."

"I . . . I'm sorry," I said searching again for the waiter.

"You're not the first," Fabian said. "When he saw the playbill for our upcoming performance, he wouldn't talk to me for three days."

"They didn't even put my name on the page," Fabian added in that squeaky Elmo voice.

"You might want to apologize," Fabian told me in his normal baritone voice, his handsome face looking very serious.

"But . . . I did."

"Not to me. To Marshmallow." As Fabian spoke, the sock puppet nodded its cotton head slowly. For a brief moment I wondered if somebody had substituted something else for the Benadryl. After a quick glance around to make sure nobody was in earshot, I leaned forward, looking at the sock puppet's wrinkled face, and said, "I'm sorry," in the same tone of voice I used with my four-year-old. Fabian and his sock puppet sat silent for a moment; then the puppet's mouth moved and Fabian squeaked, "Apology accepted."

Fabian smiled. "Well, I'm glad we have that out of the way. I sometimes wish he didn't have such an artistic temperament, but I suppose that's what makes him so talented."

At that moment, thankfully, the waiter materialized at my left elbow. We must have been an interesting sight: between Fabian's sock puppet and my balloonlike face, we looked like we were ready to run away to the circus . . . or had recently escaped. "Can I get you something to drink, ma'am?" the young man asked me.

"Another one of these, please," I said, pointing to my drink. Benadryl or no Benadryl, I needed it.

"Very good, ma'am," he said, then turned to Fabian, studiously ignoring the bright-orange-and-white puppet peering over the table like a periscope. "And for you, sir?"

"Scotch on the rocks for me," Fabian said, "and a Shirley Temple for Marshmallow."

"With extra cherries, please," the sock puppet piped up.

"And a straw, I presume?" the waiter inquired as if there were nothing unusual about a sock puppet ordering a Shirley Temple with extra cherries.

"Please," squeaked Marshmallow. I resisted the urge to beg the waiter to hurry. A moment later we were alone again: Fabian, me, and Marshmallow the sock puppet.

"What's your show about?" I asked, resisting the urge to scratch my cheek. My face felt like it was on fire.

"It's kind of a romance," Fabian told me, chucking Marshmallow under its chin. "The story of how we met, and how our relationship developed . . ."

"Romance?" I asked. "Between you and the pup—I mean, Marshmallow?"

"Exactly," he said, and began describing how he and Marshmallow had met outside a Laundromat in South Austin. As he recounted their past—they'd "met" five years ago—Marshmallow chimed in with salient details he'd forgotten. Was this split personality disorder? I found myself wondering. I could see why he was successful as a performance artist; it was a little like having a front-row seat at the insane asylum.

"Marshmallow's looking very crisp for five years old," I said.

"He takes grooming very seriously," Fabian said. As he spoke, the host seated another couple a few tables away from us. The woman shot a curious glance in our direction; I wasn't sure if it was because of my swollen face, or the fact that my dinner partner had a sock puppet, but I just smiled politely and she looked away.

Fabian was detailing the process by which they washed Marshmallow's hair (Woolite and cold water) when the waiter shimmered up to the table with our drinks. As I fell on my gin and tonic, Fabian positioned the straw between Marshmallow's pipe cleaner lips before taking a sip of his own scotch. The waiter lingered for a moment. "Have you decided yet?" he asked.

"I think so," I said, anxious to get this evening moving. I ordered the small sirloin, medium rare, and Fabian went for the filet.

"And for your friend?" the waiter asked, nodding toward Marshmallow. I had to give him tons of credit for keeping a straight face.

"He had a big lunch," Fabian explained. "I think we'll share." Marshmallow nodded sagely. "If you could just bring a second plate, that would be perfect. And a bottle of Cakebread Cabernet, please."

"Very good," the waiter said, and shimmered away, leaving me very glad I wasn't picking up the tab. My cursory glance at the wine list had revealed no bottles under fifty dollars.

The three of us were alone together. Again.

There was an awkward silence. "So," Fabian said. "I understand you enjoy karaoke?"

I almost choked on my drink. "I what?"

"Your profile," he said. "You said you like karaoke."

"Oh yes," I said, taking another swig and feeling a bit woozy. I really was going to have to take a closer look at that profile. "How about you?" I asked, trying to turn the conversation away from myself.

"I'm not very good at it, but Marshmallow does a terrific rendition of '9 to 5,'" he said. As he launched into another monologue about Marshmallow, there was a high-pitched giggle from the nearby table. The two lovebirds were leaning into each other, and he was stroking her left hand with his right. There was no ring on her ring finger, I noticed. Another divorcée?

"Margie?"

My eyes jerked back to Fabian, who was looking at me expectantly. "Sorry," I said. "I took some Benadryl, and it's making me a bit foggy. What?"

"I was asking about your last major relationship," he said.

"Oh," I said. "I was married. It didn't work out."

"I'm sorry to hear that," he said. "I've been through a few of those myself."

"What happened?" I asked, although I was pretty sure I had a good idea.

"They wanted to kick me out of the bedroom," Marshmallow announced.

"Ah," I said. My phone buzzed. I fished it out of my purse and looked at a text from Blake. "Crap."

"What's wrong?"

"My daughter lost her pig, and she's having a meltdown," I said.

"She has a pig?" Fabian asked. "Kind of a weird pet."

That was pretty rich, I thought, coming from a man who took a sock puppet on a date, but I just smiled. "It's a sweet pig."

"House-trained?"

"We're working on it," I said. Nick had taken to calling her Tinkles thanks to her penchant for urinating in the middle of the living room rug. I texted back, suggesting Blake take her out for ice cream, and asking where my mother was.

It's not working, the text came back. *She wants to talk to you.*

"Will you excuse me for a moment?" I asked, and got up without waiting for an answer. I walked past the couple on the way to the ladies' room; they were huddled together, and he was looking at her as if he couldn't wait to get through the main course so he could have her as dessert. I dialed as I walked; Blake picked up on the second ring.

I could hear Elsie moaning in the background.

"I'm so sorry to bother you," he said, "but I was hoping you could talk with Elsie. She just finished reading *Charlotte's Web*, and now she's falling apart."

"Where's my mom?"

"I told her to go to yoga and I'd take over."

"Thanks," I said. "Put Elsie on."

A moment later, I heard Elsie's whining on the other end of the line. "Are you okay, sweetheart?" I asked.

"I miss Twinkles!" she sobbed. "Can we go get her from Bubba Sue's house?"

"Not now," I said, resolving to redouble my efforts to find the wayward pig. Why had I told her she was at Bubba Sue's house? What would I do if I couldn't find her? "Why don't you take a nice, warm bath and ask Daddy to get you some ice cream?"

"But I want Twinkles," she cried. "And my fry phone."

"I'm so sorry sweetie," I said, and there was a clunk. "Elsie!"

"She dropped the phone," Blake said. "How are . . . er . . . things going?"

"My date brought a sock puppet named Marshmallow," I said, feeling a little strange talking about it with my husband. "It's more of a threesome than a date."

"A sock puppet named Marshmallow?" he repeated. "Frank knows that guy. He's got a one-man show coming up, doesn't he?"

"Marshmallow wasn't too crazy about the description on the play-bill, apparently."

"You know how to find the nut jobs, don't you?" he asked.

I bit my tongue. At least I wasn't dating a former Christian gay-reform counselor who had morphed into a Madonna impersonator.

"Anyway, what do I do about Elsie?" he continued.

"Take her to ice cream," I said. "I'll be home in a couple of hours."

"Where is Twinkles, anyway?"

"I lost her at Zilker Park," I said. "But don't tell Elsie."

"How did you lose her?"

"She took off after a sausage," I said, declining to mention that the sausage had been stuffed into a shamrock sock and attached to a naked man with a rainbow tattoo on his stomach. "Anyway, I've got to get back to my date. Just take them out for ice cream and try to distract her with stories."

"What happened to the fry phone, by the way?"

"It's a long story," I said. "I've got to run. Good luck."

"Are you going to get another pig if Twinkles doesn't show up?"

"Can we not talk about this now?" I asked.

"Right. Go back and enjoy your date. Tell Marshmallow I said hi."

"You're the one who wanted me to start dating," I pointed out, and hung up. I stepped into the ladies' room and confirmed that the Benadryl had done nothing to reduce the swelling. At the rate things were going, my eyes would be swollen shut before dessert. I splashed some water on my face, reapplied cortisone cream, and headed back to the table.

The steak arrived at the same time I did. It smelled delicious; if nothing else, I thought, at least I'd get a dinner that didn't involve cauliflower or kale.

"Thanks," I told the waiter as he drifted back toward the kitchen, and picked up my fork and knife. I'd cut my first piece when I realized Fabian hadn't picked up his utensils.

"Do you mind cutting up the steak for us?" he asked. "Marshmallow doesn't like to hold the knife in his mouth."

I looked over at Marshmallow, whose mouth was clamped around the straw. Half the Shirley Temple was gone. I hoped it was Fabian who had drunk it.

"Um . . . Sure," I said, reaching over and cutting his steak into bits, wondering how I had gotten into this situation. When I'd finished reducing the filet to manageable pieces, I returned to my sirloin.

"Would you mind putting some pieces on Marshmallow's plate?" he asked.

"Fine," I said, pushing a half dozen steak pieces over to Marshmallow. "Enough?" I asked.

"A few potatoes, too, please," Fabian said in that squeaky voice. I dished some out for each of them and then returned my attention to my own plate, trying not to watch as Marshmallow dipped down and began picking up bits of steak in its mouth and pretending to chew them. I was starting to understand the need for Woolite.

"Is everything cooked to your satisfaction?" the waiter asked as Marshmallow dug into the scalloped potatoes.

"It's delicious," I said, and Marshmallow nodded enthusiastically. The couple nearby turned to watch, not bothering to try to look as if they weren't staring, and I chewed my steak methodically. At least I wasn't home trying to console an inconsolable six-year-old, I tried to tell myself, but it didn't help much.

I had just finished cutting up Fabian's asparagus when my phone buzzed. It was a text from Peaches. *How's it going?*

Don't ask, I texted back, and put the phone in my purse as Marshmallow reached down and picked up a chunk of filet. The puppet was quiet during dinner, thankfully. Marshmallow's approach to dining appeared to be to masticate the food and then spit it back out onto the plate. By the time we were done, Marshmallow was covered in cheese and steak juice, and the plate in front of the puppet looked as if someone had regurgitated. In a way, I supposed, someone had.

"Shall we split dessert?" Fabian asked.

"No," I said, too fast. I could only imagine what Marshmallow would do with a crème brûlée. "I've probably got to get home; my daughter's having a rough night."

His eyes narrowed. "I didn't know you had kids, by the way."

"I have two of them," I said.

"You didn't mention them in your profile," he said frostily.

"You didn't mention Marshmallow," I replied with a smile.

There were a few moments of stony silence. "How long have you been divorced?" he asked.

"I'm not yet, actually. Just separated."

Fabian recoiled. "To be honest," he said, "I don't see us being much of a match, anyway. Marshmallow's not enamored of you, and that's kind of a deal breaker for me."

"It's kind of mutual, I'd say," I said, trying not to be offended that I'd been dissed by a sock puppet. "I'm not into hand washing sock puppets, so it's probably for the best."

Fabian looked stricken.

"She hurt my feelings. And I have to go to the bathroom," Marshmallow squeaked. Or rather, Fabian did, out of the corner of his mouth. People were very strange, I decided.

Fabian shot me an apologetic look. "If you'll excuse us," he said.

"No problem," I told him, finishing the last of my steak as Fabian got up and headed to the restroom with Marshmallow. The other couple looked as if they were smothering giggles as he passed. I couldn't blame them.

My phone buzzed, and I retrieved it from my purse; it was Blake. *It's not working.*

The ice cream didn't work?

She only wants her fry phone or Twinkles, he replied.

I'll be home soon, I responded.

My phone rang as soon as I hit "Send." It was Pansy.

"Margie, you've got to help me," she said.

"What?"

"They came to the house and arrested me. I'm in the Travis County Jail."

"Do you have an attorney?" I asked, gripping the phone hard.

"I do, but all he does is estate planning."

"Probably not too helpful," I said. "Does your husband know?"

"No," she said, "and he's in Toronto right now. I've got a neighbor taking care of Isabella, but how am I going to explain this to her?"

"Let's worry about getting you out for now," I told her. "I'll see what I can find out about getting you out on bond . . . and I'll look into a criminal defense attorney."

"Criminal defense attorney? Oh my God," she said. It had sunk in. "It's going to be all over the paper."

"What did they arrest you for?"

"Murder," she said. "It's going to destroy my reputation."

Since Texas was a capital punishment state, it might destroy a whole lot more than her reputation, but I decided not to bring that up. "Like I said, if it comes to it, I'll testify about how I found you."

"That would be so humiliating!"

"Let's just hope it doesn't come to that, then. I'll make a few calls," I promised.

"Please. Hurry."

Peaches didn't answer when I called, so I texted her and started Googling bail bond companies. As I took a swig of my water—I'd ditched the gin and tonic—the waiter appeared at my elbow.

"The gentleman with the sock puppet told me this is for you," he said, handing me the check.

"What?"

"He just picked up his car from valet parking," he said. "He instructed me to add it to the bill."

"He's gone?"

"Were you not planning on picking up dinner?" he asked. "He told me it was a celebration of his upcoming show."

"I'm tempted to go with a dozen rotten eggs," I said as I opened the check and just about fell out of my chair.

"I'll take care of that whenever you're ready," the waiter said respectfully, then withdrew to the other side of the dining room. Placing himself, I noticed, between me and the door.

I fished my credit card out of my wallet and slipped it into the check holder, trying not to think about my upcoming bill. Once I got the Pansy situation taken care of, Peaches and I were going to have a long talk—and I was done with Match.com.

I'd rather be single than buy another Shirley Temple for a sock puppet.

CHAPTER FIFTEEN

I couldn't get Pansy out, and Peaches was no help with a defense attorney.

"I called around," she said. "The only one I can get in touch with is Fred Arundel."

"Isn't he the one on the billboards on Highway 71?"

"The one with the dreadlocks and the guitar? That's the one."

"Something tells me Pansy's going to be wanting someone a little different."

"Hey. You see what you can come up with."

She had a point. Finding a criminal defense attorney wasn't exactly like asking around for a math tutor. "I'll ask Blake," I said, wondering why I hadn't thought of it earlier. "Hold off on Fred for now."

I hung up and called Blake.

"She's still crying," he said.

"I'll be home soon. Hey," I said. "Know any good criminal defense attorneys?"

"Oh no. What did you do this time?" he asked.

"Not for me," I said. "A friend is in jail."

"Who?"

"Promise you won't tell anyone."

"Promise."

"Pansy Parker."

"Pansy Parker? The PTA president?"

"That's the one," I said.

"What did she do? Run someone over with her Escalade?"

"Not exactly," I said. "Besides, she drives a Suburban. At any rate, do you have some names? She's in the Travis County Jail right now and needs to get home to her kid."

"What's she in for?"

"I can't tell you," I said.

"This has something to do with that dead personal trainer, doesn't it?"

"Client privilege," I told him. "Do you have a name?"

He sighed. "It'll all be in the papers tomorrow, anyway, but here you go." He reeled off a few names and numbers.

"Thanks," I said.

I got lucky on the third call—a lawyer named Margaret Chance. "I usually don't take calls this late, but in this case . . . I'll head down now."

"How long until she's out?" I asked her.

"I don't know," the attorney said. "I'm going to see if I can push for a fast hearing, but I'm afraid it will be expensive."

"They've got money," I said.

"I'm leaving for the jail now," she told me.

"Thank you so much. Tell Pansy I said hi," I said. "And please get her out."

"I'll do what I can," Margaret said.

• • •

When I'd gotten home, managed to placate Elsie, said good-bye to Blake, put the kids to bed, and thrown a load of laundry into the washer, I cleared a path through the Duplo blocks in the living room and went to the kitchen table to open my laptop.

I grabbed a pencil and a legal pad and pulled up Tristan's Facebook page. There were a few condolence messages, apparently from clients, but no family listed. I cruised through his Timeline, which was largely a bunch of ads for LifeBoost and personal training tips—not exactly riveting reading—then looked through his friend list.

He was a big fan of IronAbs Gym, where he was part owner and evidently spent a lot of time. I probably needed to check it out; while I was online, I clicked over and sent an e-mail requesting a personal training appointment with Sylvester, who was listed as co-owner. I wasn't too excited about the exercise, but I figured it wouldn't hurt to ask some questions. And maybe I'd be able to find out something that would help me recover Frances's money—and Elsie's fry phone.

Frances Pfeffer was near the top of Tristan's friend list. I clicked to her page; it was mainly family pictures, and most of her posts were inspirational memes about how women didn't need a man as much as they needed a hot-fudge sundae. I couldn't say I disagreed with her, but I suspected she was more interested in hot personal trainers than hot-fudge sundaes. I clicked back to Tristan's page and pored through his friend list. The venture capitalist Steven Maxwell was on the list, but his Timeline was private, so there was nothing helpful there.

Who else might have wanted him dead? I wondered. Pansy's husband, Mark, was a definite possibility. I ran a search on his name and found one matching profile in Austin. There was no picture, and nothing helpful.

Next was Phyllis, who had not looked too happy at the Passion Party when we were talking about Tristan, making me wonder if perhaps she, too, viewed Tristan as an extracurricular activity. To my surprise, Phyllis's profile was decidedly un-momlike; where many other women with kids had posed family portraits as their profile pictures, she had taken a picture of herself in a low-cut black dress and a seductive pout. Most of the rest of her photos were similar. There were a few photos of her two kids, who were all pink cheeks and cherubic smiles, but most of them seemed to focus on Phyllis—and although she was married, there was not a single shot of her husband. I added her name to the list, then chewed on the end of my pencil. How many moms had Tristan been sleeping with? I wondered. And were they all funding his business?

After a moment of staring at the legal pad, I picked up my cell phone and called Becky.

"Hi, Margie. How's Mr. Big?"

"I haven't even looked at it, to be honest. Pansy Parker just called; they arrested her for murdering Tristan Prescott. And Frances Pfeffer is holding Elsie's fry phone hostage."

"Frances has Elsie's fry phone?" Becky asked.

The PTA president had been arrested, and Becky was asking about the fry phone? "Did you hear what I said about Pansy?"

"Yes," she said. "To be honest, I'm not surprised about that, after what I heard today . . . but what's up with Frances?"

"She wants me to do a job, but she can't pay for it, so she's holding the fry phone ransom."

"What does she want you to do?"

"Find some money," I told her. "But I'm not sure how to do it."

"You really need to get a few extra fry phones on eBay, Margie."

"I search every day," I said glumly.

"So," Becky said brightly. "Do you think Pansy did it?"

"No," I said. "And I'm worried . . . If she goes to jail, her daughter's on her own."

"You really think she's innocent?"

"I do, actually."

"Why do they think she killed him?"

"It's a long story," I said.

"You know something, don't you?"

"Well, Pansy hired me to find out what really happened. So I was hoping you could tell me who else Tristan was sleeping with."

"I'm not the person to ask; Janelle's the one who knows who's sleeping with who."

I wrote Janelle's name down on my yellow legal pad. "I'll ask her to coffee," I said.

"Drinks might be better," she said. "It doesn't take much lubricant to get her talking. Maybe she'll tell you who she has in mind for her ménage à trois."

"Are you hoping she'll ask you?" I asked.

"God, no," she said. "Oh—Michael mentioned he saw you the other night."

"Yeah," I said. "When I was out with Trey. He was with a gorgeous woman named Jicama or something."

"Salima," she corrected me. "Yeah. They've been dating for about a month."

Something in my stomach twisted.

"I don't like her nearly as much as you, though," Becky reassured me. "Did you know she organizes her underwear by color?"

I was lucky if my underwear even made it into my dresser drawer. And I didn't want to think about how Becky had come by that information.

"He should be seeing you. I think he's still carrying a torch for you."

"I don't know," I said. "Salima's really pretty."

"He's not the one for her," Becky said. "Hopefully it'll flame out soon and he'll ask you to dinner."

"He did, actually," I said.

"When?"

"Not long after Blake moved out," I said. "But I wasn't ready."

"You goof. I told you—you snooze, you lose!"

"I'm not even divorced yet!"

"But you're dating chicken-legged soccer coaches," she pointed out.

"That was Peaches's doing," I reminded her. "And it wasn't nearly as bad as my dinner with Marshmallow the sock puppet." I told her about my latest dating escapade.

"Wow. Well, at least you got a free dinner," she said.

"Wrong. He skipped out and left me with the check."

"Makes me glad I'm still married," she said.

"Thanks."

"Oh . . . Sorry about that," she said. "I'm sure it will get better. How's Elsie liking school, by the way?" she asked, changing the subject.

"She seems to be adjusting okay," I said.

"I'm so glad you got her out of that awful private school. By the way, Zoe wants her to come over for a playdate tomorrow," she said. "Why don't I take both kids and you can take Janelle out for a drink?"

"I've got dinner at my in-laws' tomorrow at seven, but I'll send her an e-mail and see if she's up for an afternoon margarita."

"Plan on being the designated driver," she recommended. "And bring lots of cash."

"If I have any left, I will," I said glumly.

• • •

Blake might not be a great husband, but he certainly had great contacts in the legal world. Pansy was out by the next morning and on the phone with me.

"You've got to find out who killed him," she said.

"What did you tell them?"

"Nothing until the attorney showed up. And the attorney told me that was a good policy, so I just said I didn't know anything. I'm just so glad the neighbor was able to take Isabella last night."

"Is she okay?"

"She has no idea what's going on. Of course, once last night hits the papers, it'll be a different situation."

"Does your husband know anything?"

"Not yet."

"And you didn't say anything about the phone?"

"Nothing," she said. "I just hope they don't find our fingerprints all over it. I cleaned up the Passion Party toys, so that shouldn't be a problem, at least."

"Wait a moment. *Our* fingerprints?"

"You had the phone in your hand, too," she reminded me, and my stomach lurched. Just what I needed—another link to a dead body. "So, what's the next step in the investigation?"

"I'm going to meet with Janelle and see what she knows," I said, pushing my worries aside. "Is her gossip reliable?"

"It is, unfortunately," Pansy said.

"Any other moms who might have wanted to do him in?"

"Not that I know of," she said.

"And still no idea of what killed him?"

"No," she said.

Terrific.

• • •

Janelle jumped on the chance for afternoon drinks, and we arranged to meet at the Grove, a swanky wine bar on the west side of the town. Blake had the kids, so after I slathered my still-swollen face with cortisone cream, my mother and I spent the morning canvassing Zilker Park, putting up new flyers and dangling pepperoni slices in hopes of enticing Twinkles to make an appearance. When we weren't calling Twinkles, my mother was holding forth on Prudence.

"I know it was her idea to send Elsie to that private school," she said. "I can't believe she's going to bake cupcakes with her."

"Lots of people eat cupcakes," I pointed out. "I eat cupcakes."

"I know. But it's so unhealthy! And I swear she's doing it just to compete with me for the kids." She took a deep breath.

"The kids love you," I said, scanning the underbrush for signs of pig habitation. "And they love their other grandma, too. You each bring different things to the table."

"Well, she brings nothing but processed carbohydrates and shortening," she said. "And I hate to think of the chemicals in her perfume; it's so bad for their little lungs."

"They seem to be holding up okay," I said.

"I just hate to see them corrupted that way," she said.

I resisted the urge to roll my eyes; I was pretty sure my mother-in-law felt the same way about my mother's "eat green sludge" dietary campaign.

"I know you both have very different approaches to life," I conceded. "But how do you think she's corrupting them?"

"What do you think? She's luring them with sugar," she said. "Do you have any idea how addictive sugar is?"

"I do, actually," I said, thinking of the Snickers bar in my purse.

"Plastic toys, too. The off-gassing is terrible. And those clothes she buys Elsie. So frilly and stiff. How is a kid supposed to move in something like that!"

"Elsie never wears those clothes," I said. "They get in the way of her dog collar. So I don't know why you're worried."

"It's the point of the thing," she said.

"It's got to be tough for Prue; she's always been the only grandma in town, and now you're living with me."

"But . . ."

"Can we talk about something else?"

"Sure, honey," she said with a sigh. "I've been meaning to ask. How was your date?"

I never thought I'd say it, but I found myself looking forward to drinks with Janelle.

• • •

I dropped my mom off at home a few hours later. We hadn't seen a hint of Twinkles, and I still had a few hours before meeting Janelle, so I decided to cruise by Frances's house. Was it considered burglary if you were reclaiming your own property? I wondered briefly as I drove by slowly, scanning the house for signs of life.

I couldn't see into the garage, but there weren't any cars out front, so I decided to go for it.

Once the minivan was parked a few houses down, I strolled toward Frances's house, which looked like something out of *Stepford Wives, Austin Edition*. The grass was so tidily mowed it looked like someone had measured each blade with a ruler, and unlike my house, the windows had been polished to a mirrorlike shine. Despite the ninety-degree "fall" weather, an enormous autumnal wreath that looked like it had been commissioned by Martha Stewart graced the massive front door.

Since Frances was officially my client, I decided to try the front door first. If she was home, I'd beg. If she wasn't, I'd see if I could figure out a way to break in.

I pushed the doorbell button, launching a flurry of Westminsteresque chimes. They were met with a volley of yappy barks . . . thankfully, nothing that sounded too large and menacing. No one came to the door. I tried it, but it was locked. It was worth a shot.

The privacy fence gate, thankfully, was not locked. Glancing around to make sure no one was watching me, I ambled up to it, then opened the gate and slipped into the backyard.

Unlike my yard, which was a meadow of weeds, Frances's backyard was as neat as the front; when I'd been here last, it had been dark, so I hadn't gotten the full measure of it. A children's playscape occupied half of the backyard, and the other half was the same emerald-green carpet of grass as was in the front. I was thankful for the privacy fence as I walked over to the french doors in the back of the house and peered through the window, hoping to spot the fry phone.

I was in luck. There was a red plastic cube, right in the middle of the kitchen island; unless I was mistaken, I had located the fry phone.

The only problem was that there was a massive black poodle standing between the island and me, baring a mouthful of teeth in what looked like a snarl.

I pushed down the handle—the door was unlocked—but the dog advanced a few steps, growling, as I cracked the door open. "Good dog," I crooned as I shut the door quickly and fished in my bag for some stale Goldfish. I found them and proffered the open foil bag through the glass. He seemed interested for a moment, but then his eyes returned to mine, and his lips curled back farther. I could see his entire body vibrating with a growl.

If I could get him out the back door, I could slip into the house and then exit through the front of the house.

The only problem was getting him out the back door.

I emptied the few stale Goldfish from the bag onto my palm, then opened the door enough for him to sniff them. He snapped at my hand, and I jerked back, dropping a few Goldfish on the patio, but then he started sniffing.

"You want some?" I cooed. The teeth became less apparent, and the sniffing intensified.

"Come on," I said, and tossed one through the crack in the door. He gobbled it up, then looked back at me with what I hoped was a more positive glint in his eye. I took a deep breath and scattered the rest of the Goldfish behind me, then flattened myself to the side of the house and yanked the door open.

The dog bounded out the door and inhaled a Goldfish from the far end of the patio, then turned back to look at me. I was already halfway through the door and closing it behind me before he seemed to realize what he'd done and lunged at the glass, slamming into it just as I closed it behind me.

I took a big shaky breath and then hurried over to the island to retrieve the fry phone, only to discover that the red toy I'd spotted wasn't a fry phone at all; it was a plastic car.

As the dog hurled itself at the glass door, I scanned the kitchen. I opened a few drawers. There were lots of neatly folded napkins, but no fry phone.

As the dog launched into barking, I left the kitchen. Where could the phone be? I did a cursory glance around the living room, then headed down a hallway leading to what appeared to be the kids' rooms.

Unlike the rooms in my house, these two looked like they'd been decorated by an interior designer and were uninhabited by children. No piles of toys. No discarded clothing. Just a neat set of bins, labeled with hand-lettered cards and filled with toys that actually matched the label.

I actually stopped for a moment to admire it, wondering what magic Frances had that I didn't, before I started sorting through the bins and opening drawers, disappointed to find nothing but alphabetized books and folded socks.

I had exhausted the kids' rooms and was heading into the master bedroom when there was the sound of a car door slamming. I opened the blinds facing the front walk; to my dismay, there was a woman heaving a vacuum cleaner out of her trunk.

The housekeeper. It explained so much.

I sprinted out of the bedroom to the kitchen. The black poodle was still throwing himself at the door and barking his head off.

I ran to the refrigerator and opened it, but the only thing in there was celery and LifeBoost. I opened one of the bottom drawers and found a wedge of brie. As I closed the fridge and hurried to the back door, I could hear the key being put into the lock.

The poodle was practically foaming at the mouth now. But I had no choice.

I threw the door open, holding the cheese up like a talisman, and hurtled outside just as the front door opened. I glanced back to see a surprised-looking woman staring at me; at the same time, I felt a wet mouth closing on my hand.

I released the cheese and raced to the gate, praying I wouldn't feel his teeth on my behind. Thankfully, the cheese seemed to keep him occupied for at least a few moments. I was just closing the gate behind me when the poodle came loping around the side of the house, still barking.

As I hoofed it to the minivan, I didn't dare look back. I threw myself into the driver's seat, praying the van would start. It did, thankfully, and I peeled out of Coventry Lane like a teenager on her first day learning how to drive stick.

• • •

Janelle turned up at the Grove wearing four-inch platform heels and a red cotton dress that looked like it had fit well about twenty pounds ago.

"Margie!" she said, pulling me into a boozy-smelling hug. "This is so fun! I almost feel like I'm single again!" she announced, scanning the assembled middle-aged diners with a predatory eye before realizing what she'd said. "Oops. I guess you are single now. Sorry about that."

"It's okay," I said, smoothing down the maxi dress Blake used to refer to as my tropical muumuu. I'd gained a few pounds stress eating the last few months, so I was selecting my outfits from the waistband-free section of my wardrobe.

"What happened to your hand?" Janelle asked, looking at my bandaged finger; the poodle's teeth had broken the skin a bit.

"Oh, I had a run-in with my cat," I lied.

"I hate cats," she said bluntly. "But your pig is cute. Do you want to sit at the bar?"

"Sure!" I said, and followed her as she wobbled over to a table next to the window. She hiked herself up onto one of the stools, and I slid onto the one across from her.

"There are some pretty hot guys here," she said as she flagged down the waiter. "Might be a good place to pick up dates. I hear you went out with Trey the other day, by the way."

"I did," I confirmed.

"Not love at first sight?"

"Not exactly."

"He's a jerk," she said. "I don't know what Michaela saw in him."

"Who's Michaela, again?"

"His ex," she said. "She can't stand soccer now; part of the reason they broke up was that he was pushing their daughter all the time."

"It wasn't his sparkling personality?"

Janelle rolled her eyes. "I know, right? I heard he was filing a lawsuit against the league for not putting his daughter onto the select team," she said. "They moved another girl up two years, and Trey thought his daughter was more talented. He claimed it was favoritism."

"But he's still coaching for the league," I said.

"I know. And he's a maniac. We all keep joking about slipping a few Xanax into his drink. He gets almost, like, 'roid rage sometimes; I feel bad for his daughter."

"Does he take it out on her?"

"She's either the best soccer player since Ronaldo or a total screwup," she said. "She missed a shot on goal during practice two weeks ago, and he made her do fifty push-ups on the spot."

"Um . . . She's six, right?"

"Exactly," Janelle said. "There are some pretty narcissistic parents in this part of the world. Totally living through their kids."

"How old are your kids, by the way?" I asked.

"Oh, Mindy is six, like Elsie, and her older sister is about to go into middle school. She's got the first dance coming up, so she and I are

117

doing the Atkins diet together. We've got the dresses narrowed down; she wants a sheath dress, but she looks so much better in a strapless, so that's what we're going to get."

"Ah," I said. Self-reflection was evidently not a strength for Janelle. "Who's she going with?"

She shrugged. "I don't know yet, but we're renovating the house with a huge staircase—perfect for prom pictures. I think I might sign Mindy up for Pilates classes, too; she's getting a little tubby around the middle."

I couldn't help but glance down at Janelle's own less-than-trim waistline. I'd seen all the girls on the soccer team; none of them were what I'd term *tubby*.

"Hey," I said. "I noticed Phyllis seemed a little upset the other night when we were talking about Tristan. Did they know each other?"

"Like in the biblical sense?" she said, winking. "Oh, totally. They were like bunnies for a while, I hear. He was over there every afternoon before school was out."

"Isn't she married?"

"Yeah, but I don't think that matters."

"You said they were like bunnies. Did that change?"

"I don't know if it's true, but someone told me he started turning up at Pansy Parker's house recently."

"Who told you that?" I asked.

"Oh, everyone knows it," she said, and my heart sank. Had "everyone" mentioned this to the police yet?

"Hey, why are you so curious about this, after all?"

"I'm learning about how to do investigations," I told her. "It's practice, I guess."

"Sure you're not working for someone?"

"Of course not," I said, thankful that the waitress arrived with the margaritas. But only seltzer for me—I wasn't planning on drinking today—but I was looking forward to what I might hear if I lubricated Janelle a little bit more.

"Ooh, these watermelon ones are *good*," Janelle said. "Hey . . . Have you given Mr. Big a whirl yet?"

"I, uh, haven't tried it yet, to be honest."

"When you do, let me know what you think. I'm getting kind of tired of Mr. Reliable," she said.

"I'll let you know," I told her.

CHAPTER SIXTEEN

After drinks with Janelle—I limited myself to seltzer water—I went home and made some attempt to tidy the house. Blake had dropped the kids off, and my mother was attempting to get them to eat celery sticks with cashew butter; it was not going well. As I attempted to corral the Duplo blocks, I found myself wondering about Phyllis. Did she know that Tristan and Pansy were involved? And if so, would she kill over it?

I didn't have much time to mull it over, though; we were due at Blake's parents' house for his dad's birthday dinner. I was dreading the trip to my in-laws', but at least we weren't going to eat squash casserole, I told myself. And my dog bite didn't look like it was getting infected. On the downside, I spent the afternoon trying to console Elsie, who asked about both Twinkles and her fry phone at thirty-second intervals. I'd had no luck on either—not a single call from the flyer, except for a pig breeder asking if I wanted a replacement (not)—and was feeling like the mother of the year.

As we drove to my in-laws' house, Elsie was growling in the back-seat, looking as if I'd told her it was her last meal on earth. I had suggested I could drop the kids off and leave, but Prue insisted that we all come. "Bring Connie, too," she said. "I'll make a pot of lentils for her."

"Are you sure?" I asked.

"Absolutely. You're still family, no matter what," she said. "Besides, Philip insisted."

"Probably because he's still hoping to get you back together," my mother had said when I told her about the invitation. "I'll make a kale salad to bring. It'll be good to spend some family time!" She bit her lip. "I wonder if he'll bring Frank?"

"I doubt it," I said. "Philip knows they're interested in each other, but I don't think he knows they've moved in together . . . Although Blake spends so much time with Frank, I think he's going to have to spill the beans soon."

"I wonder, do you think Frank waxes?"

"Don't remind me," I said.

"I know it's hard that they're . . . intimate."

I hadn't been thinking of that, but now, thanks to my mother, I was. "I was thinking of my Pretty Kitten gig, actually." I told her that Peaches had set me up as a fake receptionist to see why the business was losing money.

"I can't wait to hear how that goes."

"Me neither," I said, once again wondering if I'd chosen the wrong career.

We arrived at my in-laws' at six thirty; my mother had put on her best blue caftan for the occasion, and had a small gift in hand. "What did you get him?" I asked.

"Oh, just a little something," she said. I'd bought him a box of golf balls and a golf humor book (I was on a budget these days), and the kids were primarily interested in the cake.

"Will it be pink cake?" Elsie asked. Pink frosting was a rare exception to the white-foods rule.

"I doubt it, honey," my mother told her. "Besides, all that food coloring is bad for you."

"I hate pink," Nick announced. "I want chocolate."

"It's Grandpa's birthday, so we'll get whatever kind of cake he likes," I reminded them. "Do you have your present ready?"

"We do," they said. I'd framed a snapshot of the kids for him, and they'd both made cards.

Blake had evidently arrived before us; his gleaming BMW was parked at the curb. As the kids spilled out of the van and trotted to the front door, my mother gave me an encouraging look. "Ready?" she asked.

"As ready as I'll ever be," I said, thankful that my father-in-law had a fully stocked bar and that I'd brought a designated driver. Something told me I was going to be relying on both.

My mother-in-law answered the door, looking once again like an escapee from *Leave It to Beaver*. "Constance! I'm so glad you could make it," she said, then spotted my face. "Oh my Lord. I've heard about those chemical peels, but . . . are you okay?"

"It's poison ivy," I said.

"How did you get poison ivy all over your face?"

"It's a long story." It didn't seem the right time to go into the whole Shamrock Streaker and runaway pig thing. "Thanks for inviting us," I said by way of changing the subject.

"I brought a salad," my mother said, proffering an earthenware bowl filled with what appeared to be yard trimmings.

"Lovely," my mother-in-law said, her expression unwavering. I had always admired that about her. "Come on in. Philip will get you a drink."

We followed my children into my in-laws' beautiful, perfectly maintained house. I set my purse down on the hall table and followed Prudence down the cavernous hall to the living room.

"What's your poison?" my father-in-law bellowed as we walked into the double-height space. The kids had already disappeared into the back of the house, where the television was, and Blake was looking slightly traumatized. There was a poststorm feel in the air that made me wonder what exactly we'd just missed, and Phil's ruddy face and ebullient voice gave me the impression he'd started happy hour a wee bit early. "I was just getting Blake another scotch. Gin and tonic, Margie?" he asked.

"Sure," I said, feeling like a drowning person being offered a life preserver. I'd cut back on the Benadryl that afternoon, knowing I'd be needing something stronger. "That would be great."

"How about you, Constance? Can I tempt you with a tipple?"

"I have my wheatgrass juice, thank you," she said, holding up a mason jar full of what looked like pond scum.

"Well, if you change your mind, let me know," he said as he added a huge dollop of gin to a tall glass and waved the tonic water over it. He then squeezed in a lime and handed the drink to me before pouring about half a bottle of gin into his own glass.

"I got the kids settled in with a video until dinner, so we can talk. How's Elsie doing?" Prue asked as we sat down on the couches.

"She likes her new school," I said. "And she seems excited about the new soccer team."

"Terrific." Prudence beamed.

"Did you know that personal trainer guy who ended up dead?" my father-in-law asked. "I heard he was into some kinky stuff. Must have had some eight-by-ten glossies on someone."

"I don't think they use eight-by-ten glossies anymore," I said reflexively.

"Fine. Sex tapes, or some kind of perversion," my father-in-law said, his eyes darting to Blake, who blushed and took another sip of scotch. *I might not be the only one needing a designated driver tonight,* I thought. I hoped Frank wasn't working.

"What are people saying about Tristan?" I asked.

"Why?" Phil asked, narrowing his eyes on me. "Are you mixed up in that, too?"

"I'm sure she's just curious, Philip," Prue said, rescuing me.

"They're saying he's a money-hungry glad-hander, that's what they're saying. Putting together some shady business. I've heard other things, too . . . Apparently he was playing the field a bit."

"Philip!" Prudence chided him.

"It's okay," I told Prue. "What have you heard?" I asked, hoping Prudence hadn't shut him down.

I needn't have worried. "I heard he's into those hot Pilates moms," he said, "if you know what I mean."

"Philip!" Prudence repeated. "Really!"

"It's human nature, sweetheart," he said, taking another big swig. "Men like hot women. Thank God I'm married to one," he said with a lecherous wink in her direction. Prue turned red, and Blake looked as if he wished he could be swallowed by the Ethan Allen sofa. My mother, on the other hand, was enjoying the show immensely. She took a long swig of wheatgrass juice and leaned forward expectantly.

"So you think a jealous husband did him in?" I asked.

"Maybe. Or it could be some funding deal gone south. He was gambling big on some drink company. He just got funding, but was waiting to hear if they could get a second bottling plant."

At that moment, there was the sound of running feet in the hall and growling. There was a humming noise, and I heard Nick yell, "Stop growling or I'll cut your tail off!"

Blake and I exchanged glances, and he stood up.

"I'll go check on the kids," he said, looking grateful for the excuse to leave the living room.

He didn't have time to get there, though. The humming noise grew closer—it sounded a little like an electric toothbrush on steroids. As we all watched, Elsie bounded into the living room on all fours, followed a moment later by Nick, who was brandishing a glowing Mr. Big, the anatomically correct vibrator Becky had given me at the Passion Party.

"Nick is chasing me with a lightsaber," Elsie complained as I vaulted out of my chair and yanked Mr. Big from my son's chubby hands.

My mother-in-law looked as if she might go into cardiac arrest as I flipped the switch to "Off" and attempted to shove the thing into my pocket. Unfortunately, it was an exercise in futility, since it just made me look like I had testicles coming out of the side of my shorts.

"Where . . . Where did you get that?" she asked my son.

"Mom's purse," he said cheerily as Blake, Prudence, and Phil stared at me, eyes wide.

"It's a funny-looking lightsaber," Nick said. "What are those balls for?" he asked, pointing at my pocket.

"It's not a lightsaber. It's . . . It's for drain clogs," I said. "They keep it from falling down the sink. I'll just put this back now. But no more going through Mommy's purse!"

Nick's eyebrows squinched together. "You know, it kind of looks like a—"

"How about some chocolate milk?" my mother-in-law sang out. "Come on, sweethearts. Let's go into the kitchen!"

"I want vanilla," Elsie growled.

"Vanilla it is, then," Prue said, and disappeared into the kitchen with Elsie crawling at her heels and Nick looking longingly back at my bulging pocket.

• • •

After the Mr. Big incident, dinner didn't start off with what you'd call a convivial atmosphere. Blake looked about as comfortable as a centipede on roller skates, my mother was eyeing the roast beef as if Prudence had arranged a dead fawn on a platter, and Phil was on his fourth drink by the time we sat down. I was a little worried about my mother-in-law; she was still looking like I might need to pull out the smelling salts at any moment. Things didn't improve when the kids started eating.

"No steak?" my father-in-law asked as Elsie finished piling her plate with macaroni and cheese and bread.

"I'm more worried about the lack of vegetables," my own mother piped up as she forked a wad of kale salad.

"She eats lots of fruit," I volunteered.

"Are Popsicles a fruit?" Nick asked as my mother-in-law spooned boiled peas onto his plate.

"There's fruit in them," I told him.

"And sugar, and food coloring, and goodness knows what else. I'll tell you what; let's make some homemade Popsicles this week!" my mother announced, sounding like an aging Mary Poppins.

"The kids can always make them here," my mother-in-law said in a tight voice. "Maybe next weekend they can spend the night, and we can make cupcakes together!"

Elsie looked up from the mountain of macaroni she was building. "Vanilla?"

"Of course, darling," Prue said, casting a glance at my mother. "You can have all the sweets you want when you're at Grandma Prue's house. What's a grandma if she doesn't spoil her grandchildren?"

My mother put down her fork. "So, good grandmothers poison their grandchildren?"

Prue looked at the salad. "I suppose that could be construed as poison."

"Mother!" Blake and I said simultaneously. At least we were in agreement on one thing.

Both mothers closed their mouths, but neither looked repentant. The tension between the two women had been growing ever since my mother moved in with me, and I was afraid the battle lines were being drawn. As the children looked around the table with wide eyes, I took another sip of my drink and cut Nick's steak into manageable bites. On the plus side, I told myself, looking hard for a bright side, I wasn't cutting up meat for a sock puppet. And I wouldn't be stuck with the bill.

There was nothing but the sound of forks and knives on plates for a while. It was Elsie who broke the silence. "Mom lost Twinkles."

Philip put down his fork. "You what?"

"She's visiting Bubba Sue," I said to Elsie.

"I don't believe you," Elsie said, fingering her collar. "I think she ran out the door like Bubba Sue did."

"How's school going?" Blake asked, tossing me a questioning look.

"Fine," she said. "But soccer wasn't very good. Twinkles tried to eat Coach Trey's shorts."

"She what?"

"He wasn't being very nice to Elsie, and Twinkles was being protective," I said.

"Coach Trey looked like a tomato." Nick giggled. "And he said some very bad words to Mommy. Like f—"

"Nick!" Blake interrupted.

"Those aren't words to repeat," I said, putting one hand on his chubby leg.

"But you said them this morning!" Nick protested.

There was a strained silence in the dining room again.

For a moment, I was almost nostalgic for squash casserole.

CHAPTER SEVENTEEN

"There are you headed today?" Becky asked me when I called her the next day. Frances had sent me another photo of the fry phone, this time dangling over a Vitamix blender. I deleted it and wondered how I was going to find Frances's money. Maybe today's trip would help, I thought.

"First, I'm going to look for Twinkles, and then I've got an appointment with IronAbs this afternoon," I said. "I signed up for a personal training session so I can grill Tristan's partner."

"Or he can grill you," she said. "I've heard that place is brutal."

"How bad can it be?"

. . .

I was reflecting on that as I passed two stick-thin women arrayed in Lululemon clothes. Their derrieres looked like halved bowling balls. I pulled my T-shirt down over my paint-splashed bike shorts and adjusted the scrunchie in my hair as a young man with chiseled everything held the door open for me. I'd spent another hour that day with no luck at Zilker Park, had received another text of Elsie's fry phone posed in an envelope addressed to Uzbekistan, and wasn't particularly looking forward to what was in store for me now.

"Thanks," I said as I walked into a reception area that looked like it should belong to the Four Seasons.

"May I help you?" asked the young man behind the desk.

"I've got an appointment with Sylvester," I said.

"Just have a seat," he said politely. "He'll be right here."

I sat down on a wooden chair that, while attractive, was less than comfortable, and looked up when Sylvester swept into the lobby. He looked a little like a life-size Malibu Ken.

"So," he said, giving me a quick up and down. "What's your usual training regime?"

"Umm . . . primarily refrigerator pose," I joked. "And spoon curls."

His handsome brow wrinkled. "Spoon curls? I haven't heard of those."

"I was kidding." Nothing. "You know . . . eating ice cream?" I pantomimed it.

"Oh," he said, his brow clearing. "That stuff is terrible for you. Dairy, sugar . . . and then there are all the additives. I'm a big fan of frozen coconut milk with a bit of stevia. With a little unsweetened cocoa powder? It's delicious!" His eyes grazed over me. "You're interested in a meal plan, too, probably . . . but let's get started first, shall we?"

"Sure," I said, swallowing hard and following him to a stationary bike. I'd been in a dominatrix's dungeon before. As I looked around at the contraptions arranged in the room, I found myself wondering if I might not prefer the dungeon to the workout room. "This is a nice place," I lied. "How long have you been in business?"

"We opened about six months ago," he said, positioning me on the bike. I glanced around the room. Although the place was expensively decorated, except for a lone blonde in a black catsuit doing something that looked mildly pornographic on a rubber ball, it was practically deserted.

"You're the owner, right?" I asked Sylvester, who looked a little less perfect close-up. He was still fit, but his skin was a bit craggy; it looked like the sunbathing had started to catch up with him.

"I am," he confirmed. "Now. I'll just warm you up for ten minutes, okay? And then we'll take it from there." He adjusted the resistance to a point where it was barely possible for me to move the pedals, and hit "Start." "I'll be right back," he said, and left me alone with my bike.

I pushed the pedals around for about forty-five seconds, regretting the two chocolate-cream donuts I'd grabbed on the way, then cranked back the resistance and pedaled a little more. But my legs hurt, so I cut the resistance to zero and pedaled at what I'd consider a leisurely pace. I didn't know what exactly I was in for; I decided to pace myself. Sylvester had disappeared through a door toward the front office. As I checked to see if the resistance could go below zero, the blonde finished with her rubber ball and strutted in my direction, checking herself out in the mirror and sucking in her nonexistent stomach as she crossed in front of the row of machines.

"Hi!" I huffed as she got within a few machines of me. She gave me a curious look but didn't slow down. "What do you think of this gym?" I tried again. "I'm thinking of joining."

"You are?" she asked in a dubious tone of voice. "I guess you have to start somewhere," she added.

"How's the management?" I asked.

"Well, one of them died the other day," she said.

"Really. What happened?"

"Someone killed him," she said.

"That's horrible." I blinked and tried another leading question. "Why would someone do that, I wonder?"

"Oh, Tristan had lots of enemies," she said.

"How do you know?"

"I dated him for a while," she said. "He was connected, but . . ."

"But what?"

"He had a habit of bilking people," she said. "I figured it would catch up with him eventually. I figured he'd go to jail, though, not . . ." She shivered.

I thrust out a hand. "I'm Margie, by the way. Margie Peterson."

"Geneen Trautwein," she said.

"Can I take you to coffee sometime?"

She made a moue of distaste. "I don't drink coffee."

"Right." No coffee. I could tell donuts were out. "Maybe a green smoothie or something?" I suggested. She stared at me. "You know, to ask you more about the gym?"

She narrowed her eyes. "Are you hitting on me?"

"Of course not!" I said. She looked offended. "I mean . . . not that you're not gorgeous, but I'm straight. Totally. Honest."

She glanced up at the clock. "I guess I'll be here for another hour . . ."

"Maybe when I'm done with my workout, then," I said, as Sylvester emerged from the office.

"I'll meet you downstairs at the juicing station," she said.

"Right. Thanks, Geneen."

"How are we doing?" Sylvester said with a fake, toothy smile as he walked over and glanced at the machine. "What happened to the resistance?"

"I cranked it down at the end," I lied. "I didn't want to overexert. Since it's just a warm-up."

"Well, then. Are you warm?"

I nodded, feeling a sudden wave of apprehension. "What's next?"

"I thought we'd start with some sprints," he said, leading me over to a treadmill.

"So," I said. "I hear you lost your business partner."

"I did," he agreed, the toothy smile gone.

"I'm so sorry . . . That must have been terrible. What happened?"

"They're still looking into it. Anyway . . ."

"Had you known each other long?"

"It was a business arrangement," he said shortly. "Let's get you going. Do you run?"

"No," I said.

"Jog?"

"Uh, no."

"How about resistance training?"

"What's that?"

"Do you lift weights?"

I gave him a weak smile and attempted humor. "Do grocery bags and laundry baskets count?"

An expression of something like disgust passed over his handsome face. "Let's see what you can do. We'll do some interval training for starters."

"Interval training?"

"It'll help burn that excess flab," he said, glancing at my middle. "We'll spend some time at top effort, and then a short cooldown."

"I can do that," I said. I could ask questions during the cooldown, I decided. "This seems like a great location for a gym," I said, trying to get back to the real point of my visit. "High rent, though."

He ignored my comment. "Let's get you started, then." He fiddled with the controls, and then hit "Start."

"This isn't so bad," I said as the treadmill ramped up.

"Sylvester!" someone called from the office.

"It's all programmed, so you're good to go. I'll be right back," he told me.

As he headed back to the office, the treadmill increased in speed until I was jogging. It kept going; I grabbed the bars on either side and upped the pace, lungs burning already. The belt continued to speed up, making a loud whirring noise. I ran faster, but was losing ground; and still the belt was speeding up.

I didn't think about much of anything for the next minute—which felt more like a century—and when the belt finally slowed down, I gasped for breath, thankful to be walking again. I wasn't a fan of inter-vals, I decided. I'd have a chat with Sylvester when he came back.

Unfortunately, I hadn't taken more than three breaths and about fifteen steps before the belt started speeding up again. I struggled to keep up with it, glancing over my shoulder to see what was behind me—something like a torture device with knobs and bars sticking out all over it—and motivated myself with images of my body impaled on an exercise machine.

I was on the third round, hanging on to the handles and barely able to breathe when Sylvester materialized at my shoulder. "How are we doing?"

"Off," I gasped. "Dying."

He squinted at me. "You're purple. Maybe we should take it down a few notches."

He hit a button, and the belt slowed a fraction. "Off," I repeated. "Are you sure?"

I nodded hard, and he punched another button. The belt slowed to a stop, and I bent over double, my breath sounding like I was sucking air through a straw.

"We'll do some more in a few minutes," he said. "In the meantime, let's do some kettlebells."

"Kettlebells?" I wheezed.

"It's not cardio," he said. "You'll be fine."

I levered myself off the treadmill, feeling like a ninety-five-year-old trying to get out of a hospital bed, and crab walked after him to a serene-looking green mat in the corner. He swung a kettle-shaped weight the size of an anvil off a metal rack and plopped it in the middle of the mat. "Grab that," he said.

I grabbed the handle and pulled up, but nothing happened.

"Pick it up," he prompted.

"I'm trying," I sputtered, and hauled up on it again. It moved a fraction but did not lift from the floor.

He sighed. "We'll try this one, then," he said, and plopped a slightly smaller one next to it. I wiped sweat and tears from my eyes and reached for the handle, deciding I was going to be charging Pansy hazard pay.

CHAPTER EIGHTEEN

By the time Sylvester was done with me, I had learned nothing, but caused what I hoped wouldn't be irreparable damage to every part of my body except—possibly—my skull.

"Same time next week?" he asked.

"I'll . . . I'll call when I have my schedule," I said, and limped toward the stairs, hoping Geneen hadn't given up on me.

He nodded and turned back to the office; I got the feeling he could tell I wouldn't be signing up again soon. If this was how he handled incoming clients, I thought as I hobbled down the first flight of stairs to where a swanky silver sign read "Roots Café," no wonder the place was dead.

Geneen was waiting for me, looking dewy and disturbingly fit as she perched on a chair in the corner with a mason jar of water.

"How was it?" she asked.

"Terrifying," I said, and squinted up at the menu above the bar. "What can I get you?"

"I'll just have a LifeBoost," she said.

"I'll be right back," I said, and went to place an order with the bored-looking college-aged employee behind the bar. She looked up from breaking off her split ends and gave me a dull smile. I couldn't help but notice a piece of kale stuck to her braces.

"Can I help you?" she asked.

"Two LifeBoosts, please," I said.

She gave me a vacant stare. "Slim, or Focus?"

I glanced back at Geneen. "Slim," she said.

"What she said."

The young woman slid two glass bottles filled with green sludge across the counter to me. "That'll be eleven dollars."

"Excuse me?"

"Eleven dollars," she repeated.

"For two drinks?"

She nodded.

"Are they multipurpose drinks?" I asked. "Do they do my laundry and clean my kitchen, too?"

She looked confused. "Uh . . . I don't think so."

I fished in my wallet for cash and put it down on the counter. "I'll need a receipt with that, please," I said. I was definitely charging this to Pansy Parker. With a bottle in each hand, I waddled stiff legged back across the floor, feeling like John Wayne in a green-juice shootout.

"Thanks," Geneen said as I handed her one of the bottles and levered myself onto the chair next to her.

"What's in this, anyway?" I asked, inspecting the murky drink.

"I don't know, but it makes me feel great," she said, opening it up and taking a swig. I squinted at the back of the bottle. *Proprietary blend of herbs* was listed as the fourth ingredient; it was bottled in East Austin. I opened it up and took a careful swig.

"Gritty," I said. And green. Very green.

"It's fiber," she said. "It's good for you."

I took another sip, trying to ignore the weird taste, and focused on Geneen. "So," I said. "Tell me about the gym."

"What do you want to know?"

"Well, what happened to the owner, for starters? Was there some kind of argument between the partners?"

"Oh, Tristan was a big thinker. He was always a pie-in-the-sky kind of person. I was surprised he managed to get this place built." She lifted her drink. "Same with this . . . but this stuff is like magic. I'm telling you."

I squinted at the bottle. "What do the drinks do?"

"I've dropped five pounds since I started drinking them . . . They just fill me up so much that I'm not hungry. And I've got so much energy, too! Apparently he's got some mix of Chinese herbs that works wonders."

I took another tentative sip, trying not to wrinkle my nose. "So this drink stuff is . . . was . . . his business, too?" I asked.

She nodded. "He got funding from Steven Maxwell."

"I've heard the name before. Who's that?" I said, as if I had no idea.

"You don't know Steven Maxwell?" she asked. "He's one of the big venture capitalists in town. Everyone wants to hit him up for money. Tristan was training him and apparently talked him into funding LifeBoost."

"Looks like it was a good bet," I said.

She nodded. "It's selling like gangbusters. Everyone loves it; Tristan was thinking of taking it national."

"So it's just in Austin?"

"For now," she said. "It gets bottled in Austin, and apparently he's got some herbal company in China that makes his special blend. It's sad that he died when he did; things were finally starting to turn around for him."

"Do you know who inherits his interest in the gym and the drink company?" I asked.

"He never said," she told me. "You seem more interested in Tristan than the gym," she remarked. "Are you with the police or something?"

"No," I said. "Just wondered how this place keeps going when there seems to be nobody here."

She snorted. "That's because Sylvester charges so much for his training sessions."

"They're brutal," I said. "It's like paying to be tortured."

"You get used to it," she said. "And you do get into terrific shape. I think I could crack walnuts between my butt cheeks these days."

I wasn't quite sure how that constituted a useful skill, but I didn't ask. "So you and Tristan dated."

"Only for a little bit," she said. "I think he was a little kinkier than I was . . . Plus, he wasn't really looking for a long-term relationship. He was great in bed, though, I'll give him that." She got a dreamy look in her eyes for a moment, then sighed. "Such a waste."

"I'm sorry," I said.

She shrugged. "It was a while ago; he was a nice guy, though. At any rate, the gym is nice . . . not crowded, lots of machines, and if you do the training, you'll be in terrific shape." She took another sip of her drink and looked at her sparkly-cased phone. "Thanks for the drink, but I've got to run."

"Thanks for talking with me," I said. "Can I get in touch with you if I have more questions?"

"Sure," she said, fishing a card out from the back of her phone. It was sleek and silver: *Geneen Trautwein, Interior Design*. "If you ever need help with designing your home or office, let me know. What kind of work do you do, anyway?"

"I'm a mom," I said.

"I hope your husband makes a mint, then . . . Otherwise, the dues here will kill you," she said.

"I'll bet," I said vaguely, and unfolded myself from my chair, wincing as I straightened. Before attempting to walk, I took another sip of my drink. It tasted terrible, but I was parched after my little episode with Sylvester; besides, I'd spent almost six dollars on it. Plus, Geneen said it was magical. I could use a little magic in my life about now. "Thanks for talking with me," I said.

"Sure," she said, watching as I shifted to the other foot and winced again. "It gets easier after the first month or two."

"Month or two?" I asked. I wasn't sure I was going to be able to push the gas pedal in the van, much less turn the steering wheel.

"Take turmeric," she advised me. "Otherwise, you're going to be in major pain for the next two days."

"Thanks for the tip," I said, shuffling toward the stairs. I didn't know about turmeric, but ibuprofen was definitely in my future.

CHAPTER NINETEEN

Unfortunately, the swelling did not go down fast. After a day of nursing my face with cold compresses and ibuprofen, I still looked like a tomato. I dropped the kids off the following morning and spent the day doing what I could from home and dodging my mother's suggestion that I try a turmeric mask (which I declined, figuring it would turn me from red to orange), and just hoped it would get better quickly on its own. When it was time to pick Nick up from school, I grabbed the rest of the LifeBoost I'd stuck in the fridge—I could use a little boost, to say the least—and piloted the van toward Green Meadows school. I had just taken the last swig of the LifeBoost and pulled into the parking lot when my mother called.

"Margie, I'm so glad you picked up!" she said.

"Hi, Mom. I'm just about to get Nick; I'll meet you at home."

"I'm worried," she told me. "I'm at Austin Heights, but I can't find Elsie."

"She's supposed to ride home with us today," I said, feeling my heart pound.

"I went to the pickup area, and she's not there. When I checked her classroom, the teacher told me she'd gone outside with the rest of the kids, but she's not there."

"Did Blake get her?" Odds were low, since it was still office hours, but I didn't know what else to think. A wave of anxiety welled up in me . . . Where was she? Was she hiding in one of the bathrooms? Had she had something bad happen and slipped out of school during the day?

"I texted him, but I haven't heard back," my mother told me.

"I'll call him," I said, hands shaking. "Did you call Prue? Sometimes she comes and spends the afternoon with Elsie."

"No," she said, her voice tight.

"I'll call her, too," I said. I hung up and dialed Blake with trembling hands—no answer—and then my mother-in-law. Her voice mail picked up after the third ring, and I left a frantic message. I called again, then texted.

Where could Elsie be? I turned over the possibilities as I went to get Nick; I didn't like most of them. I scanned the crowd of four-year-olds waiting to be picked up, but my son wasn't there. I tried not to run to his classroom; when I yanked the door open, Mrs. Bunn, the extremely solid director of the school, was waiting for me.

"Where's Nick?" I asked, starting to panic. Had someone kidnapped both kids?

"Mrs. Peterson, I'm so glad to see you," the director said in a placid, self-satisfied voice. Mrs. Bunn—also known as Attila the Bunn—gave me a disdainful look.

"Is everything okay with Nick?"

"He was involved in an altercation with another boy today," she sniffed.

"But he's okay?"

"He is, at least. The other boy has a red mark where your son struck him." Her chins wobbled as she lifted them in a disapproving manner.

At least he was okay, I thought, feeling my heart thundering in my chest. "What happened?"

"Evidently the other boy said something about Nick's father wearing a dress, and your son hit him on the nose with one of the pink graduated-tower blocks." She sniffed. "It was very upsetting. Those blocks are building tools, not projectiles. Or . . . *weapons*." She pronounced the word as if it contained only four letters.

I resisted the urge to roll my eyes. "I'm sorry that happened. We'll talk about using words instead of blocks."

"He reported that his sister simply growls to communicate," she said. "Have you consulted a mental-health professional for her?"

"We're making an appointment," I lied. It was on my list, but Blake wasn't on board.

Attila arched an eyebrow at me. "Is everything okay in your household?"

"My husband and I are separating," I said. "It's been a bit stressful. But I really have to run . . ."

She sighed. "Families just aren't what they used to be."

"It wasn't on my agenda, either," I snapped. "We're doing the best we can. Where is he?"

"He is in time-out in the main office," she said. "But as I'm sure you're aware, this isn't the first time this has happened this semester."

"We're working on it," I told her. "Now. My daughter is missing, so I need to get him and head to Austin Heights." I regretted saying it as soon as the words left my mouth.

"Your daughter is missing?"

"I'm sure Blake picked her up instead of my mother—they've got so many involved grandparents we sometimes have a mix-up—but I really have to get going."

She peered at me. "There's something green hanging off your nose."

I raised my hand and discovered a partially disintegrated leaf—a little something from the LifeBoost, I imagined. "Thanks," I said.

"We will discuss this more tomorrow," she pronounced as I hurried out of the classroom and sprinted toward the office.

Nick's eyes were red and swollen, and he was sitting with his arms crossed in the corner of the room. "I'm here, sweetie," I said. "But we have to go and track down your sister."

"I don't want to come back here," he said, his eyes welling with tears. "I hate Mrs. Bunn."

"Let's talk about it in the car," I said, holding out my hand. After a moment, he reached up and grabbed it, then trailed me to the car as I dialed Blake and Prue frantically, hoping that someone had tracked down Elsie.

I had just left Blake another message when Peaches called.

"What's up, buttercup?" she asked.

"Everything," I said. "My client spent time in jail, Elsie wasn't there when my mom went to pick her up, and I'm still coming up empty on my cases."

"So, no fry phone, either?" Peaches asked.

"Why is there a clown car behind us?" Nick asked. I glanced into the rearview mirror. Sure enough, it was a bright-red car covered in white polka dots.

"I don't know, honey," I said.

Peaches was still talking. "How did your date go?"

"Expensive," I said. "He and his sock puppet left me with the bill. He bought a seventy-dollar bottle of wine."

"Ouch," she said. "Want me to track him down and we can egg his house?"

"First, I have to find Elsie."

"Any luck on Twinkles?" she asked.

"No," I said glumly. "But I did get some info on Tristan. I'll tell you once I've got Elsie."

"I'm sure you'll find her."

"Mommy, you shouldn't talk on the phone and drive," Nick piped up from the backseat.

"I'm sorry, honey . . . You're right." The light in front of me turned yellow, and I touched the brake. "I'll call you later," I told Peaches, and hung up just as the car behind me plowed into the back of the van, pushing me into the intersection.

• • •

There was a clatter from behind me as I whirled to check on Nick. "Are you okay, sweetie?"

"That was scary," he said, tears leaking down his face.

I looked up; a Land Cruiser was bearing down on us from the left. "Hang on; I have to get out of the intersection," I said. As I turned to the right, leaving my bumper behind me, the clown car from behind me sped up, then zipped past me and away.

But not before I got to see the plate.

MRSHMLW

"Fu—" I began, then realized who was in the backseat. "Oh, honey. I'm sorry. Pardon my French."

"It's okay, Mommy," he said in a small voice. "I don't speak French."

I pulled over to check Nick more thoroughly—he was upset, but I didn't see any blood or bruises—then hurried back into the intersection to retrieve my bumper before turning to look at the back of the van.

I cringed; it wasn't good.

But I was pretty sure I knew who was responsible.

I tried to open the back of the van, but the door was crunched closed. Instead, I slid open one of the passenger doors and wedged the bumper between the backseats. As I closed the door, I dialed Peaches again.

"Any luck?" she asked.

"None," I said. "But I've got a license plate for you to look up. I've got to find Elsie, so I'll call the police later . . . Let me know when you've got the plate info," I said. I told her the letters and signed off. I was half-way to Austin Heights before she called me back. I jabbed "Speaker."

"You're not going to believe this," she said.

"Let me guess. Fabian?"

"Exactly."

"He just plowed into the back of my van and took off," I said.

"I guess sock puppets aren't conducive to good driving," she said.

"They're not so good with eating steak, either."

"Ew," she said. "I assume you haven't heard anything about Elsie?"

"Nothing yet," I said, feeling my stomach twist.

"She'll turn up."

"God, I hope you're right." I gunned the minivan, hoping the bumper was the only thing missing, and hurtled toward Austin Heights Elementary, praying that my phone would ring. My heart was racing, and not just because I'd been rear-ended by Marshmallow the sock puppet.

My daughter was missing.

CHAPTER TWENTY

By the time I got to Austin Heights, my mother had mobilized all the school staff and a local trooper. I had unbuckled Nick and together we had hurried to the front office. The teacher, Mrs. Wilson, was looking teary-eyed and distraught, and my mother was pale.

"Did anyone see her after she left the room?" the trooper asked.

"She just went out with the rest of the kids," Mrs. Wilson said. "I feel so terrible."

"Did you look on the playground?" I asked, scanning the soccer field behind the school and wondering if she might be on the swings.

"We checked," my mother said. "Any word from Blake?"

"I've left two messages," I said.

"Is there anyone else who might have picked her up?" the trooper asked.

"We've tried to reach her father and her other grandmother, but no one is answering," I said.

"Anywhere else she might have gone?"

"Have we checked the bathrooms?" Mrs. Wilson suggested.

"Let's go," I said, my heart thumping out a staccato rhythm in my chest.

"Is Elsie okay?" Nick asked, sounding scared.

"She's probably just hiding, honey," my mother said, glancing at me. "Why don't you come with me and we'll check the bathrooms?"

She led him away, and the trooper looked at me. "Are you on good terms with your husband?" he asked.

"What? Yes!"

"You're not separated?"

"Well . . . we are, but . . . why?"

"Sometimes the other parent is responsible when a child disappears."

"Are you saying you think Elsie might have been kidnapped? There's no way that Blake would take Elsie. That's crazy!"

"Are you sure? I should probably call it in . . . We can have someone go to his office—and his place of residence."

"No," I said. "Let me make one more phone call." I grabbed my phone and dialed Prudence again. She picked up on the third ring.

"Prudence, it's Margie. Do you have Elsie?"

"I was just about to call you back; I didn't mean to cause a crisis," she said. "I thought we'd get mani-pedis after school today."

I felt faint with relief and looked up at the trooper. "My mother-in-law has her."

"Thank God," the whey-faced teacher breathed.

"Is everything okay?" Prudence asked.

"The police are at the school and were about to send someone to Blake's office," I said. "Next time, could you at least text me?"

"I thought I did. Hold on," she said. I heard her asking Elsie what color polish she wanted; a moment later, she got back on the phone. "What time should I have her back?"

"We eat at six thirty," I said. "Please make sure she gets her homework done, if she has any."

"We'll do that right afterward," she said. "Ta for now!"

I hung up the phone, feeling like I could use a stiff drink and a three-day nap. "She forgot to text me and tell me she was picking Elsie up."

My mother hurried over just as I finished talking. "We found her," I said.

She echoed the teacher. "Thank God. Where is she?"

"Prue picked her up."

"Without telling me?" My mother's usually smiling face turned dark. "She scared us all half to death!"

"I know," I said.

"This is just part of her plot to win them over, isn't it?" she said.

"Mom." I nodded toward Nick. "Can we talk about this later?"

She gave me a curt nod that told me we'd be talking about the subject at some length. "What's she doing, taking her to a candy store?"

"They're getting mani-pedis," I said.

"At her age? All those chemicals . . . and the objectification!"

"Mom . . ."

"Right." She turned to the trooper. "I'm sorry for the trouble."

"I'm sorry, too," I said. "We need to work on communication, apparently."

"It's no worries," he said. "I'm just glad everyone's okay."

"Me too," I said, but my heart was still racing.

• • •

"I can't believe she did that!" my mother said when we were back at the house.

"She just wasn't thinking," I told my mother.

"She's going to ruin your children," my mother warned. "It was her idea to take them to Holy Oaks, and see how that turned out. If Prudence has her way, they'll be soaked in sugar and artificial food coloring and decked out in designer clothes made by overseas slave laborers."

"I'll talk to her," I promised, my head still spinning. I pulled a package of chicken breasts out of the freezer and filled a pot with water to thaw them, then called the insurance agent.

"Again?" he asked when I described what had happened to my back bumper. My minivan had been through quite a bit over the past year.

"I know," I said. "But I got the plates; he took off after he hit me." I relayed the information, then clicked over when the phone beeped.

It was Pansy.

"Any news?" she asked when I picked up.

"I'm making progress," I said.

"God, I hope so. You know who did it?"

"No, but I have some leads," I said. "Are you doing any better?"

"I'm still recovering from being behind bars. It was horrible," she told me. "I can't go back there. I never should have gotten into that affair. I'm such an idiot."

"I'll do everything I can to help," I promised.

"Look—I've got to go pick up Isabella. Let me know what you find out, okay?"

"I will," I promised, then hung up and called Peaches.

"Did you find Elsie?" Peaches asked.

"Prue had her," I said. "It's another battle in the war for the grand-children's hearts, I'm afraid."

"Your life is never dull," she said. "Find anything else out?"

I told her what I'd learned at the gym that day. "I don't know what LifeBoost has to do with anything, but his partner at the gym didn't seem too happy with him, and it sounds like his new business was taking off. Any way to find out who benefits?"

"I'll see what I can find out," she said. "Oh—got a lead on the Shamrock Streaker, by the way. I was talking with one of my friends at Southside Tattoo—he remembers doing the tattoo, but can't remember his name. He promised he'd look through the files for me."

"Are you sure it's the same one?"

"How many rainbow tattoos on men's abdomens can there be?"

"This is Austin," I reminded her.

"True. But at least it's a lead. Oh—you're scheduled to go to the waxing salon. I told her you'd be in tomorrow at nine," she said.

"Our location?"

"No, silly. The one on the east side."

"Fine. Will you run a search on Sylvester Bachman for me and see if you come up with anything?"

"Like prior poisoning convictions? To be honest, I'm not sure why you're so interested in helping this PTA lady out."

"It's for her daughter," I said. "She's got Asperger's, and her dad's never around. If something happens to Pansy . . ."

"I got it," she said. "I'll see what I can find out. In the meantime, tomorrow at nine."

"Talk to you later," I told her, and hung up. I had a very bad feeling about tomorrow.

And as usual, I was right.

CHAPTER TWENTY-ONE

"Why are you wearing all black, Mommy?" Nick asked as I dropped him off at Green Meadows the next morning. The last thing in the world I wanted to do was spend my day at the Pretty Kitten, but Wanda wouldn't be put off.

I adjusted the black T-shirt—it was a bit too small and kept rolling up—and smiled at Nick. "It's kind of like a uniform. I have to go work at a beauty salon," I said.

"What kind of beauty salon?"

"The kind where they take off extra hair," I said.

"That's weird," he said. "People pay money for that?"

"They do."

"How do you take off the hair?"

"You put wax on it and then rip it off."

"Are they bad people?"

"Who? The people getting the hair taken off?"

"Yeah. Is this instead of jail or something?"

I stifled a snort. "Some women like to take the hair off their legs. Some people shave, and other people wax."

"So will you be ripping hair off other ladies?"

"Not today," I said.

I dropped him off and headed east, hoping Peaches had told me the truth and I wouldn't be trapped in a room slapping wax onto another woman's privates. I'd heard the moaning from a distance; I didn't want to get that close.

I arrived at the satellite location of the Pretty Kitten five minutes late. I paused to apply another coat of powder to my still-swollen face, and then trotted up to the front door.

The woman behind the desk looked up when I walked in and peered at me over her horn-rimmed glasses. She wore an ill-fitting black 1950s-style shirtdress with a round collar, short bangs, and a black wedge cut. I would be willing to bet my savings account (all fifteen dollars of it) that she had at least two pairs of thrift store mom jeans in her closet at home.

"Sorry I'm a few minutes late," I said. The decor was similar to the one near Peachtree Investigations, only not quite as well kept up; there were smears on the glass in the front, and two lipstick-marked coffee cups on the side tables in the waiting room.

"No worries," the woman said. She didn't introduce herself, but her name tag said *Yvonne*. "Your first client isn't here for another fifteen minutes."

"My first client?" I asked. "I thought I was just supposed to do the desk."

"We don't need help with the desk," she said. "Wanda told me you'd be taking care of clients."

"But—"

"It's super easy," she said. "I'll take the first one, and I'll let you brush up on the manual. You've done this before, right?"

"Not really," I said.

She waved away my concerns. "You'll be fine. Just brush the wax on the same direction as the hair, use the strips and pull the opposite direction, and put on lots of numbing cream. Oh, and talcum powder, first."

"Surely there's more to it than that."

"Well, you might want to hold the skin taut," she said. "Otherwise it might tear."

I cringed. "Are you sure I can't just do the front desk?"

She sighed. "You'll have to learn that, too, I suppose," she said. "Let me show you how it works."

She ran me through the process of ringing someone up. Thankfully, one of my summer jobs had been at a Gap in the mall, so at least I knew my way around a cash register. "And here's the appointment calendar," she said, pulling up a book with handwritten entries. It was a loose-leaf binder—easy to replace pages, I thought.

"It's not computerized?"

She shook her head. "Got it?" she asked.

"I think so," I said.

"And here's the tutorial," she said, pulling up a YouTube video on the computer. "I'll just show you the place, and then you can watch the video. You'll be a pro by the time your first client comes in."

I seriously doubted it, but trailed her through the salon without saying anything. There were three treatment rooms, all done up in leopard print, black leather, and hot pink—it looked more like a bordello than a waxing salon—and as we went, she very quickly talked me through the details. "Here's the wax, here are the waxing paddles—throw them out between uses; no double dipping!—and here are the strips for pulling. Use as few as you can; they can get expensive."

"But isn't it better to do small areas?" I asked. Becky had told me that once.

"Oh, the quicker, the better is my theory. Like ripping off a Band-Aid. Anyway, here are the gloves—you'll want to wear those—and the tweezers are in the jar over there."

"Tweezers?" I asked.

"For the hair that doesn't come up with the wax," she said, looking at me as if I were a moron. "Haven't you ever had a Brazilian?"

"Uh, no," I said.

"Bikini wax?"

I shook my head.

"Good Lord. You're like back in the Dark Ages. I'll bet you could lose things down there," she said, nodding toward my nether regions. "Anyway," she continued as I blushed a deep red, "most of them come in trimmed, but if they haven't, you'll want to trim to about one-quarter inch. They'll cover that in the tutorial. The easiest ones are people who have been waxing for a long time. First timers hurt the most." She picked up a tube of numbing cream. "You'll want to slather this on before and afterward, and tell them they can use ice packs and ibuprofen if it's really bad."

"How long does it hurt?"

"Depends," she said. "Redheads have the lowest pain tolerance. We usually ask if they've taken ibuprofen before we get started. Anyway, here are the towels. If you want, maybe you can watch the first procedure. The client's name is Mirabelle—she's a professional woman, so I'm sure she won't mind."

"Professional?"

"World's second-oldest profession," Yvonne said with a bawdy wink. "Well, then, I think you're ready to go."

I was far from ready, but I just smiled and nodded and prayed the day would go quickly. I was only here until two. How bad could it be? I thought as I followed Yvonne back to the front desk and sat down to watch the tutorial.

To my relief, it didn't look that bad. The woman in the video just slapped on some wax, patted on a strip, and lifted. Things seemed to get a little bit dicey in the loose-skin area, but it looked manageable. And the woman on the table didn't scream at all—either that, or they muted the sound.

I had watched it a second time when the front door opened and a short, curvy woman walked in.

"Hi," she said in a deep southern drawl. "I've got a nine thirty?"

"Hi, Mirabelle," Yvonne said as she came to the front. "Come on back."

"Do you want me to come back with you?" I asked.

She glanced at her watch. "Cerridwen isn't here yet, so I don't have anyone to work the front desk. Knock when she shows up."

"What time is Cerridwen supposed to be here?"

"Nine," she said as she led Mirabelle to the back. "Did you trim?" she asked as they walked.

"Didn't need to," Mirabelle said before they disappeared into a treatment room.

While they were in the back, I kept busy by acquainting myself with the front desk—and the computer. It was odd that they didn't do scheduling on the computer, I thought. Out of curiosity, I checked the browser's history. Evidently Yvonne was into fashion; she'd spent a lot of time on the Nordstrom website, and had placed several orders for shoes. Or someone had.

The front door opened, and I closed up the history tab and smiled. The woman didn't smile back. "I've got a nine thirty," she said.

"Okay," I said, looking at the calendar. Only one name was written down for nine thirty. "What's your name?" I asked.

"Diane," she said.

No Diane on the page. "You're not on the calendar," I said, "but I'm sure Yvonne can fit you in as soon as she's done."

"I don't have time to wait," Diane said, her lower jaw jutting out. Her graying hair was cut short in something between a buzz cut and a bowl cut. She wore a pair of lime-green polyester pants that looked strained almost to the breaking point and a pink plaid shirt that was dotted with a constellation of bleach stains. In short, she was the last person on the planet I expected to want a Brazilian wax.

"Which services are you here for, then?" I asked, hoping it might just be mustache removal, or something like plucking a few beard hairs.

"The whole shebang," she said.

"The Brazilian?"

She nodded.

"All right, then," I said. "If you'll just have a seat, I'll go back and check on Yvonne."

"I said I don't have time to wait," she complained. As she spoke, another woman walked in. She didn't look a day over sixteen and had a thick braid of black hair that made me more than nervous about what might be down south.

"I'm Stacy. I have a nine-thirty appointment." she said.

"So do I," Diane whined, "and there's no one here to take care of me."

"Well I have to be somewhere by ten thirty, so I can't wait," Stacy said.

"Just have a seat and someone will be with you shortly," I said politely, hurrying around the desk and scooping up the coffee cups. "Can I get you something to drink?"

"Coffee," said Diane, crossing her arms over her ample middle.

"Coconut water," replied the young woman with the five-pound braid.

"I'll be right back," I announced, realizing I had no idea where the drinks were. I hurried to the back and was relieved to find a coffeemaker— but no brewed coffee. I tossed some grounds into a filter, poured in enough water for four cups, and hit "On." Then I opened the dorm-size minifridge under the counter.

No coconut water. But there were several bottles of water and some LifeBoosts in there. I grabbed one of each and trotted back to the front. "Coffee's brewing. We're out of coconut water, but I've got water or LifeBoost." I offered the braided woman both bottles; she grabbed the green murky one.

"I've been meaning to try this," Stacy said. "Thanks."

"When is my appointment?" Diane asked.

"I'll be right back," I told her, and scurried to the back, where I knocked on the closed treatment door.

"Hang on a moment," Yvonne said. There was a short shriek, and a moment later the door opened wide. "What?" she asked. Behind her, spread-eagled on the table, was Mirabelle. I averted my eyes.

"Um . . . There are two people up front who say they have nine-thirty appointments," I said.

"Who?"

"Stacy and Diane," I said.

She sighed. "I'll be up in a few minutes," she said. "I'm almost done here." She closed the door on me, and I headed back to the front.

"She'll be just a few minutes," I reassured the two clients. As soon as I finished speaking, another person walked in the door.

"Hi," he said, then did a double take. "Margie."

"Frank," I said. It was my husband's boyfriend. "What are you doing here?"

He turned a deep, scarlet red. "Umm . . . I have an appointment."

"For a Brazilian?" I blurted. The two women looked up from their phones.

"Um . . . Yes. I'll just sit down over here," he said, looking as if he'd like to be just about anywhere else in the world than the Pretty Kitten with his boyfriend's soon-to-be-ex-wife. He looked very dapper in a pink shirt with a striped tie; his shoes—leather and very shiny—looked expensive. The only thing indicating his alter ego was his shapely arched eyebrows. I was trying not to stare at him, trying not to imagine him in a Madonna outfit, and trying very hard not to think of him kissing my husband.

"Can I get you a drink?" I asked, addressing a spot about three feet to the right of his well-coiffed head.

"No," he said quickly, and buried his face in a *Cosmopolitan* magazine.

I sat back down behind the desk and attempted to look busy.

"It's 9:38," the gray-haired woman complained.

"We'll be with you as soon as we can," I said, double-checking the calendar. Only one appointment was booked, but there were three people in the front office expecting to be served—and only one professional waxer on duty. At least I had plenty to report to Wanda.

"Is anyone else working?" the braided woman asked. I was about to answer when the front door opened and a blast of musk perfume entered the shop, followed by a globe-shaped redhead with about a tube of red lipstick on.

"Sorry I'm late," she sang out, adjusting her extremely brief skirt. She looked at me. "You must be the new girl."

"I'm Margie," I told her.

"Cerridwen," she said with a sweet smile.

"I'm so glad you're here," I told her. "These two ladies both have a nine-thirty appointment, and Yvonne is with a client."

"I was here first," complained Diane.

"But I have a ten-thirty appointment at my Pilates studio," said Stacy. "I can't afford to wait."

"I'll take you right away," Cerridwen said to Diane, "and we'll get it figured out." As she spoke, Yvonne and Mirabelle emerged from the back; Mirabelle was waddling and looked as if she had just spent a few weeks riding bareback. Which I guess, in a way, she had.

"Thank goodness," I breathed. "I'll go ahead and check Mirabelle out."

"I'll take care of Stacy," Yvonne said, stepping in front of me. "Why don't you take this gentleman back?"

"What?"

"It'll be fine," she said.

"But . . ."

Frank turned white. "But Blake told me you're a private investigator. He didn't tell me anything about waxing."

Yvonne turned sharply. "What?"

"It didn't work out," I said, blushing. "Otherwise, why would I be here?"

She didn't look convinced.

"I've got Diane," Cerridwen said.

"I guess I'll have to take Frank, then," I told her, anxious to move on before Yvonne started questioning me. "How about I prep him and get things going, and you can come in when you're done with Diane?"

"I guess that'll work," Cerridwen said.

Frank looked like he was about to faint. "But . . ."

"You'll be fine," Yvonne told him. "Everyone here's seen it all before anyway."

"Let's go," I said, forcing a smile that must have looked more like a rictus and leading him to the treatment room in the back.

CHAPTER TWENTY-TWO

N ow," I said. "You're here for . . . well, the whole shebang, right?"
I asked, hoping he'd changed his mind.

He turned scarlet. "Yes," he said. "Hot pants show everything."

"Right," I said. "Uh, why don't you just get changed . . ." The video
had showed paper underwear, but I didn't see any paper underwear in
the room. "Did you . . . er . . . trim?" I asked, just as the woman in the
video had.

"Yes," Frank said, his face the shade of an angry tomato.

"Right," I said. "I'll, uh, be right back, then." I hurried out of
the treatment room, not sure which one of us was more relieved, and
listened.

"It's a fifteen percent discount with cash," Yvonne was saying to
Mirabelle.

"I've always got cash," Mirabelle said, winking at her.

As I listened, the cash register opened and closed, and Yvonne and
Mirabelle set another appointment for about four weeks away. I slid
back down the hall as the front door jingled closed, and gently knocked
on Frank's door. "Ready?" I asked.

Silence.

I knocked again.

"Can I just wait for Yvonne?" he called through the door.

I turned to Yvonne, who was walking down the hall. "He wants to wait for you," I said.

She rolled her eyes. "Why don't you just prep him and start on the legs? I'll take care of the rest when I'm done with Stacy."

"But—"

"Do you want a job, or not?" she asked.

"Fine," I said, and turned to the door. "I'm just going to do the legs," I said, and opened the door.

Frank was lying on the table looking like he was expecting to be drawn and quartered. He was obviously a regular; he had less leg hair than I did—and nicer legs, too. Not a lot of cellulite, and absolutely no saddlebags. "This is so embarrassing," he said.

"It's fine," I said, although it was anything but. "Why don't I just put the numbing cream on and we'll go from there."

I reached for the tube on the counter and squeezed some into my hand. "So, what event are you prepping for?" I asked, hoping light conversation would make the whole process less mortifying for both of us.

"The Austin Heights fundraiser," he said. "I'm performing."

"Ah," I said, my hand hovering over his muscular calf. I took a deep breath and smeared some on; he jumped as if I'd electrocuted him. "Where is it?"

"At Steven Maxwell's house," he said.

"Steven Maxwell? The venture capitalist?"

"Yeah," he said. "He does a lot of fundraisers; he's a really good guy."

"I hear he funded a drink company not long ago."

"LifeBoost?" he asked. He relaxed a little as I slapped on more numbing cream. The conversation seemed to be working to distract him, at least so far. I wasn't so sure it would work as well once I got north of his knees. "Yeah. It's been selling really well. Blake and I—" He suddenly realized who he was talking to. "Oh. Sorry."

"No," I said. "It's okay."

"Really?"

No, it wasn't okay, but what was I going to do? My husband was gay. Even if I had the hairiest legs on the planet, it wouldn't make Blake be attracted to me. I could be a lot of things, but a male Madonna impersonator wasn't one of them. "I'm glad you two found each other," I told him. "He's much happier since he met you."

His face broke into a smile. "Is he? I know we were both trying to turn straight, but once we met each other . . . It was like it was destiny."

I tried not to roll my eyes. I was getting kind of tired of hearing about Journey to Manhood, which perhaps could more accurately have been named Journey to Falling in Love with Someone Else's Manhood. I never had understood how a long, intimate weekend of group hugs and emotional sharing with other repressed gay men was supposed to turn someone straight. Evidently Frank and Blake hadn't gotten it, either.

"I'm sorry," he said. "I shouldn't be talking about this. But I hope someday I can really get to know your kids . . . Frank talks about them all the time. He says you're a great mother."

I swallowed hard. It was weird to think of Blake confiding things about me to Frank . . . but I was touched that he'd said something so kind. "You're kidding me, right?"

"No," he said. "I know things didn't work out for you two romantically, but he thinks you're awesome with the kids."

"Really?"

"He's trying to repair things with them a bit now," he said. "He told me he was so preoccupied with what was going on with himself that he wasn't really . . . available. I think he's trying to make amends."

"Huh," I said. He had been more open since the two of us split up, as if a different personality was coming out.

As I applied a smear of numbing cream to his inner thigh, he said, "I hope I get to be a part of their lives sometime. I mean, not now, obviously . . . but they seem like really great kids."

"They are," I said. "Thanks." My hand moved a little farther north, and he jerked upright, almost losing his towel.

"Tell me the truth. You're not a waxer, are you?"

"No," I confessed. "I'm still a private investigator. I'm working undercover for the salon owner, to see why profits are suddenly down."

"Good thing, too . . . That woman is a nightmare. I'll tell you what," he said. "This isn't my first rodeo. Give me that tube of numbing cream; I'll put it on, and do the talcum powder, too, and that way we're both off the hook."

I felt like I was about to faint with relief.

"She always takes cash—says it's a fifteen percent discount that way—and never gives me a receipt. I'll ask her for one today, if you want, and we'll see what she does."

"Really?"

"Really," he said.

"That would be a huge help," I said. "Thank you. One more thing—where can I get tickets to the gala?"

"Why?"

"Steven Maxwell is involved peripherally in a case I'm looking into."

"The death of Tristan Prescott?" he asked.

"How did you guess?"

"It's all over the papers," he said. "Besides, you asked if Maxwell was an investor in LifeBoost, and I know whose company that is." His eyes glinted. "I didn't just fall off the turnip truck, you know."

"Obviously not," I said. "What do you know about Steven Maxwell?"

"I heard through the grapevine that he's had some bad investments lately. And I know he was gambling big on the LifeBoost thing. Something about the secret blend of ingredients . . . I've got two friends who have lost a lot of weight on the drinks, but they're basket cases."

"What do you mean?"

"Jumpy," he said.

Had I been a little on edge yesterday? I wondered. Granted, Elsie had been lost, but could my reaction have been more than just fear over my daughter? Even if it had been, though . . . What did that have to do with what happened to Tristan?

"Do you know anything else about the trainer, Tristan Prescott?" I asked.

"He's bi," Frank said.

"How do you know?"

He shrugged. "The gay community is small."

"Did he have any lovers that you know of?"

"I'll ask around," he said. "And I'll get you the tickets to the gala; I always get a few freebies. You want one, or two?"

"Two," I said. I could have Becky or Peaches go with me, I decided. I wasn't sure what I'd find out, but maybe I could determine if Maxwell was linked to Tristan in some way other than the business. "And if you can find out anything else about Tristan, that would be great."

"I'll see what I can do," he said. "Now hand me that numbing cream."

I gave him the tube and the talcum powder and headed out to the hallway, a bit startled to realize that I didn't hate Frank after all. In fact, I kind of liked him.

I walked back to the front desk and glanced at the calendar, flipping forward to the next month and scanning the entries. No sign of Mirabelle's name. I was starting to understand why the Pretty Kitten wasn't raking in the cash.

It was because Yvonne was raking in the cash.

I was flipping back to the current week when there was a blast of floral scent, and Yvonne said from behind me, "Looking for something?"

I jumped. "Just learning the ropes," I said quickly.

"Is the client ready?" she asked.

"Yes," I said. "All numbed and powdered and ready to go."

"Why were you so squeamish about him?"

"He's . . . Well, he's my husband's boyfriend."

Her eyes widened for a moment, and then she smirked. "I can see why you wouldn't want to get that close and personal. Why don't you clean the bathroom, then?" she asked. "The toilet brush and cleaner are in the back room. I'll take care of checking out clients."

"Were those walk-ins?" I asked. "They seemed to think they had appointments, but they weren't in the calendar."

"That's why we fired our last assistant," she said. "She was terrible with keeping track of appointments. I'm sure we'll get it squared away."

As she spoke, I noticed a small spiral notebook sticking out from the pocket of her apron. A secondary calendar or record of transactions? I wondered.

"Now. Why don't you get started on the bathroom? And I'll deal with Frank." She squinted at me. "Is he really your husband's boyfriend?"

"He is," I said. "Why do you think I'm looking for jobs in waxing shops? I'm getting a divorce."

"That must have been awkward," she said.

"It was fine," I told her. "He's actually a nice guy."

As she disappeared into Frank's treatment room, I walked to the back of the shop, thankful that I wasn't the one ripping the hair off Frank's privates. I found the back room easily; it was a jumble of supplies. I found the toilet brush and cleaner hidden behind a stack of empty boxes. Bathroom hygiene did not appear to be a priority at the Pretty Kitten, leading me to wonder about other hygiene practices. I poked around until I found a pair of rubber gloves, then took out my phone to snap a shot of the messy supply room—just to show Wanda—and then headed out to find the bathroom.

I was right about my bathroom-hygiene suspicion. I was a working single mother with a four-year-old boy whose aim was less than ideal, and our facilities were still exponentially cleaner than the women's loo at the Pretty Kitten. Wishing I had a gas mask, I sprayed everything down liberally and stepped outside to catch my breath and let things "marinate" for a few minutes.

Frank was just coming out of the treatment room when I closed the bathroom door. He gave me a quick wink and walked gingerly down the hallway. If his act included dancing, I hoped he had good painkillers; his gait reminded me of when I visited my grandmother in an assisted-living facility.

As Frank settled up with Yvonne—he, too, paid cash and got a discount—the front bell rang, and an older man walked in. I paused; something about him was familiar. Closing the bathroom door, I walked up to the front of the salon and listened as he signed in.

He gave his name as Elwood.

"Full wax?" Yvonne asked.

He nodded. "The usual," he told her.

"I'll take him!" I sang out.

Yvonne turned around and looked at me, surprised. "Are you sure you know what you're getting into?" she asked in a low voice.

"Of course," I said, pulling off my yellow rubber gloves. Thankfully, another client walked in just then, making the decision easier for her. "Which room is free?"

"Number three," she said, shrugging. "Good luck."

"Follow me, sir," I chirped, leading him down the hall before Elwood could have second thoughts.

"Go ahead and get ready," I told him. "Towels are in the corner."

"You're a new girl," he said, leering at me, then narrowing his eyes a bit. "Have I seen you somewhere before?"

"Probably here on one of your visits," I said, closing the door of the treatment room behind me.

Unless I was very mistaken, I was about to wax the Shamrock Streaker.

CHAPTER TWENTY-THREE

When I walked back into Elwood's treatment room a few minutes later, he was stretched out under a towel. "Ready?" I asked.

"I love it when I get a new girl," he said. I glanced down; the towel seemed rather tentlike. Terrific.

"So, the whole shebang, or just the . . . er . . . bikini area?"

"I can take care of my legs," he said. "But I need a little help going hairless down below, if you know what I mean."

"Right," I said, reaching for the numbing lotion and wishing it were a bottle of whiskey. I wasn't sure how much waxers got paid per hour, but I was pretty sure it wasn't enough. I gloved up and then squirted some of the lotion onto my hand. "Ready?"

"Can't you tell?" He winked.

I took a deep breath and reached for the towel, inching it down his abdomen . . . to where a rainbow tattoo arched down toward Elwood's tentpole.

"You can just take the towel off altogether if it's easier," he suggested.

"Oh no," I said. "It's good." I smeared on some of the numbing cream. "You know, I think I've seen a tattoo like this somewhere before."

"The ladies love it," he said.

"I can only imagine," I said. "Like the ladies at the Zilker Park Garden Club?"

The tentpole sagged. "What?"

"I knew I'd seen you somewhere before," I said.

"You . . . You were the one," he said.

"That was me," I said. "Now. Are you ready?"

"I . . . I think I've changed my mind," he said, clutching his towel to him. "I think I have to go."

"Oh, but it'll be so much fun!" I said. "Are you sure?"

"Absolutely," he said.

"Well, you'll still have to pay a cancellation fee, I'm afraid . . ."

"You won't . . . You won't tell anyone, will you?" he asked.

"About your garden club visit?"

"It's not just the garden club," he said.

"You frequent other ladies' clubs?"

"No, it's not that! It's . . . there's this woman I like."

"You know, you could always just ask her out," I suggested.

"I'm too shy," he said.

I looked down at him. "You're kidding me, right?"

"No," he said. "She lives in my building. I've admired her for a while, but I know she's way out of my league."

"What's her name?"

He sighed. "Willhelmina," he said.

I blinked at him. "Willie?"

"You know her?"

"I do," I said.

He reached up and grabbed my arm; his face was almost as pink as mine now. "Don't tell her it's me," he begged. "Please. I'd die of embarrassment."

"You run in front of a plate glass window wearing a sausage-stuffed shamrock sock and a unicorn mask, and you're too embarrassed to ask a woman out on a date?"

"It's complicated," he said. "If you tell her, I'll sue your pig."

I bit my lip. "She's still missing."

"Have you tried baiting her with Hickory Farms sausage?"

"Good idea," I said. "Look. I'll cut you a deal. Either you tell her, or I do."

"What?"

"She's got to know. If you tell her, you can confess that you think she's beautiful and just wanted to get her attention. If I tell her, she thinks you're some kind of weird pervert." Not that he wasn't, but I'd leave it to Willie to decide what to do with him.

"I can't!"

"You can."

"What about the pig?"

"You didn't get hurt, did you?"

"It was porcine assault!"

"Do you really want to admit to the authorities that you were streaking at the garden club?"

"I wasn't totally naked."

"You were after Twinkles got to you," I pointed out.

"All right," he said. "Fine."

"I'll go get Yvonne to do your waxing," I said. "One week, okay?"

"One week," he said.

"What's your number?" I asked. "I'll find out what her favorite restaurant is. You can ask her out after you spill the beans."

"You don't think she'll turn me down?"

"I'll put out a feeler," I said.

"Thank you," he told me. "What's your name?"

"Margie," I said.

"Margie," he repeated as I pulled a pen out of my apron pocket, and we used waxing cloths to exchange numbers.

"If it goes well, I'll help you find your pig."

"I'll take you up on that," I said, handing him the number. "I'll grab Yvonne."

"I'll be waiting," he said.

"One last thing, though. If you start dating Willie, you have to stop exposing yourself to the ladies."

"If I can expose myself to Willie, that's all I'll need."

"And I hope you like pot roast," I said, thinking of Willie's culinary approach to wooing men.

"It's my favorite." He beamed as I walked out and flagged down Yvonne.

"Done?"

"He requested you," I said. "He said you've got a natural touch."

She rolled her eyes. "Dirty old man," she muttered, and I wondered if setting him up with Willie was such a good idea. I knew I'd told him I wouldn't reveal who he was, but I wasn't going to send her out with the Shamrock Streaker without her knowing, either.

The dating pool was awfully shallow, I thought as Yvonne pushed past me in a cloud of cheap perfume. Maybe staying single wasn't such a bad idea after all.

• • •

I managed to escape the Pretty Kitten without having to wax anyone's privates, and with enough information to make Wanda very happy—or at least much better informed. I left a message for Willie to call me back—another case closed—and fielded a text from Frank. He was dropping the tickets off in my mailbox that afternoon.

I dialed Blake. "Would you mind keeping the kids tomorrow night?" I asked.

"I can't," he said. "I have to go to a benefit."

Duh. Of course he was going to see Frank perform. "I'll be there, too."

"Why?"

"It's linked to something I'm working on," I said. "What about your parents?"

"My mom said they're going out that night, too," he said. "Is Connie free?"

"I'll ask her," I said. "Man, I feel like I'm out every night lately; I hate it." I sighed. "I guess I can always ask Peaches."

"You're kidding me, right?"

"Becky might be a better option," I agreed.

"If you don't have any luck, let me know. One of my partners has a teenager who babysits."

"Thanks," I said, reflecting that Blake was a better husband now that we were separated than when we were together. My heart twinged, but I pushed the feeling aside. "I'll text you and let you know," I said as I got into the van, glancing at the bumper still wedged between the seats.

Another thing on my list, I thought. A list that for some reason seemed to grow, but never shrink.

CHAPTER TWENTY-FOUR

O f course I'll take the kids," my mother said when I asked her to watch them while I went to the fundraiser.

"Great," I said. "It doesn't start until eight; I'll take them to soccer practice first."

"Perfect," she said. "Where are you going?"

"A benefit for Austin Heights," I said.

"Ah," she told me. "By the way, how did your waxing salon experience go?"

"Ummm . . . It was interesting," I said.

"Did you have to do the deed?"

"No, thankfully. But I may have solved two of my cases . . . and I had to clean the most disgusting bathroom I've ever seen. I'm not sure which is worse." I glanced at my phone. "Shoot," I said. "Elsie!" I called. "Are you ready for soccer?"

She danced into the room wearing a pair of soccer shorts and a pink tutu.

"Are you sure Coach Trey is going to be okay with that?" I asked.

"He told me not to wear my collar," she said. "He didn't say anything about a tutu."

My mother and I exchanged glances, and I shrugged.

At least she wasn't complaining about Twinkles or the fry phone.

• • •

Coach Trey was already yelling when we arrived at the soccer field a few minutes later. Nick had stayed home with his grandma, and Elsie had refused to take off her tutu. She loped out onto the field, kicking her pink soccer ball in front of her, as I took my spot among the moms on the bleachers. Pansy, I noticed, was absent, but Janelle was splayed out on the second bleacher, looking like happy hour had started early—like around noon.

"You made it!" Janelle said, waving her half-empty Frappuccino at me.

"I did," I said, taking my seat on the bleachers and looking at the team.

"We're the Red Avengers!" Trey barked at the girls. "What's our cheer?"

"Take no prisoners," the girls said in a halfhearted chant.

"That's right," he said, then spied Elsie. "What is that?" he asked, pointing to her sparkly tutu.

She jutted out her lower jaw. "It's my tutu."

"Take it off."

"No," she said.

"How are you going to kick a ball in a skirt?" he yelled at her.

I couldn't hear Elsie's verbal response, but everyone saw her physical response. As we watched, her foot shot out, making contact with the pink ball and launching it directly—and at high velocity—at the coach's crotch.

"You little . . ." He doubled over, clutching his crotch, while the rest of the team looked on with a mix of horror and mirth. Elsie ran over and retrieved her ball, then joined her companions, who took a step away from her.

"Ouch. What are you going to do about that?" Janelle asked me.

To be honest, I wasn't quite sure—he had asked the question, after all—but it looked like I should probably do a bit of damage control.

I got up and shuffled over to where Trey was writhing on the ground, moaning.

"Are you okay?" I asked.

"She's off the team," he said.

"What? I don't think you can do that."

"I just did," he said.

"It was an accident," I said.

"You were kind of yelling at her," Becky said, coming up behind me. "Besides, you've been looking for another forward. It looks like you might have found one."

He looked up at her and grimaced.

"You can't get rid of her," Becky continued. "We won't have any subs."

"Fine," he said, then turned to glare at my daughter. "But I'll be watching you," he said in a menacing tone.

"Maybe if you were a little nicer to the girls, morale might improve," Becky commented. "Anyway . . . Do you want us to take over practice?"

"I've got it," he growled, slowly getting to his feet. "Five laps," he barked, walking crablike to the sidelines.

"Who turned you into Xena: Warrior Princess?" I asked Becky as we walked back over to the sidelines.

"He's a jerk," she said. "He deserved it. By the way, any word on Pansy?"

"I've got a few new leads," I said.

"Gossip has been all over town today," she said. "Poor Pansy."

"What do you know about LifeBoost?" I asked.

"Michael was negotiating a shipping contract for them just the other day," she said.

"Really?" I asked. "Do you think he could get me into the bottling company or something?"

"Why?"

"I have a feeling what happened to Tristan may have had something to do with LifeBoost. And I heard Steven Maxwell invested in it," I said. "He's got an event tonight, and I'm going after soccer practice."

"Wow. Any word on Twinkles?"

"No," I said. "Thanks for asking. And Frances keeps sending me awful pictures of Elsie's fry phone."

"Like what?"

I looked down at my phone. There was a new text: a picture of someone, presumably Frances, dangling the fry phone over a wood chipper. I showed it to Becky.

"That's awful!" she said.

"I know. And I have no idea how to find out where her money is. If she did invest in LifeBoost, I'm hoping there are some documents at Steven Maxwell's house that show it."

"You're going to rifle through his office while you're at his party?"

"You have any other suggestions?"

She was quiet.

"Well?"

"I'm thinking," she said.

"Right. Let me know if you come up with anything. Until then, I'm going with Plan A."

"Be careful," she said.

"I've invited Peaches."

"Oh God."

"Yeah. And Blake's boyfriend is performing."

"Performing what?"

I sighed. "He's a Madonna impersonator. 'Like a Virgin' is his specialty, according to Blake."

"Man, I wish I could go. I'd love to watch that show . . ."

We returned to the bleachers and watched the kids on the field. Trey handed his daughter a bottle of LifeBoost; she chugged it and handed it back to him. "Talk about a stage mom," someone said. "You'd think she was his only child."

"He's got a son, right?" another mom asked.

"Yeah, but he's not into sports, so his dad doesn't want anything to do with him," Becky said. "Honestly, I'm not sure his daughter's into sports, either, but he doesn't give her much of a choice."

"She's pretty good, though," I said, watching as Brianna wove among her teammates like a fox among a bunch of chickens. She snagged the ball from Zoe and put it smack in the center of the goal. "I wonder why she didn't make the Rec Plus team?"

"I think it's because her father pissed off the league director," Becky said. "He's got the social graces of a water buffalo."

"I noticed," I said, watching Elsie, who was picking dandelions. The coach glanced at her, looked like he was about to bark something, then caught me watching and kept his mouth shut.

A moment later, Brianna stole the ball and streaked by everyone again. And then, suddenly, she put her hands to her chest and stopped.

"What's going on?" I asked.

"I don't know," Becky said, standing up. "She looks like she's having trouble breathing or something." As we watched, the girl's legs buckled, and she fell to her knees.

"Brianna!" Trey was racing across the field to his daughter, who crumpled to the ground just as he got there. "Help!" He looked up wildly. "Someone call 911!"

• • •

As Phyllis dialed 911, the rest of us hurried across the field.

"What's wrong with Brianna?" Elsie asked.

"She's not feeling very well," I told Elsie as Trey crouched over his daughter. "We're going to take her to get checked out."

"Let's do a few drills," Becky said, taking charge of the situation. "Why don't we practice taking shots on the goal?" she suggested, and together we herded the girls over to the other end of the field. As we cycled them through the line, letting each girl take a shot and then stand in the goal, our eyes drifted over to Brianna. It seemed forever before the whine of a siren came; all of a sudden, there were two fire trucks and an ambulance, and EMTs were rushing across the field to the prone form on the ground.

The girls faltered, but Becky kept them moving. As they loaded Brianna onto a stretcher and carried her to the ambulance, everyone just stopped and stared. "Keep going, girls," Becky said, and she and I hurried over to the gaggle of moms who'd been surrounding Trey and Brianna.

"What is it?" I asked.

"Tachycardia," Chantal said. "Her heart rate was super high. They don't know why; they're taking her in to make sure she's okay."

"Did they say if she's going to be all right?" I asked.

Chantal shook her head. "They didn't say anything. I don't think they know what's going on." She glanced over at the bottle on the ground. "I wouldn't be surprised if it was that weird combination of Chinese herbs. Those things are totally unregulated, and he gave them to her like they were lollipops. Said they 'boosted her performance.'"

"I think it may be time to call practice for the day," Becky said. She walked back to the girls and brought them over.

"What's wrong with Brianna?" they asked.

"They're taking her to find out," Becky told them. "We're going to end practice early, since her dad went with her. Does everyone have a parent here?"

Most did; Becky and I called the remaining two parents, and as the girls dispersed, she looked at me. "That LifeBoost does make me kind of hyped up," she said. "Do you think maybe that's what caused it?"

"All I've heard is that it's some proprietary herbal blend. Maybe some kind of epinephrine?" I suggested. "Wasn't there something named ma-hwangsomething a few years back that was a stimulant?"

"I think so," she said. "Do you think maybe that's what did Tristan in?"

"It's possible," I said. "I haven't heard anything about an autopsy."

"Me neither." She shivered. "I hope Brianna is going to be okay."

"Where's the bottle she was drinking from?"

"Over there on the ground," she said. I walked over and picked it up, then walked to the bleachers.

"Is she going to be okay?" Elsie asked.

"I hope so," I said. "At least they got her to the hospital quickly."

"I'll bet it was those awful drinks," Janelle said. "I had one the other day, and I felt so jittery I almost punched someone who tapped me on the shoulder. Do you think they're overloaded with caffeine, like those Monster drinks?"

"They make me feel kind of high-strung, too," Chantal said. "I drank one at dinner the other night and didn't get to sleep until three. But I read an entire book while I was up and reorganized the linen closet while I was at it."

"I know," another mom said. "I just get tons of stuff done, and I'm never hungry. It really is like a magic drink. I'm not sure I'd give it to my kids, though. You just never know what's in that stuff."

"Isn't it going to be distributed nationally?" Chantal asked.

"I thought it was just local," Janelle said.

"They were in negotiations to expand it to another bottling company," someone said. "My husband said something about it the other day. Now that Tristan Prescott's gone, though, I don't know where things stand."

"I think Dr. Flynn was consulting on it."

"Dr. Flynn? Isn't he a neurologist?"

"That's the one," another mom said. "It was hush-hush, but we saw them meeting a few times. I wouldn't be surprised if there was some kind of kickback."

Dr. Flynn was definitely someone I needed to talk to—even Blake's mom had mentioned him once when we were talking about Elsie—but from what I'd heard around town, it wasn't going to be easy to get an appointment. "I hear he's got a long waiting list for patients," I said.

"He does, but if you let him know you know another patient, they'll squeeze you in earlier."

"Good to know," I said. I was thinking of getting Elsie checked out anyway; it might be a way to kill two birds with one stone, so to speak.

"It's super convenient; he's got his own pharmacy on the premises, so they can fill your prescription right there at the office. And it's in the neighborhood."

"No wonder he's got a waiting list," I said. "I think I'll make an appointment for my daughter."

"Why? Is she having problems?"

"Just a checkup."

"He'll give you a scrip for ADD drugs if you ask," a mom I recognized from the PTA meeting—Sarah Soggs, I remembered—said. "They made a huge difference when my daughter took the SAT."

"You have a high schooler?"

"No . . . She's in fifth grade, but you can never start too early."

"Right," I said. "So she doesn't have ADD?"

"Of course not," Sarah said. "But since everyone else is getting chemical help, why shouldn't she? Things are so competitive these days. It's important to get them into the right activities and the right classes early—and SAT scores are really important."

I blinked at my daughter. I was mainly worried about her eating with a fork—not learning algebra and analogies. "What about just being kids?"

"I know," Chantal said wistfully. "It's nothing at all like it was when we grew up. But it's a different world, isn't it?"

Only because we made it that way, I thought as I collected Elsie and headed to the car. As we left the field, my daughter looked up at me. "Is Brianna really going to be okay?"

"I'm sure she is," I said, hoping I was right.

CHAPTER TWENTY-FIVE

My mother and Blake were chatting happily in the kitchen when I got home.

"Brianna fell over on the field, and they took her to the hospital," Elsie announced.

"Wow. Do they know why?" Blake asked.

"I haven't heard," I said. "Hey—who was that doctor your mom was recommending we see?"

"Dr. Flynn?"

"That's the one," I said. "I got another recommendation for him tonight. I think I'm going to make an appointment."

"I still think there's nothing wrong," Blake said, "but I guess it can't hurt. I just don't want her labeled with anything."

"I agree," I said. And even if he did prescribe Elsie some kind of strange drug, that didn't mean I had to give it to her.

• • •

By the time Becky was finished dressing me up for the gala, I could barely breathe. "I hate Spanx," I said. "I'm afraid if I sit down, I'm going to cut off all circulation to my legs."

"You'll get used to it," she said.

"Not having circulation in my legs?" I asked.

"The compression," she said. "Besides, at least you won't be tempted to overeat!"

"Right," I said as I tottered down the front walk and levered myself into the minivan.

Steven Maxwell's house was enormous. It had stuccoed walls and an orange tile roof and was about the length of a city block. At first I thought it was a La Quinta, but there wasn't a parking lot and there was no Denny's in front of it.

Peaches was standing on the vast front porch waiting for me when I walked up to the entrance. I hardly recognized her; she was in a black sheath dress with a fairly tasteful-looking pearl necklace. Only the hair, which she'd redyed tangerine orange, and her six-inch leopard-print platform wedges told me I was looking at my boss.

"You finally made it," she said, taking a last drag of her e-cigarette before tucking it back into her bra. "I was wondering if you'd been swallowed by your dishwasher or something."

"No such luck," I said, adjusting my navy skirt and wishing I'd let Becky talk me into something a little more glamorous. Compared to the women in fashionable summer dresses I saw filing past me, I felt like I'd just come from a shopping trip at the Salvation Army.

"Where's your buddy, Becky?" Peaches asked as we sailed through the massive front door together.

"She had to watch the kids tonight," I said as she surveyed the living room. It looked like the inside of a Spanish mission church—not just in decor, but in size—with tall stuccoed walls and arched windows. Except the back of the house, which seemed to have one of those massive glass walls. It was currently open, letting both the sound of jazz music and the tastefully dressed middle-aged guests drift back and forth from the patio to the living room. If that's what you called the hangar-size space we were standing in.

"This is some pad," Peaches said. "And he lives alone?"

"Single, from what I hear. New hair color?"

"I figured I should touch it up before this shindig. Is he looking for a girlfriend?" she asked, reaching up to adjust her hair. It was so orange that I felt the urge to avert my eyes.

"What about Jess?" I asked, referring to her on-again, off-again boyfriend.

"I was kidding," she said halfheartedly, then practically tackled a young woman carrying a platter of wineglasses. "Got any Shiner?" she asked.

"Just Chardonnay and Merlot, I'm afraid," the young woman said. "You could ask at one of the bars, though." She nodded toward a skirted table tucked outside beneath a palm tree.

"Bars? Plural?" Peaches asked.

"Yes, ma'am," the young woman said.

"Well, I'll take one of these to start with," she told the young woman. "And then we'll toddle over that way," she told me. As we lightened the woman's tray by two glasses, Peaches reached down and tugged at her hemline. "I feel so frumpy in this outfit."

I looked down at my too-long navy skirt. "You're kidding me, right?"

"Well . . . relatively speaking, anyway. We really need to take you shopping before your next date."

"If they're anything like Marshmallow and his sidekick, I'll pass. By the way," I said, "since I'm going to be busy tomorrow, would you track down the receipts from the PTA and make sure they match what's in the register? I'll drop the file at the office."

"Got it," she said.

That was one thing sorted, I thought. I looked around the lush backyard, which was the size of a football field—only a football field that a landscape architect had been allowed to turn into a tropical Disneyland fantasy. Bunches of colorful red and orange flowering plants with glossy leaves ringed the manicured grass—the guy's watering bill must have been insane, I thought, since none of the plants looked equipped for dry Austin summers—and tiled fountains tinkled here and there, flanked by lush green foliage and about ten types of palm trees. Giant swathes of bougainvillea decorated planters on the back deck. If I tipped one over, I thought, I could probably maim someone.

White-clothed tables were arranged on the back porch and the green stretch of grass not far from the infinity pool; a small jazz band played soft music, and black-tied waitstaff milled through the sparkling crowd, offering tidbits that were mostly declined by the skeletal but fabulously dressed attendees.

And by me, unfortunately. I'd already put enough stress on the seams of my underwear; I wasn't sure they could handle even a miniature flauta, no matter how temptingly golden it was. I was considering disappearing into the bathroom to de-Spanx myself; then I remembered that without the Spanx, I looked a little like a can of Pillsbury biscuits that had popped its seams, and looked longingly at a bowl of *queso* instead.

"I'm going to get in line," Peaches said. "See you in a few?"

"I'll be checking the place out," I said.

I headed back inside. As I strolled around looking for Steven Maxwell's office and trying to find an opportunity to sneak upstairs, I heard a familiar voice from behind me. I turned to see my husband.

"Blake!" I said, smiling at him. He was with two middle-aged men I didn't recognize.

He excused himself from the conversation and walked over to the side of the room with me. "Are you sure you're okay being here? The performance is going to be by—"

"Frank," I supplied. "I know. He got me free tickets."

"Where did you see him?" Blake asked, surprised.

"I . . . ran into him," I said, deciding there was no need to tell him of my gig as a waxer at the Pretty Kitten. "It went fine. He's very nice."

Something like relief washed over Blake's face. "I'm glad you think so."

A familiar, whiny voice caught my ear; I looked over to see Trey Volker and winced.

"What?" Blake asked.

"Elsie's coach is here," I told him. "I'm afraid Elsie's soccer career may be short," I said. "He's still irked over the tutu incident. I kind of had a disastrous date with him, too."

"Him?" Blake asked.

"Yeah," I said. "I told him he needed a personality transplant."

Blake burst into laughter. Trey glanced over and spotted me; his eyes narrowed. Blake and I both smiled and waved; he turned red and made a beeline for the bar.

"He was about to kick Elsie off the team, but Becky intervened."

"Good to have friends in high places," he commented.

"It is," I admitted. "Hey . . . Do you know anything about Maxwell?"

"I know he's had a couple of bad deals lately," he said. "He invested millions in a tech company that declared bankruptcy six months later. Apparently the 'new' technology had already been introduced by a rival three months earlier."

"Ouch," I said.

"He needs a big win," Blake said. "It costs a lot to maintain all of this."

"I'll bet," I said.

I was about to ask him if he knew anything about the bottling company when he said, "Oh my God."

"What?"

"Look." He stabbed a finger at a familiar couple. His parents.

"What are they doing here?" I asked.

"I don't know," he said.

"Do they know Frank's performing?"

"If they don't, they will soon," he said. Although he was coming to terms with his new "lifestyle," it was still proving a bit of a challenge for his parents—particularly his father.

"Let's go this way," I said, turning to the left and tugging him behind me. We had gotten about five steps before I ran into Trey, who had taken a step backward to check out a twentysomething who was wobbling back and forth on a pair of pink platform wedges.

"What are you doing here?" he asked.

"Supporting the elementary school," I said. "How's your daughter?"

"Better," he said.

"Any idea what caused it?"

"We're still figuring that out," he said, darting his eyes to the side. "Maybe too much caffeine." Something told me it wasn't just caffeine that was the problem.

"Is she going to be okay?" I asked.

"They're keeping her under observation, but they said she's probably fine."

"I'm so glad," I said.

Trey suddenly seemed to notice Blake, and his eyebrows went up a bit.

"I'm sorry, I haven't introduced you. Have you met my husband?" I asked.

He blinked. "Husband? I thought you were separated?"

"We are." Blake extended his right hand. "I'm Blake. I understand you're coaching Elsie's team?"

"I am," he said.

"Who's this?" Peaches asked, toddling up with a Chardonnay in one hand and a Shiner in the other.

"You know Blake, of course. And this is Trey Volker," I said to Peaches.

She glanced down at his slacks. "He's wearing pants, but I'm guessing you're right about the chicken legs."

"Pardon me?" Trey asked.

"I hear my daughter's got quite a foot," Blake said, changing the subject—not that it helped. "Sounds like you've got yourself a forward."

Trey turned red. "Your daughter's got some serious discipline problems," he said. "If it were up to me, she wouldn't be on the team at all."

"Good thing it's not up to you, then," Blake said mildly.

Trey didn't seem to know what to say, so he harrumphed and walked off.

"I can see what you mean about the personality transplant," Peaches said.

My husband grinned at me. "Must have been a fun date."

"It kind of went downhill after I told him I'd seen bigger legs on a newborn fawn," I said, and he laughed.

"Margie?" I turned to see Willhelmina staring at me, bright eyed. "Is this your new beau?" she asked, looking at Blake.

"This is my husband, actually," I said.

"He's a looker, isn't he?"

Blake blushed.

"His boyfriend is a lucky man," I said, trying to ignore the twist in my gut. "And you've met Peaches."

"I have," she said. "Terrific shoes."

"Yours are pretty awesome, too," Peaches said, pointing at her blingy gladiator sandals. They were topped by peacock-blue harem pants and a zebra-print tunic with about six sparkly necklaces. Willie's hair was growing back in now that the cancer treatments were done, and she had dyed her cropped hair copper. She and Peaches were almost a matched set.

"I can't do heels anymore, but I do what I can," Willie said. "Any luck on the streaker?"

"Sort of," I said. "I should have more for you by the end of the week." That would give Elwood time to work up his courage.

"I'm not sure if Martha will be happy or disappointed," she said. "I think the heart attack she had when that streaker came by was the most exciting thing to happen to her in years!"

I glanced over and realized Prue had spotted us. She said something to Phil, and his face lit up as he looked over at us. "Uh-oh," I said to Blake. "Here they come."

"Blake! Margie!" Prue seemed delighted to see us together, and she pulled me into a more enthusiastic hug than I'd ever received. "I'm so glad to see you both!"

"Patching things up, finally?" Phil asked, beaming, and slapped Blake on the shoulder. "I knew it was just a phase."

"Ummm . . ."

"We're not here together, Phil," I said, rescuing Blake.

"No?"

"No," Blake said. As he spoke, Frank came up behind him, wearing shorts and a pink button-down shirt. He gave Blake a peck on the cheek; Blake turned a bit pink, but Frank turned to his parents and greeted them with a smile. Frank might have been a gay-reform-camp counselor a few months earlier, but once he came to terms with his sexuality, he certainly embraced it.

My father-in-law, on the other hand, looked like he was about to suffer a coronary. "How dare you!" he asked.

"Dad," Blake said, putting a hand on his arm.

My father-in-law jerked away. "Don't touch me," he said to his son, and then turned to Frank, who had turned pale under his pancake makeup. "You've just completely . . . perverted my son. I don't even know who he is anymore. He used to be a family man, with a wife, and, and now, he's consorting with . . . freaks." He spit the last word out, and I took an involuntary step back.

"Philip," my mother-in-law said. "This is not the time or the place."

Blake stood paralyzed. Frank looked from Blake to his father. "I should go," he said, and turned away, weaving through the crowd of onlookers.

"Follow him," I said to Blake without thinking.

He stood frozen for another moment, then turned to me and said, "Thank you." Without another look at his father, he turned and plunged through the crowd, calling Frank's name.

CHAPTER TWENTY-SIX

B lake. Come back," his father ordered.

My husband didn't even glance over his shoulder.

"Margie," Willie said, putting a hand on my arm and breaking the strained silence. "I have someone I'd like to introduce you to." She turned to my in-laws. "It was nice to meet you," she told them, then led me away.

"I'm sorry that happened while you were there, but thank you," I said to her. "I appreciate the rescue."

"I can see now that the pot roast was never going to work," she told me, reaching up to touch her cropped hair. "Besides, I wasn't kidding. I do have someone I want you to meet." She pulled us up to one of the bars and tapped a man on the shoulder. "Elwood?" she said. "I want you to meet a friend of mine."

He turned around and dropped his drink on the stone patio.

"Nice to meet you," I said, thrusting out a hand and trying not to grin.

He opened and closed his mouth like a hooked fish for a moment.

"Elwood?" Willie asked. "Are you okay?"

"Fine," he said, recovering himself. "You just looked . . . familiar."

I'll bet, I thought, and turned to Willie. "How do you and Elwood know each other?" I asked.

"It turns out we live in the same building," she told me. "He stopped by the other day and told me he had an extra ticket to this shindig. I'm always up for a night out on the town, and it turns out we have a lot in common. And I promised to make him pot roast!" she added, winking at me.

I looked at Elwood, who was still looking somewhat stunned. "I have a feeling there's more to this man than meets the eye," I said.

He blanched. There seemed to be a lot of that going around tonight.

I watched Elwood out of the corner of my eye. He wiped a bead of sweat from his brow.

"Where are you sitting?" Willie asked me.

"Probably not with my in-laws," I said, glancing back toward where we'd had our little conversation. Neither of Blake's parents was in evidence.

"Maybe we could sit together!" Willie suggested. Elwood choked, and Willie slapped him on the back.

"Thanks for the invite," I said. "I may take you up on it."

"I hear there's going to be a great Madonna impersonator tonight," Willie said. "I hope she does 'Material Girl.' I always liked that song."

"We'll see!" I said, thinking that it was turning out to be quite an exciting night.

Elwood moved a few steps away to replace his drink, and I took the opportunity to touch Willie's sleeve.

"There's something I have to tell you about the case," I said in an urgent voice.

"Margie, relax! It's your night off . . . We'll talk business tomorrow." She looked over at the buffet table. "Oh, look. The food's out. Let's go get some!"

"But—" Before I could say anything else, Elwood was back. "I'll let you two go . . . but come see me before you leave," I said. I wasn't going to let her go home with Elwood until she knew what she was getting into.

"The invitation to join us is open!" she said.

"Thanks. By the way," I added, "what does Steven Maxwell look like?"

"He's over there," Willie said, pointing to a tall, slightly paunchy man in slacks, with skin the color of drywall. He did not look like a regular consumer of LifeBoost . . . or even sunlight.

"So his investments haven't panned out recently?" I asked.

"Not at all," she said. "String of bad luck. It's a good thing LifeBoost is going so well, or there might be a 'For Sale' sign out front."

"Thanks, Willie. Nice to meet you, Elwood," I said, turning to her companion, who was still looking slightly sick. I glanced back at my friend. "Catch you later?"

"Promise," Willie said as she grabbed Elwood by the arm and hauled him toward the buffet line.

I snagged a fresh glass of white wine from a passing waiter and drifted over toward Steven Maxwell, who was talking with a few tanned, fit men who, unlike the venture capitalist, looked like they spent more time on the golf course than in the office.

"I hear the company's expanding. Is it too late to ante up?" one of the men was asking as I walked by.

"There might still be some opportunity," Maxwell replied. "Call my office and set up an appointment, and we can talk about it."

"My wife swears by the stuff," another one of them said. "She's lost ten pounds in a month."

"It is pretty amazing," Maxwell said.

"Who was the doctor who came up with the formula?"

"It was Flynn, wasn't it?" the first man asked. "I saw him a few minutes ago. He looks like he could use some of his own medicine." He chuckled.

"And it looks like the company founder had a little too much of it," another said. "Although I hear he was getting some on the side, and that's what did him in."

"If you're gonna go, that's not a bad way to do it," one of the other men said.

"Have you all had dinner yet?" Maxwell asked. He didn't seem too anxious to talk about Tristan, I noticed. Or LifeBoost. "The shrimp is amazing; I had a little bit earlier." He put a hand on one of the men's shoulders. "I look forward to meeting with you this week. Now, if you'll excuse me . . ."

He headed toward the house, scanning the crowd. I followed him, watching as he nodded at several of the partygoers, and then put his hand on the arm of a short, stout man who was wearing a suit that looked like it might have fit him ten years ago. Maxwell said something in his ear; the stout man's smile faded, and he excused himself from his companions. I drifted behind them as together they headed into the house.

I walked inside after them, watching as they disappeared down a short corridor to the left of the cavernous entry hall. I lingered a moment in the hall, then nonchalantly followed them, stopping when I heard voices through an open door.

"Who did you tell?" Maxwell asked.

"I didn't say anything," the shorter man spluttered.

"The guy I was just talking to knows you consulted," he said. "The deal was no connection, remember?"

"It's not connected. There's no paper trail. I promise."

"It's your company ordering it, isn't it? Of course there's a paper trail!"

"Yes, but it's not being shipped to the plant. It gets shipped elsewhere, then delivered locally."

I crept closer, hoping to hear more, but the door slammed shut. I turned around and headed back down the hall just in time to see Pansy walk through the front door on the arm of a man I presumed was her husband. He looked like he was attending a funeral; I was guessing she finally let him know she'd been arrested.

"Pansy," I said.

She gave me a tight smile. "We'll talk later," she said.

"What are you doing here?"

"Keeping up appearances," she said, raising her chin and beaming at a rather startled-looking woman across the capacious living room.

As I walked through the living room behind her, I heard snatches of a few conversations. They weren't particularly complimentary. I looked around for a friendly face. Blake was nowhere in evidence, his parents had vanished, and Willie was deep in conversation with the Shamrock Streaker. I found myself browsing the silent auction items and watching Pansy as she attempted to strike up conversations with a series of women, all of whom suddenly found something else to do. I was about to go and find a table when Janelle materialized behind me.

"Margie!" she bellowed. "I thought that was you. You had any one-on-one time with Mr. Big yet?"

"Uh . . . No," I said, blushing. "Where's your husband?"

"He's home with the kids," she said. "Did you hear about Pansy? I can't believe she killed her personal trainer! I always thought they kind of had something going . . ."

"She what?" I asked, as if I had no idea what she was talking about.

"Didn't you hear? They arrested her for killing Tristan. From what I hear, they broke up because he was seeing some other woman, and she killed him because she was jealous. Dumped his body in the parking lot of his gym. But who'd have guessed she'd be jealous of Phyllis?"

"Phyllis must have been really upset," I said.

"She was," Janelle told me.

"Did she suspect anything was going on between Tristan and Pansy?"

"Oh, how could she not know?" she said. "We all did."

"And she wasn't jealous?"

"Of course she would have been!" Janelle said. "She wanted him all to herself." Her eyes darted to Phyllis, who was wearing a sacklike dress that didn't scream *adulteress*.

"Are you sure they were together?"

"Well, you never can be sure, but that's what I've heard."

"Was he seeing anyone else?" I asked.

"Frances, of course."

"Oh?"

"You think Frances killed Tristan Prescott?" she announced. A half dozen people turned to stare at us.

"No. I was just asking. So," I said. "It seems like all of Austin Heights is here tonight."

"It does. This is the place to see and be seen," she told me. "Plus, it's all for a good cause: the Austin Heights Education Foundation."

"Right," I said. "And there's entertainment, too?"

"Oh yes," she said. "Austin's the live music capital." As she spoke, there was a crackling sound from the backyard stage. I looked over to see Maxwell behind the microphone.

"Good evening, ladies and gentlemen," he said. "Thank you so much for coming out to support the Austin Heights school district."

CHAPTER TWENTY-SEVEN

Peaches sidled up to me as I stood there. I excused myself and together we walked to a spot a short distance away from the stage. She looked remarkably subdued in a black dress with only a moderately plunging neckline. "Find anything out?" she asked.

"A few things," I said, telling her about the conversation I'd heard.

"Where was his office?"

"First floor," I said. "Down the hallway to the left of the front door."

"Wanna go check it out?" she suggested.

"Let's go together," I told her. "I'll stand guard at the end of the hallway."

Together, we made our way through the crowd in the living room, most of whom were now paying attention to Maxwell, who was going on about the school district and children.

"This is some house," Peaches murmured, touching the frame of what looked like an original painting. "How much do you think this is worth?"

"I have no idea," I told her. "Probably more than my minivan."

"I've bought bagels that were worth more than your minivan," Peaches said. "It looks like there used to be more," she said, pointing to a few empty nails on the wall.

"Maybe he's redecorating," I suggested.

"I hope he picks something better than this," Peaches said, stepping back to look at the red and yellow-green splotches on the canvas. "This way?" she asked, pointing to the short hallway.

"Yes," I said.

"I'll stand guard," Peaches said.

"I thought I was supposed to stand guard?"

She shrugged. "You need the practice more than I do," she said. "Besides, I'm kind of hungry." She waved to a young woman with a plate of bacon-wrapped shrimp. She finished off her glass of wine and exchanged it for two shrimp on a napkin.

"Really?" I asked.

"It'll be more natural than just standing here," she said, popping a shrimp into her mouth. "Go while he's talking. I hear there's a Madonna impersonator, and she's terrific. You won't want to miss her."

"That would be Blake's boyfriend," I told her.

"Huh. Well, maybe you will want to miss it."

"I haven't decided yet," I told her, then drifted down the hallway, feeling my palms turn clammy. At least I wasn't breaking in, I told myself; after all, I did have a ticket to the event, even if the invitation hadn't said anything about rifling through the owner's drawers.

As Peaches leaned against the wall at the end of the hallway, washing her shrimp down with a Shiner Bock, I turned the doorknob and let myself into the office. I hated snooping in other people's stuff; I'd ground Elsie and Nick if I found them doing what I was about to do. Which was unfortunate, since it was kind of an occupational hazard.

The office was bigger than my living room, with a massive mahogany desk in the center and a massive studded leather chair. The walls were covered in dark wood bookshelves populated with expensive knickknacks and a few old hardcover book sets that appeared to have been bought by the yard. The door might have been unlocked, but the desk drawers weren't. I tried them all, and then felt underneath them for taped-on papers or anything else exciting, but came up empty. My sandaled feet sank into the thick rug as I looked around the room. I wasn't sure what I was looking for, but it didn't appear to be here.

I did a quick search of the bookshelves, just in case, but all I found was a dead cockroach hiding behind a diminutive globe . . . and almost as much dust as there was carpeting my own shelves. Housekeeping could use some work, it seemed.

I was about to head for the door when I heard Peaches from down the hall. "Oh, I'm sorry I got in your way. Are you the owner of this place?" she asked.

There was no answer . . . and the footsteps were coming closer. There was a glass door to the front porch; I ran across and tried it, but it was stuck.

"This is a nice place you have here!" Peaches bellowed. "How long have you lived here?"

The reply was gruff . . . and right outside the door. I had two choices: have Steven Maxwell find me in his office, or hide. My eyes fell on the massive mahogany desk. I sprinted across the plush rug, twisting my ankle as I rounded the corner of the desk, and shoved myself into the knee well of the desk, which was about the size of my closet at home.

And about as dusty, I realized as I crawled to the back of the desk and stifled a sneeze.

"Are you sure you can afford this party?" a male voice asked from somewhere in the study.

"They're paying me for the venue," said a voice I recognized as Maxwell's. "I've got another deal about to happen, anyway; I'd sell, but I've got to keep up appearances. If the expansion goes through as planned, I won't have to worry about it."

"Any public offering or buyout interest on LifeBoost yet?" the other voice asked.

"I've gotten a few calls," said Maxwell. "But I'm not sure that would be in our best interest." A pair of black slacks and expensive loafers appeared, and then their owner deposited himself on the leather chair. I crouched farther back in the well of the desk, disturbing more dust. My nose started to run, and the urge to sneeze was unbearable.

"What are you going to do about it?"

"Haven't decided yet."

"Is Prescott's death a problem?"

"No," he said. "He wasn't a majority shareholder. He just had the idea; he only had a small share, although he was starting to make noise about wanting more. It's kind of convenient what happened, really. He was a liability."

"Because of the ladies?"

"Not just the ladies," Maxwell suggested. "But he couldn't keep his mouth shut if you taped it." The man crossed his legs and leaned back in his chair. I could see his face now; I just prayed he didn't look down.

"I hear demand is way up," the other man said. "Are you going to be able to keep up with it?"

"The plant's got capacity, and we're talking to two more, but it's sourcing the ingredients that might be a problem."

"How secure is your source?"

"Pretty good, I think . . . but the volume could be an issue."

"What about the FDA?"

"Supplements aren't regulated," Maxwell said. "I don't see a problem with that."

"What about the girl?"

"What about her? You're dealing with that, remember?"

"Of course."

"Any interest in the house, by the way?" another voice asked.

The answer was almost a growl. "How do you know about the house?"

"I know people," the man said.

"It's supposed to be kept quiet."

"I won't say anything. Promise."

"Good," Maxwell said, and then wheeled closer to the desk. "What about the other issue?"

"It'll be taken care of," said the first man.

"It needs to be done quickly," Maxwell said.

"It will be done by tomorrow. I promise."

"There's a lot riding on it," Maxwell warned.

"You don't have to remind me," the man answered. "I promise, it's as good as done."

"Good," Maxwell repeated. "We're going into two new markets next week, and there's a publicity push. It's got to be clean."

"Message received," the man said. There were footsteps; apparently the men left the office. Unfortunately, Maxwell didn't go with them. He pulled his chair under the desk, leaving his knees about half an inch from my face. The sneeze that had been threatening to explode welled up in me. I pinched my nose hard and tried to think of something other than sneezing. Like being found under Steven Maxwell's desk in an extremely compromising situation. I pressed myself more tightly against the back of the desk, hoping he would go and rejoin the party.

Instead, his phone rang. He picked it up on the second ring. "Maxwell," he said gruffly.

After a moment of silence, he said, "Wrong number."

I was about to sneeze when the door burst open.

"Can I help you?" Maxwell asked.

"This isn't the ladies' room," I heard Peaches say. "It's awful nice, though. Look at all those books! You must be a big reader."

"This is my private office," he said shortly, standing up.

Peaches evidently didn't take the hint, because a moment later I saw her leopard-print wedges sinking into the carpet as she pretended to examine the bookshelves. "Wow. You read this stuff?"

"I'd like you to leave now," Maxwell said in a tight voice.

"Sure," she said. "But will you show me where the bathroom is?"

"It's right by the front door."

"Can you show me?" she asked. "I'm a little bit turned around."

He stifled a sigh that I totally understood. "Follow me," he said.

A moment later, I heard her say, "Ooh, you've got strong arms. Do you work out?" as her wedges shuffle-clomped down the hallway. The sneeze I had been holding burst out of me.

"What was that?"

"What was what? Oh, look at this artwork. It kind of looks like lemon pudding with a splash of strawberry sauce. How much did that cost you, anyway?"

"The ladies' room is this way," he said firmly, and the clomping moved farther away. I unfurled myself from the back of the desk and crawled out into the room, then hurried toward the door. I was walking down the hallway when Maxwell reappeared, looking annoyed. He looked at me for a moment, as if trying to place my face. I smiled and moved past him, heart pounding, glad when he didn't stop me, and grabbed the first glass of wine I saw.

Peaches joined me two minutes later.

"You made it out," she said. "Sorry about that. Where were you, under the desk?"

I sneezed again and brushed my skirt off. "Me and a couple dozen dust bunnies," I said. "His housekeeping could use some work."

"Find anything out?"

"Maybe," I said, and reported what I'd heard.

"I wonder what the problem is?"

"I don't know," I said. "And everything was locked down."

"Think there's another office?"

"I doubt it," I said. As I spoke, the first bars of "Like a Virgin" came from the backyard. "I think that must be Frank."

"Are you up for it?" Peaches asked.

"Why not?" I said. "How many women get to watch their husband's boyfriend prance around in hot pants?"

It wasn't just hot pants, as it turned out. When we walked out, Frank was wearing a replica of Madonna's cone-studded bustier. He was very convincing—even down to the beauty mark penciled in above his lips. I glanced around the crowd; there was a mixture of horror, amusement, and fascination, just like the ladies' garden club when the streaker appeared. Speaking of streakers, Elwood was still looking nervous and stricken. Our eyes met as Frank launched into the opening lines, and his nostrils flared like those of a startled horse. I was guessing he hadn't broken the news to Willie yet.

I turned my attention to the stage, where Frank was prancing around in six-inch silver heels that looked a lot like something Peaches would wear. I scanned the crowd for Blake—he was toward the back of the crowd, looking both proud and embarrassed—then looked for my in-laws, hoping they weren't here. My father-in-law had some heart issues, and this might tip him over the edge. I found myself wondering whose idea it was to have a female impersonator at a school fundraiser.

Frank was just sliding across the stage, legs splayed, when there were two pops. A light near the front of the stage exploded into a shower of glass. Frank's eyes widened beneath the false eyelashes. He paused for a moment, lipsticked mouth wide open in an *O* of surprise, and then put a hand to his shoulder. Blood seeped through his fingers, and as music blared through the speakers, he crumpled to the stage.

CHAPTER TWENTY-EIGHT

F rank!" Blake vaulted onto the stage and knelt over the fallen performer as the music continued to blare. Everything else seemed frozen. Blake grabbed the microphone from the stage and yelled, "Call 911! He's been shot." There was mass panic from the crowd, and as he dropped the mic, the speaker squealed.

He pressed a hand to Frank's bleeding shoulder. I grabbed my phone and called 911; Peaches jogged to the stage, somehow managing not to kill herself as she vaulted up the steps.

"Where did the bullet come from?" she bellowed over the music.

"Behind the stage," Blake said.

"Got it," Peaches said, then reached in her spangled purse and pulled out a gun before disappearing into a wooded area behind and to the left of the stage.

As I finished giving the details to the dispatcher, I scanned the crowd. Pansy was there, near the front of the crowd, but there was no sign of Blake's parents. A sick feeling bloomed in my stomach; had Blake's father gone crazy and shot Frank?

No, I thought. It wasn't that. It was something else. Maybe something involving LifeBoost.

But what?

I shoved my phone back into my purse and hurried to the other side of the stage, hoping whoever had shot Frank didn't still have bullets in the gun and wishing I had something other than a vibrator as a weapon.

The music shut off suddenly, along with the lights. There was a momentary silence and a rustle of leaves ahead of me. Adrenaline pulsed through me as I dropped into a crouch; behind me, there was a sudden buzz of voices, as if someone had flipped a switch. I reached in my purse for Mr. Big—I figured I could always club someone over the head with it—and crept behind a gnarled oak tree. As I crouched behind the trunk, there was another rustle, and footsteps came closer. I held my breath and raised Mr. Big over my head as a person stepped out from behind the tree.

"Holy shit!" Peaches yelled as I brought the enormous vibrator down on her head with a crack.

"Oh my God," I said. "I'm so sorry." The impact had turned the appliance on; it was now glowing and buzzing.

"Why do you have that thing in your purse?" she asked. "You do know that's not what it's for, right?"

As she spoke, there was a loud rustle from behind her.

We looked at each other. "Go get him," she said, handing me the gun.

"But . . ."

"Just go," she said.

I took the gun and raced through the brush after the other person, trying not to think about the fact that I had had no training in shooting a gun—ever—whereas my opponent at least knew enough to hit Frank in the shoulder from something of a distance.

"Stop!" I yelled, as if that were going to help, and followed the crashing sound as it rounded Maxwell's mansion, heading toward the street. I got one glimpse of the person—whoever I was chasing was wearing a hat and sunglasses—and had just gotten to the driveway when Janelle stepped in front of me.

"Margie!" she said, grabbing my shoulders. "Slow down!"

"I can't," I said, brushing her off.

She grasped at my sleeve. "Where are you going?"

I looked to see the person dodge between two cars and sprint toward the street. "Let go!"

"Is that a gun?" she asked. "Are you chasing someone?" She grabbed my sleeve tighter. "Is that the shooter? You should really call the police—it's dangerous!"

I yanked my arm away from her. There was a ripping sound, but at least I was free. I sprinted up the road just in time to see a white SUV peel out. The driver gunned the engine and disappeared around a corner before I could even catch the make of the car.

I turned back, stifling a number of colorful obscenities, to see Janelle. "Did he get away?" she asked.

"Yes," I said shortly.

"How exciting," she said. "Maybe I should be a private investigator. Do you think I'd be a good one?"

I looked at her bloodshot eyes and the askew straps of her too-short dress and grabbed my torn sleeve. "No," I said shortly, and marched back into the house, hoping Frank was going to make it.

• • •

The EMTs wheeled Frank into the ambulance about thirty minutes later, with Blake climbing in behind him.

"Is he going to be okay?" I asked.

"They think so," he said. "It nicked his shoulder, but didn't hit the lungs or heart." He glanced back at Frank, whose bustier was making the blue blanket look like a very small mountain range. "He was lucky."

"I saw the shooter, I think," I told him.

"Who was it?"

"I couldn't tell, but whoever it was drove a big white SUV. Do you have any idea who would have wanted to hurt Frank?"

He shook his head. "Neither of us do," he said. "He wondered if it might be my dad . . ." He trailed off and looked around him. Thankfully, no one was in earshot.

"Where is he, anyway?"

"My parents left before the performance," he told me.

"It's been a rough night. I'm glad he's going to be fine, though."

"Ma'am?" One of the EMTs touched me on the shoulder. "We have to get this man to the hospital."

"Right," I said, then turned to Blake. "Have you talked to the police about setting a guard on him?"

"I will," he said. "Speaking of police . . ." He nodded behind me, and I turned to see Detective Bunsen.

"You," he said in a resigned tone of voice. "How are you mixed up in all of this?"

"The victim is my husband's boyfriend," I said. "I hope you'll put a guard on him."

"Your husband's . . . Never mind," he said with a sigh. "I think we have to have a talk."

"I guess so," I said, and as the ambulance wended its way through the parked cars on the street, Detective Bunsen and I headed into the house.

• • •

It wasn't a convivial meeting, but it was nice not being suspected of murder for a change. I didn't mention eavesdropping on Maxwell's meeting with his cronies, but was a bit worried when he asked about my in-laws.

"I understand there was an argument between . . . your husband, the victim, and your father-in-law," he said.

"Just a misunderstanding," I said. "It's an adjustment for him."

"I'll say," he said. "Was he in the crowd for the performance?"

My palms started sweating. "He left after the argument. Why?" I asked, as if I had no idea.

"Does he own a gun?"

"I don't know," I said, even though I was well aware that he was a member of the NRA. "You'd have to ask him that."

"He doesn't appear to be here," he told me.

"I saw the shooter," I told him. "At least I think he was the shooter."

"How do you know that?"

I told him about our chase through the woods.

"Why did you chase him?"

"It seemed like the thing to do," I admitted. "I like Frank."

He gave me a doubtful look. "Did you see a gun?"

"No, but the shot came from behind the stage. Why else would someone be back there?"

"Yes. Why would you be back there? Were you really that concerned for your husband's boyfriend's . . . welfare?"

"What?" I asked. "You're not seriously suggesting I shot him?"

"May I see your purse?" he asked me.

I reached for it automatically, then remembered what was inside, and felt my face turn red.

"Don't you need a warrant?"

"I don't think it'll be hard to get one," he said. "We can do this now, or we can do it in a couple of hours; it's up to you."

"I can explain," I said, feeling mortified as I handed my bag to him.

He peered inside, and his eyes widened. I didn't know if he was looking at Mr. Big or Peaches's gun, but it didn't really matter.

"I think you'll have to," he said. "I'm sorry, but I'll have to take this as evidence."

"Fine," I said. What else was I going to do? "But could I have my keys?"

"Not yet," he told me. "We need to talk some more."

"There's nothing else to say," I told him. "I was watching the performance. I saw Frank get shot, and I raced behind the stage to see who it was."

"Do you have anyone who can attest to you being in the audience?"

"Peaches," I said.

"Other than your boss—or partner, or whatever you call her."

"Willie saw me, I think," I said. I gave him her full name, and he wrote it down.

"Most people would run the other way from an active shooter," he said.

"You're probably right," I said. "It must have been the Chardonnay."

"I think we need to chat some more, Mrs. Peterson," he said. I groaned.

It was going to be a long night.

CHAPTER TWENTY-NINE

I wasn't wrong. It was at least three hours before I managed to get my wallet and keys back—they kept my purse and its contents—and was able to call Blake.

"How's he doing?" I asked as I pulled out of the subdivision.

"He's awake," Blake said.

"Thank goodness," I said. "Did they station a guard at his door?"

"Yes," he said. "I insisted."

"I'm so sorry this happened," I told him. "I'm afraid the police think I may have done it . . . but I promise you, I didn't."

"I know, Margie," he said. "You've been pretty amazing through all of this."

"Thanks," I said, meaning it. "I'm not going to say it hasn't been hard, but . . . I know you didn't do any of this on purpose."

"I didn't," he said. "It tears me up knowing how much I hurt you. I really made a mess of things."

He wasn't wrong, but there was no point in hashing that out again. All we could do was go forward. "Thanks," I told him, although I still felt a hollow pang in my stomach. "Just between you and me, though, I'm worried about your dad."

"Why? Did the police ask about him?"

"Bunsen asked me a lot of questions about him, and he wasn't in the audience when the shooting happened—I assume he left, but I didn't see him go. I told Bunsen I saw the shooter, but I don't think he believes me."

"This is a nightmare," Blake said.

"At least Frank's coming around," I said.

"True. But he's not going to be on stage for a while."

"Keep asking him why he thinks someone might have wanted to do him in," I said. "In fact, do you mind if I come visit and ask some questions?"

"About what?"

"About his relationship with Tristan Prescott," I said.

"The personal trainer who died?" Blake said.

"Yeah. I think he and Frank knew each other, at least a bit; I'm wondering if Tristan told him something someone wants kept quiet."

"It's worth asking, I guess," he said. There was a voice in the background. "Hang on . . . He's asking for me. Can I call you back?"

"Yeah," I said. "I'm on my way home now."

"Tell your mom thanks for helping with the kids."

"I will." I hung up and pulled onto my street. I was halfway to my driveway when a pair of headlights glared through the rear window of the van. Someone had pulled out from the curb and was right on my tail, revving the engine. I wasn't sure what kind of vehicle it was, but it appeared enormous; the headlights seemed to fill my back window.

Something told me I didn't want to risk a face-to-face meeting with whoever was driving the behemoth behind me—particularly not in my own driveway, with my kids and my mother in the house—so I turned right at the end of the street, hoping I was wrong and the car or truck or tank or whatever it was would turn left.

No such luck. It followed me, still about six inches from where my bumper usually was, as if there were a magnet attached to the back of the van.

I continued down Walsh Tarlton Lane at a relatively sedate speed, as if being tailgated by someone who was staking out my house was normal for me, and then turned onto Bee Caves Road, hoping whoever it was would pass me and keep going. I wasn't terribly surprised when that didn't happen.

My palms started sweating as I cruised toward the next traffic light. The fuel light was lit on my gas gauge; if I'd planned to drive around until my tailgater got bored, that was now off the table. And even if I were skilled at evasive driving, the van had about as much get-up-and-go as an octogenarian on tranquilizers.

The only thing I could think to do was to drive to the nearest police station; it was only a couple of miles away.

I glanced in my rearview mirror, almost blinding myself, then tilted the mirror down. As I looked back at the traffic light, it turned yellow. Under normal circumstances, I'd stop . . . but these weren't normal circumstances.

I stomped on the gas pedal. The van's engine whined in response, and the entire vehicle seemed to strain as the engine flooded with gas. The light turned red just as I hit the intersection, and for the first time, I found myself hoping I would be stopped by a cop, but I sailed through unobserved—and followed closely by my pursuer.

Crap.

It didn't matter how fast I went; the vehicle behind me was faster. I raced down Bee Caves, hoping some bored cop would stop us, but the streets were quiet. As I approached the intersection of Highway 360, my heart sank; not only was the light red, but three cars were waiting at the intersection; even if I'd been brave enough to run the light, there was no way to do it. I pulled into the right lane and slowed to a stop, leaving a good amount of space between me and the Subaru at the light and wishing the shoulder were bigger than half a car wide.

The SUV behind me stopped, its headlights practically in the van's backseat, and I readjusted my mirror, hoping no one would get out of the driver's seat.

Nobody did. Instead, the driver gunned the engine and slammed into the back of the van.

My neck snapped back and forth, and the van lurched forward until it was almost in the trunk of the station wagon in front of me. I looked back at the rear window; the SUV was backing up, and I knew it was going to hit me again. I didn't think; I wrenched the steering wheel to the side and veered onto the narrow shoulder, wincing as the undercarriage scraped on the curb. I pulled out onto the service road of MoPac, cringing as tires squealed behind me, and gunned the engine, praying that the trail of sparks behind me wouldn't ignite the gas tank.

In a heartbeat, the enormous vehicle was back on what would have been my bumper if I'd ever reattached it. And this time it didn't wait for me to stop. As I swerved into another lane, the vehicle rammed into the back right of the van. I lost control of the steering wheel for a moment, coming within inches of the guardrail before I managed to steer the van back onto the main road. The police station was less than a mile away, but it felt like a cross-country trip.

I kept one eye on the mirror and swerved from lane to lane, trying to avoid being rammed by the SUV, but it was like driving a Winnebago and trying to outrun a Ferrari—only the SUV was the size of a Winnebago. Twice more it crunched into the back of my van, seemingly undeterred by the impact.

It was gearing up for a fourth impact when the station appeared in the distance, like an oasis in the desert. As the SUV zoomed up behind me again, I swerved to the right and braked. The truck surged past me; I glanced over to see who was driving, but the windows were tinted. The truck squealed to a stop, and I hit the gas, ignoring the wheezing sound and swerving around the truck, my eyes fixed on the station.

The SUV was behind me again before I knew it. I lurched to the left and then the right, thankful that there weren't other cars on the road, then jerked the wheel to the right when I reached the entrance to the station. The tires whined, and the left side of the van floated up from the pavement so that for a long, terrible moment the van was suspended on two wheels, trying to decide whether or not to roll over.

It didn't; instead, the airborne tires hit the ground with an ominous thud. I hit the gas again and swerved so that I was just next to the entrance, then wrenched the key out of the ignition and hurtled through the passenger door. I sprinted to the glass doors of the station just as the truck pulled in behind me; I yanked the door open and hurled myself inside.

The dispatcher at the front desk looked up, startled. "What the—"

She didn't get a chance to finish, though, because there was a huge *boom!* outside. The glass doors shattered. A moment later, there was the sound of something heavy and metal hitting the pavement, and the squeal of tires.

Three uniformed officers raced to the front lobby as the dispatcher unfolded herself from behind the desk.

"What the hell happened?" asked the shortest of the three.

I peered around the corner at the blackened frame of the Dodge Caravan. "My minivan blew up," I told them. "Sorry about the doors."

• • •

By the time an officer dropped me off at the house, it was well past midnight.

My mother was at the front door waiting, looking pale and rattled. "Are you okay?"

"I'm fine, but the minivan is toast," I said. "Literally."

She looked past me at the cruiser, which hadn't moved from the end of the driveway. "Why are the police here?"

"They're keeping an eye on the house," I said.

"What happened?" she asked, closing the door behind me and locking the deadbolt.

"A truck followed me and rammed into me," I said. "I drove to the police station and got out just in time."

"What do you mean, just in time?"

"I mean before the van blew up."

"Oh, Margie . . . They bombed you?"

"No," I said. "The police think the impact must have done something to the fuel line, and it was ignited by sparks from some of the stuff dragging off the back of the van." I headed into the kitchen and collapsed into one of the chairs as Rufus glared at me from his perch on top of the refrigerator.

"Thank God you're okay," she said. "Why would someone do something like that?"

"That's what I've been wondering," I said. Was it related to Frank's shooting, or Tristan's death? Something told me it was . . . and that the two were connected. But how?

She peered out the window. "Are they staying?"

"They are," I said. "Whoever followed me was parked on the street; they know where I live."

"I hate to suggest it, but do you think it might be time to take the kids somewhere else for a few days?"

"Like Blake's?" I asked.

"Or your in-laws'," she suggested.

After the confrontation with Blake tonight, I wasn't sure that was the best idea . . . but I didn't want the kids to be in the house if it wasn't safe.

"Maybe it's a good thing we haven't found Twinkles. On the other hand, it may be kind of uncharitable of me," my mother continued, "but I'd love to see your mother-in-law with a pig in her house."

"Assuming we can find her." With everything that was going on, I hadn't had time to look for her—or to go after the fry phone. "Besides, I'm not sure how well that will go over."

"That's right," my mother said. "Prue might turn her into bacon. Poor little thing . . ."

She wasn't little, but I didn't mention it. "Blake isn't on great terms with his parents right now," I said.

"No?"

"Someone shot Frank at the party tonight," I said. "I don't know if Phil is on the suspect list yet, but I wouldn't be surprised; he and Blake and Frank had a big argument at the party, and several people heard it." I didn't mention that the police had also questioned me. I figured the blown-up minivan was enough disturbing information for one night.

"I can drive the kids to school tomorrow," she said, "but what are you going to do about a car?"

"I don't know," I said. "I'll call the insurance company in the morning."

"I'm glad we've got someone watching the house," she said. "I don't like how dangerous this job is for you."

"Me neither," I told her. "But it beats waxing people's genitals for a living."

"Are you sure about that?"

I thought about it for a moment. "No," I said, and headed to bed.

CHAPTER THIRTY

O f course I didn't have rental coverage on my minivan.

"The investigator will have to inspect the vehicle," the insurance agent droned as I cut up an apple for Elsie.

"The police impounded what's left of it," I told her.

"Oh." Silence. "Was there another vehicle involved in the accident?"

"Yeah. A giant truck rammed into me repeatedly from behind. The theory is that it damaged the gas line, and the sparks from the trailing metal ignited the fuel."

"So there was another vehicle involved," she intoned. "Did you get the license plate?"

I sighed and arranged the apple slices on a plate, then added a gluten-free tortilla. "No."

"The other vehicle didn't stop?"

"No. And honestly, I was more concerned with not dying than taking down license plate numbers."

"So you don't have insurance information from the other vehicle."

"Look, I think people who attempt vehicular manslaughter usually don't stop to exchange info," I pointed out. I was testy, but I hadn't slept well, and I had no idea how I was going to get around. There was a beep on the other line. "Hang on," I told the insurance person, and switched over.

"I got you a car," Peaches said. I'd called her first thing and told her what had happened on my way home.

"Thank God."

"You might want to wait until you see it to start thanking God."

"Why? What is it, a moped?"

"No, there's plenty of room. It's just . . . You'll see. Can you get a ride to the office? By the way, I got you a job at the bottling company," she said. "You start today; I'll call and say you'll be a bit late."

"What?"

"The one you told me about. The one that does LifeBoost. I called your friend and told him you needed a favor."

"You called Michael?" I'd told her what I'd found out about the company, but it had never occurred to me that she'd actually get me a job there. Or call Michael, for that matter.

"Yup. Like I said, you start this morning."

"That's great," I said, "but I've got a doctor's appointment for Elsie. Why can't you do it?"

"It's not my case. Besides, I can't lift heavy things. I put my back out on the mechanical bull again."

I groaned. "E-mail me the address."

"Already did," she said. "Good write-up on the Pretty Kitten, by the way. Wanda gave us a bonus."

"Has she forgiven us for the parking lot shooting?" A few months ago, someone had shot up my minivan in front of her store. They'd missed the plate glass windows, but she hadn't been happy.

"Working on it. What's the appointment?"

"Doctor Flynn's," I told her. "Evidently he consulted on the LifeBoost drink, so I made Elsie an appointment."

"That's got to make your mother-in-law happy."

"Killing two birds with one stone."

"I'll see you soon, then," Peaches said, and hung up.

I switched back to the insurance agent, but she'd evidently hung up on me. I sighed and went to wake up the kids. I wasn't looking forward to breaking the news about the van.

"Grandma's taking Nick to school, and we have to go to a doctor's appointment," I told Elsie as she chewed on her gluten-free tortilla—one of the few Grandma-approved things she would eat. Rufus, who was delighted by the absence of pigs in the house, watched her with interest from the top of the fridge; he was the only cat I'd ever met with a starch fixation.

"I made you a lunch and put in applesauce; don't forget to put everything in your backpack."

"My backpack is in the van," she said. "I did my spelling homework on the way home from school."

"Honey," I said, glancing at my mother, who was trying to feed Nick a soy sausage patty, "I'm afraid the minivan was in an accident last night."

Her eyes widened. "The minivan?"

"What happened?" Nick asked.

"It . . . Well, it had some problems," I said.

"Did the back piece fall off again?"

"No, that happened earlier in the week."

"Did something else fall off, then?" Nick asked.

"Not exactly," I said. "But on the plus side, we should be getting a new van soon!" I didn't think telling them it had blown up was the way to start the day.

Elsie looked worried. "Did you get my backpack out?"

"I didn't have time," I said.

"You can get it today, though, right?"

I took a deep breath. "I'm afraid we're going to have to get you a new backpack, sweetheart."

"But my homework is in that backpack!"

"I'll write a note to your teacher."

Her eyes filled with tears. "And my sparkly pencil case with the penguins on it!"

"We'll get you another one, sweetheart. I promise."

"And my booster seat with the *Lady and the Tramp* stickers on it?"

"We'll replace all of it," I told her, but I might as well have been talking in Swahili. Elsie had left the building; Fifi was here, and in major meltdown mode. "After school, we'll go to Target and you can pick out a new backpack."

She crawled over to the couch cushion that doubled as a dog bed and whined, "But all the good ones will be gone! And that one was special!"

"It's just an object," my mother contributed. "All objects are impermanent. Maybe it's a spiritual lesson——"

"Mom," I said. "Maybe we can talk about spiritual lessons later?"

"Everything's all wrong!" Elsie wailed. "Daddy isn't home, all we have for dinner is green goo, Mommy crashed the minivan, and now I've lost my homework and my sparkly penguin pencil case forever!"

"At least you still have Rufus," Nick pointed out.

At that moment, the cat darted over to Elsie, stole the tortilla from her hand, and took off down the hallway.

It was that kind of morning.

• • •

"You've had a pretty exciting week," Becky said when I filled her in on everything that had happened over the last twenty-four hours. We'd tucked Elsie into the backseat with her headphones on, and Becky was driving me to the office to pick up a vehicle.

"Yeah," I said. "It's been fun. We're thinking of moving the kids over to my in-laws' house until this all gets cleared up."

"You think it's dangerous for them?"

"Whoever was driving that truck knows where I live," I said. "The thing is, who's going after me?"

"Maybe someone who knows you saw the shooter at Maxwell's house yesterday?" Becky suggested.

"It's possible," I said. "But I didn't see enough to ID him."

"He doesn't know that," she said. "What's on the agenda for today?"

"Michael got me a gig at the bottling factory that does LifeBoost," I said.

"Why?"

"Because I think LifeBoost may have something to do with what happened to Tristan."

"What are you going to be doing?"

"Monitoring equipment, I think. Or quality control, or something."

"No driving forklifts, I hope. Your luck in the vehicular department hasn't been stellar lately."

"I don't have a license for a forklift."

"Like that would stop you," she snorted. "I kind of wish I had your job sometimes. All I've got today is planning my next Passion Party."

"Tell Michael thanks for getting me in at the bottling company, by the way," I said.

"You should tell him yourself." She gave me a sidelong glance. "I still think he's sweet on you."

"No he's not," I said, glancing over my shoulder to make sure Elsie hadn't taken off her headphones. "He's dating that Ximena girl."

"Salima?" she asked.

"Yeah. That."

"I don't think they're serious," she said.

"No?"

She shook her head. "You should see if he's free for drinks," she suggested.

"Even though I'm still married?"

"Really, Margie. What are the odds that you and Blake are getting back together?"

I sighed and looked at my phone, anxious to change the subject. "I'm supposed to be at the bottling company in fifteen minutes; I called to say I had car trouble."

"That's the understatement of the decade," she told me. "Is insurance covering it?"

"I don't know yet. The claims adjustor hung up on me this morning. Thank goodness Peaches found me a car," I said as we turned into the lot of the Pretty Kitten.

"Umm . . . ," Becky said. "Did she say what kind of car?"

"No. Why?"

She pointed. Parked next to the front door of the waxing salon was a giant wood-paneled station wagon entirely covered with plastic bananas attached to springs.

"It can't be," I breathed.

"I'll bet you ten bucks it is," she said. "Let's just hope you don't have to tail anyone."

CHAPTER THIRTY-ONE

"After what happened to your last rental car, this was the only one I could get," Peaches told me as we stood in the parking lot, surveying the Bananamobile. Elsie kept tapping one of the bananas and watching it bounce back and forth. "On the plus side, there's plenty of room for the kids' stuff!"

"Does it run?"

"It did this morning," she said, handing me the keys as Becky stifled a snort. "Aren't you supposed to be there at eight?"

"I'm going," I said, opening the front door and looking at the seat, which was covered in a stained material with a jaunty drunken-chimpanzee motif. On the plus side, Elsie was delighted with our new wheels, and started an animated conversation with the chimpanzees as she buckled herself in. As I turned the key in the ignition and the engine coughed, I found myself looking up at the Pretty Kitten with something like wistful nostalgia.

Maybe being a professional genital waxer wasn't such a bad idea after all, I thought as I backed the Bananamobile up, narrowly missing Becky, who was doubled over in laughter and clutching Peaches's spandex-clad arm.

. . .

At least Elsie was a fan of the bananas. My first stop was to take her to the ADHD doctor. Sarah was right. If you knew the right people, it wasn't hard to get an appointment at all.

As I pulled the bouncing Bananamobile up outside the clinic, Elsie looked up from the monkey-festooned backseat and said, "Why are we here?"

"Just to talk to the doctor," I said.

"Is he going to try to get me to take off my dog collar?"

"No," I told her. "It's just a little evaluation to see if you need help focusing at school."

"How come Nick doesn't have to go?"

"He might," I said vaguely as I opened the door, causing the bananas to wobble violently, and she hopped out.

"I like the banana car better than the minivan," she said, "but I miss Twinkles. And my fry phone."

"I know, sweetie." My stomach twisted as I looked down at my daughter; I felt like the mother of the year. Again. I smiled at a woman whose eyebrows were raised as I grabbed my daughter's hand and headed for the front door.

As we walked into the luxurious lobby, I found myself thinking that perhaps med school might not have been a bad idea. I followed the signs to the frosted-glass door that led to the neurology office. The carpet was like velvet, the chairs looked like they were straight out of a designer's atelier, and the woman behind the front desk looked like she moonlighted as a runway model. The chairs were full of moms, some with children, some without.

"Can I help you?" the receptionist asked.

"I've got an appointment with Dr. Flynn at nine."

"Sign in here," she said, indicating a clipboard on the front desk, and then handed me a sheaf of forms to fill out.

It was a good thing the waiting room chairs were comfortable, since we spent the next hour and a half in them. I handed Elsie my phone; she had just pulled up Candy Crush when it rang. It was Peaches.

Elsie handed me the phone, and I stepped out into the lobby. "What's up?" I asked when I picked up.

As I spoke, Elsie's head popped around the door.

"Mom? They called for us."

"I'll be right there, honey," I said to Elsie. I told Peaches I'd call her back and hurried into the waiting room.

The nurse gave me a big toothy smile and led us back into a small, spare room with a mural of sea turtles on the wall, what appeared to be a bath mat on the floor, a metal exam table, and two chairs.

Elsie eyed the table and growled.

"You can sit here," I said, patting the chair next to me. A moment later, there was a knock at the door, and an enormous man who was looking very official in a crisp white lab coat and gray slacks walked in. "I'm Dr. Platt," he said to me, extending a pawlike hand. "Dr. Flynn was called out of the office on an emergency. Sorry for the wait."

"I'm Margie Peterson," I told him as he enveloped my hand and shook it firmly. "And this is Elsie."

"Hi, Elsie," he said, squatting down to attempt to get on her level. Elsie scooted behind me and dug her fists into my shirt. He gave me a rueful smile and looked down at the clipboard in his hand. "What are we in for today?" he asked.

It wasn't Dr. Flynn, but on the other hand, at least it was a doctor. "Um . . . Elsie has a bit of an alternate personality," I said delicately.

"I am Fifi," she snarled from behind me. "I am not another person."

Dr. Pratt's eyebrows went up, and he peered around me to Elsie. "What would you like me to call you?"

"Fifi," she said, and began barking. Going to the doctor's office seemed to have unleashed her inner Pekingese. She hadn't gotten down on all fours in nearly a week; now, she was attempting to crawl under the exam table.

"How long has Fifi been around?" Dr. Pratt asked me.

"Oh, on and off for a few months," I said.

"Anything going on at home?"

I nodded. "Her dad is living in an apartment," I said, omitting the whole part about drag queens and Journey to Manhood.

Elsie growled menacingly.

"Ah," he said. "Is this just at home, or at school, too?"

"Mainly at home these days," I told him. "She likes to wear a collar and eat from bowls on the floor."

"Does she have a pretty healthy diet?"

"Only white foods," I said, feeling like the worst mother on the planet. It was one of those moments when you realize that what passes for normal in your house is anything but in the world at large. As if to underscore my feelings, Elsie started yipping from beneath the table.

He went through another set of questions about school performance, friends, bedtime . . . pretty much a laundry list of family things. Unfortunately, I wasn't able to answer any of them glowingly. When I was done, he peered under the exam table.

"Can we talk for a few minutes, Fifi?" he asked. "I've got dog treats."

"Dog treats?" she asked. "What kind of dog treats?"

"Hershey's Kisses . . . but you probably only like white food, right?"

"Chocolate is okay for dogs," Elsie announced. Chocolate was decidedly not okay for dogs, but I wasn't arguing. She crept out from under the exam table and accepted a Hershey's Kiss.

"Good girl," he cooed. She gave him a half smile and then scuttled back under the table, unwrapping her "treat."

"Do you worry a lot?" he asked her when she was tucked back into the corner.

She nodded slowly.

"I hear you've changed schools, and things with your mom and dad are a little bit crazy right now. Is that kind of scary?"

She nodded harder.

"Would you be willing to try something for me? To see if it helps you feel more calm, and a little less upset?"

She hesitated, then nodded.

"I'm going to write a prescription for you and give it to your mom," he said.

"What is it?" I asked.

"Fifi, do you mind if we leave you in here for a moment? I want to show your mom something," he said. "Would you like another Kiss?"

She nodded, and he handed her one, then led me out into the hall.

"She's going through a rough time, isn't she?" he asked once I closed the door behind me.

"She is."

"There could be a lot of things going on," he said. "Insurance covers preliminary evaluations, but they're just a starting point; we could do a full assessment, but they're expensive, and insurance doesn't cover them. I'm guessing the separation and the school issue are taking a toll—and it sounds like you've got a lot on your plate right now."

"You could say that," I agreed as my phone buzzed in my purse.

"Here's the number for a therapist who takes insurance," he said, handing me a card. "And if you don't mind, I'll prescribe her something for anxiety and mild depression; it might help her get through this time."

"Okay," I said. "What about the dog thing?"

"Did it start when you and your husband began having problems?"

"I think so."

"It could be just a fantasy response to a stressful situation. Let's keep an eye on it and check back in in a couple of weeks, okay?"

"Okay," I said, feeling so relieved that I didn't care at all about LifeBoost or anything connected with it.

"And if things don't improve, think about a full evaluation with us," he told me. "It's expensive, but it can be helpful."

"Thanks," I said, feeling both sad that I was being handed a prescription and hopeful that maybe we'd be able to help Elsie out. *Medication* among parents was a dirty word. Although, I thought as I surveyed the anxious-looking parents in the waiting room, evidently it wasn't that uncommon.

I went back in for Elsie, and together we walked down to the in-house pharmacy and handed over the prescription.

"Do you want to wait?" the woman asked.

"How long will it be?"

"Fifteen minutes or so," she said. "Your insurance info is in the system already."

"We'll hang out a few minutes," I said.

As we sat in the waiting room, a string of attractive women walked in to pick up prescriptions.

One of them sat down next to me, tapping her foot as she sat. She had so much energy it was making me feel nervous. "I just love this in-house pharmacy thing," she said.

"How long have you been coming here?" I asked.

"I've been seeing Dr. Flynn for years," she said. "He's just awesome. So flexible."

"I know," said another woman who was also waiting. "He's a miracle worker. Without him, I'd never fit into these shorts."

"Wait . . . He prescribes diet drugs? I thought this was a neurology practice," I said.

"Um . . . Yes," one of the women said. "But there's an added benefit of most of those ADHD meds."

"Like what?"

"I'm never hungry, and I can run for miles," the first woman said. "And since my daughter started on Adderall, her SAT scores went up two hundred points. I think she's got a shot at Princeton now."

"Really?" I asked. She sounded like Sarah Soggs.

"I know. He's a miracle worker."

"Ms. Apple?" the pharmacist called.

A thin woman got up and retrieved her bag of pills, then hurried out of the office.

A few minutes later, Elsie's name was called. I read the instructions—fish oil in the morning, meds at night—and then walked out of the practice, still surprised by the flow of women in the pharmacy. A few minutes later, I dropped Elsie off at school and called Blake.

"What's up?" he asked in a pleasant voice, despite the fact that he was at work. Another change since our marriage dissolved.

"I took Elsie to see a doctor this morning."

"How did it go?"

I relayed what he'd told me.

"How expensive is the evaluation?"

"I don't know," I told him. "I think it's at least a thousand dollars."

"Man," he said. "I always knew I should have gone to med school."

You're telling me, I thought. Blake's hourly rate was significantly higher than mine. Then again, I hadn't had to go to school to be a PI. Although I did have a certification test coming up that I hadn't studied for.

"We'll see if she improves, and go from there."

"I'm sure she'll be fine," he said.

Here's hoping, I thought but didn't say.

• • •

It was a very long drive to the bottling company. The bouncing bananas were very distracting, and at least two people snapped pictures of me as I sailed toward East Austin. I pulled into the parking lot of the plant much later than I'd anticipated. When I slammed the door, the bananas shuddered as if they were having a seizure. I glanced around the parking lot, thankful that no one could see what I was driving, trotted to the big glass door that appeared to lead to the office, and hurried inside.

"Hi," I said to the young woman behind the desk, who was halfway through painting the fingernails on her left hand a sparkly, virulent green that looked like it should have been named Princess Swamp Thing. "I'm here for my first day."

She gave me a blank look.

"Marge Peters." We'd decided on a very creative false identity. "I'm supposed to be working in the plant?"

"Hang on," she said, and stabbed at the keys on her phone with an as-yet-unpainted finger. "Roy?" she said when someone picked up. "There's some lady here named Marge who says she's here for a job."

Even from a few feet away, I heard a booming voice from the receiver. "Send her back."

She hung up and pointed to the door behind her. "That way," she said. "Door at the end of the hall."

"Got it," I said, and went in the direction her lacquered finger had indicated.

Most of the doors off the main corridor were closed, but one near the end was open. I slowed down as I passed; there was a balding man inside, drawling into a phone with his feet up on the desk. "The supplier says there should be no problem," he said. "I'm not sure whether we should cut out the middleman or not, though." As he spoke, he wheeled around, and our eyes met.

I recognized him, I realized; he was one of the men from Maxwell's party.

"Hang on a moment," he said, and covered the phone with one hand. "Can I help you?" he asked me.

"I just got turned around," I said, and scuttled down the hall to the door at the end, which—as it turned out—led to a room that sounded like the bowels of hell. A few people turned to look at me, then went back to whatever they were doing. The whole process seemed extremely complicated, from the look of the massive machinery in the middle of the warehouse-size room.

A man in safety goggles and noise-canceling headphones walked over to me. "You're late!" he bellowed.

"Sorry," I said.

"Let's get you fitted out," he said, and led me to a small room with a big plate glass window that overlooked the big room. I breathed a sigh of relief when the door shut behind me. "I'm Roy," he told me. "I'll be your supervisor."

"Nice to meet you, Roy. I'm Marge." I stuck out a hand. He crushed it so hard my knuckles popped. When he released it, I resisted the urge to inspect my fingers for fractures. "I hear you've got some experience on the line," he said.

"Pardon me?"

"On the line," he repeated.

"Oh yes," I said. "I used to work in ice cream." *When I was fifteen,* I thought but didn't add. Scooping cones for suburbanites.

"Then you know what to expect," he said in what I felt was a spirit of gross optimism. "The labeling machine's been giving us trouble this morning, so we'll start you there."

"Uh . . . fixing the machine?" That would be a disaster.

"No," he said, eyes twinkling a bit. "Putting labels on bottles. You think you can handle that?"

"Of course," I said with a confidence I didn't entirely feel. Still . . . putting labels on bottles. How hard could that be? I just hoped they didn't need them completely straight. "How long have you worked here?" I asked.

"Twenty years," he said.

"But you've only recently started bottling for LifeBoost."

"A couple months ago, yes."

"What all is in the stuff, anyway?"

He gave me a funny look. "Why do you care?"

"Just curious," I said. "I've got a friend who swears by it."

"You don't get free samples, if that's what you're asking."

"No, don't worry," I said. "Just wondering. So," I added with what I hoped was a winning smile. "Will you show me the whole bottling process?"

He glanced at his watch. "I don't have time today, and you're on the clock. Or you will be in a moment." He handed me a time card.

"You'll need to clock in and out with this," he said. "Let me show you your station."

"Got it," I said. He put his headphones back on and opened the door to the floor, and I stifled the urge to cover my ears. "Earphones and safety goggles?" I yelled.

He took off the headphones, and I repeated the question.

"Right," he yelled back, closing the door and walking over to a metal cabinet in the corner of the office. After fishing through it, he pulled out a rather ratty-looking headset and a pair of cracked goggles. I eyed the headset with apprehension, thinking maybe I'd go without, until he opened the door again.

"Do you have any antibiotic wipes?" I yelled.

He rolled his eyes and pointed to the door. I put on the headset and the grimy goggles and followed him out onto the floor, looking around the mass of machinery and trying to figure out where the drink additives were. I resisted the urge to ask; I got the feeling I'd used up my allotment of questions.

All too soon, we were at the labeling section, where two women with rather frantic looks on their faces were trying to keep up with the bottles the juggernaut next to them was disgorging. They would smack a label on the bottle and put it in a cardboard box, then grab another; they moved so fast it was almost mesmerizing.

"Here's the new hire!" he yelled at the two women, who barely looked up as they scrambled to label the bottles that were threatening to fall off the table.

"What do I do?" I asked, a little stupidly, in retrospect.

"Put the labels on the bottles," the shorter of the two women yelled back.

"Lunch is at one," he said.

"When is my break?" I asked.

"No break," he said. "These girls will show you the ropes." Neither woman looked up as he walked away.

With no other direction forthcoming, I grabbed a spool of labels and reached for a bottle. It took me thirty seconds to peel the label off the backing, and when I stuck it on the bottle, it was crooked. As I leaned down to put it into the box, the woman closest to me grabbed it out of my hand.

"Crooked," she announced, and applied another label with laserlike precision, then slid it into the box in almost one movement.

"Watch," she announced. Her hands moving so fast they were almost a blur, she snatched a bottle from the line, smoothed a label onto it, and slid it into the box. The whole process took about three milliseconds and looked almost magical. "You try," she said.

I tried to look optimistic about it, despite the fact that I had a hard time even putting bumper stickers on straight, as I attempted to replicate her movements. The result, unfortunately, looked like a three-year-old's craft project.

With a tight smile, she yelled, "Go slow. You learn."

I did go slow. I did try to learn. But by the time I'd finished one slightly crooked label, my helper had finished at least a dozen. She shook her head at me. "For now, move boxes," she announced, pointing to a pallet that was half-full of LifeBoost cases.

"Got it," I yelled, and started relocating the boxes to the pallet. "Am I supposed to glue these shut or something?"

She nodded toward a glue gun attached to a long cord. I grabbed it, opened the flap, and squeezed the gun. Nothing happened, so I squeezed harder, and a giant glob of glue shot out of the end of the gun and stuck to the floor.

"Sorry!" I yelled as the woman rolled her eyes and shook her head at me. She said something to the woman next to her and got up to get a wad of rags to wipe up the floor. I cringed as the pile of bottles grew; obviously I was nothing but an impediment on the floor today. Whoever called factory work *unskilled* didn't know what they were talking about, I decided as she expertly applied glue to two boxes and heaved them up on the pallet.

"Gentle!" she yelled, then watched me do the third box before returning to the now-overflowing pile of bottles.

"Got it!"

It was not the most successful first morning on the job I've ever had, and if I'd had any thoughts of looking around while I was working, they were dashed; I had my hands full just trying not to glue myself to the floor. When the time came for lunch, the whole line shut down. I took off my headset, but there was still a ringing in my ears.

"Now what?" I asked.

"Lunch!" the shorter one said to me, and waved me to follow her toward the break room, where everyone else was heading like bees to a hive.

"I want to look around first," I said.

"Okay, but hurry. Only half hour."

I took her at her word and practically jogged through the plant, trying to find the place where they mixed the drink concentrate. I found it after about five minutes of searching; it was near a giant vat in the back. The drink concentrate was in big plastic bags and was a lurid green; there was also a pile of smaller bags filled with something that looked like flour. I slipped my phone out of my pocket and took a picture, then looked for any shipping information. I found one address in a pile of discarded boxes—a box with a local Austin address on it—but the smaller boxes seemed to have had their labels torn off. I snapped a picture of the address I found, then searched through the boxes to see if there was anything else interesting.

"The break room is over there," a voice behind me said, startling me.

CHAPTER THIRTY-TWO

W hat are you doing?"

I turned around to see a woman about my age with a severe-looking bun and the kind of look that makes you feel like you just got caught with an overdue library book. I looked down; I had a cardboard box in one hand and my phone in the other. There was an uncomfortable silence that seemed to stretch on for several hours before I finally came up with something of an explanation. "I was looking for a big piece of cardboard to take home for my daughter to play with," I said.

Her face transformed at the mention of Elsie. "You have a daughter? How old?" she asked.

"Six," I said.

"Me too! She loves making forts with those boxes. Here," she said, coming to join me. "Let me find you a good one."

"Thanks!" I said as she grabbed a particularly big, almost-intact box.

"This looks like a good one."

"She'll love it," I said. "She likes to pretend she's a dog; that would make a perfect doghouse."

"Mine thinks she's a parakeet," the woman said, rolling her eyes. "I bought her a perch last week. I'm Marta, by the way."

"Nice to meet you, Marta. I'm Margie—I mean, Marge." We shook hands. I smiled at her.

"Hey, where's your car?" she asked as I dug through another stack of boxes. "I'll help you carry these out."

"Ummm . . . Are you sure you don't want to wait until after work?"

"Nah. These might be recycled by then."

"It's right outside, then," I told her. "How do we get out of here?"

"Follow me," she said. Together we trooped toward a door to the left of the supervisor's office—he wasn't in evidence, thankfully—and out a side door I hadn't noticed. "Which one is yours?"

I pointed to the Bananamobile, and she dropped the box she was carrying.

"Wow. Are those bananas?"

"Yup."

She picked up the box and looked at me as if I were a normal person who had suddenly taken off her mask and turned out to be an alien with a purple snout.

"I'm borrowing it from a friend of a friend, who's in a band. Honest."

"What do you normally drive?"

"A minivan. I'm just . . . having car trouble right now."

"What kind of trouble?" she asked. "My cousin's a mechanic."

"I think it's totaled," I said as I unlocked the back hatch, making all the bananas bounce.

"Wow," she said. "It's kind of mesmerizing. What do they look like when you're going sixty?"

"This car doesn't go sixty," I replied, shoving the boxes into the back of the station wagon, which was upholstered in faded plastic banana leaves.

"I'm surprised it goes at all. Those bananas can't be very aerodynamic." She tossed in the box and I slammed the trunk shut, making everything shimmy. We both stared, transfixed, until Marta looked at her watch. "Uh-oh," she said. "Almost time."

We were about to go back when an unmarked white truck drove up to the loading dock. "What's that?" I asked.

"Just a delivery," she said. "We're almost out of time . . . We'd better get back."

"Hang on," I said. "I left something in my car."

"You'll have to go back in through the front door," she warned me. "This door takes a key."

"I'm good," I said.

As she doubled back to the building, I headed back to the Bananamobile and pretended to check for something in the front seat, keeping my eyes on the truck. There were about ten boxes in the back. I hurried over to the truck and took a peek at one of them; like the other boxes, the labels had been torn off or covered with the address of the plant . . . except for half of the one on the bottom. The return address appeared to be in China, and it was addressed to a company called ScripWorks in Austin. I was about to snap a picture of what was left just as the delivery guy walked back outside. "What are you doing?" he asked.

"That's, uh, cool postage," I said, pointing to the colorful edges on the box's label. "Where did these come from, anyway?"

"I don't know," he said. "I just do the deliveries."

"Can I take a picture of this cool label?" I asked.

"Why?"

"I love foreign stuff," I said.

He shrugged. "I guess."

I took a photo as he carried a box through the loading door. As he disappeared, I looked back at the box, which was held together with paper tape. I took the car key to the Bananamobile and sliced through the tape; there was a thick plastic bag inside. I folded the lid back a bit and then tore a hole in the bag. The only thing in my pocket, unfortunately, was a doll cup I'd picked up off the floor that morning.

I filled it with powder, wrapped it in an empty McDonald's apple slice wrapper from my other pocket (embarrassing, but true), and then bent the flap back down before hoofing it toward the front entry as if nothing had happened.

"Can I help you?" the young woman at the front desk asked a second time that day.

"I was here earlier," I said.

She stared blankly.

"I'll just head back," I said. She looked confused. "I'm working on the line," I reminded her.

"Oh. Okay," she said, and went back to texting on her phone as I hurried past her down the hallway.

Evidently I was late; everyone was back at their stations, toiling away. The supervisor, Roy, wasn't in his office, so I decided to give myself a tour of the facility on my own. Walking as if I knew where I was going, I took a right toward what appeared to be a few massive soup cans that I hoped were the mixing vats. Although there were several pallets stacked along the wall behind them, there was no sign of the boxes of white powder.

"Hi!" I said, hailing a friendly-looking man with a black mustache who appeared to be monitoring something on the side of one of the soup cans.

He smiled at me.

"Is this where it all gets mixed?" I yelled in what I hoped was a friendly tone. Thankfully, it seemed a little quieter away from the giant conveyor belt area.

He nodded.

"What all goes in it?"

He pointed to the green goo on the shelves.

"Are those the magical Chinese herbs?" I asked.

"No," he said. "They keep those in a locked room. Who are you?" he asked.

"I'm new here," I told him. "Just getting a feel for the place. How long have you worked here?"

"Two months," he said. "They hired lots of people when it got busy."

"Who handles the Chinese herbs?" I asked.

"The manager," he said. "He's the only one with the key to that room."

"Where is it?" I asked.

"Why? You some kind of inspector or something?"

"No, I just started working here, and I'm just curious. Those must be some herbs!"

"That LifeBoost stuff makes me kinda jittery," he said. "I know lots of people love this stuff, but not me."

"Marge!"

I looked behind me to see Roy tapping a foot. "What are you doing here?"

"I got lost," I lied. "I hear you're the herb man!"

"Who told you that?"

The man I'd been talking to ducked his head and tried to look inconspicuous.

"Oh, someone told me that this morning. Where am I supposed to go, again?"

"Did you clock out for lunch?"

"Ah, no."

"Then you clock out a half hour before you stop working," he told me in a terse voice. "The girls were looking for you."

"The girls?"

"The girls putting on the labels."

"Oh, the women, you mean," I said.

He rolled his eyes. "This way. Don't get mouthy."

I resisted the urge to plant my toe in the middle of his ample derriere as I followed him over to the labeling area. From what I could see, they were actually doing better without me. Evidently one of the women shared my assessment; she grimaced at the sight of me.

"Are you getting the hang of it?" he asked.

"There's a learning curve," I said, "but these women are showing me the ropes. They're amazing . . . I hope you give them a raise."

"Their pay is none of your business," he said in a gruff voice. The two women looked spooked. "Get to work."

I stared at him as he walked away, then looked at the two women. "Is he always like that?" I asked when he was gone.

"Unless he like you," one woman said. "Last young woman here was always in his office. She didn't want to, but he said if she didn't, she lose her job. She has a little girl."

"She quit?" I asked as I started putting bottles in boxes.

"He fired her when she wouldn't go," the woman told me.

"That's awful!"

"She's the third one," she told me. "He likes the skinny ones. Good thing you not skinny."

My feelings were almost hurt, but I realized I was still less round than the two women I was with. Besides, unless Becky was lying, at least Michael seemed to like me as I was . . . and at least it meant I hadn't had to deal with a perverted pretend boss.

"You sure you don't want me to try again with the labels?" I asked.

They giggled. "Tomorrow," they said, and I grabbed another box.

• • •

By the time I got back into the Bananamobile and drove out of the parking lot, leaving a group of several bus riders enjoying a moment of mirth in my wake, I was bone tired and had earned a whopping eighty dollars. But at least I had a sticky bag of powder in my pocket. I called Peaches.

"I got a sample of the herb stuff," I said. "It looks more like sugar than herbs."

"I've got a friend who can analyze it," she said. "Can you drop it off here?"

"I'll swing by," I said.

"How's the car?" she asked as a lowrider passed me and honked its horn.

"I never thought I'd say this, but I miss driving a minivan."

I dropped the sample off at the office and headed home.

I might have missed the minivan, but the kids were delighted when I pulled into the driveway, bananas bouncing. The cop at the curb spilled coffee down the front of his uniform as I sailed by him, waving.

"What is that?" my mother asked as the two kids climbed over the seats.

"It's my loaner car," I said, turning to Elsie. "How did it go today?"

"Bad," she said.

"Did you give them the note I wrote excusing you for being late?"

"Yes," she said. "But I miss Twinkles."

"I'm working on it," I told her. Even though I wasn't. I didn't have time!

"I don't believe you," she said. "You lost my fry phone again, too."

My mother looked at me.

"I'm sorry, honey," I said. "I'm doing the best I can."

Which, as usual, wasn't quite enough.

CHAPTER THIRTY-THREE

The next morning, I dropped the kids off at school and drove to Tristan's apartment building, hoping to find something to tie Frances's money to LifeBoost. The place was extremely swanky; fortunately, it was also Willie's building. I parked at a meter, ignoring the stares of passersby as the bananas wobbled in the wind, and headed into the building, wondering if I'd run into Elwood.

"May I help you, ma'am?" asked the young metrosexual at the front desk, pushing his horn-rimmed glasses up on his nose. The lobby was as tony as I remembered, with a few acres of marble floor and a few very expensive and uncomfortable-looking couches.

"Yes," I said. "I'm here to see Willhelmina Bergdorfer."

"Does she know you're coming?" he asked.

"She will in a moment," I said, and pulled out my phone. He arched his tweezed eyebrows at me as I dialed and waited for her to answer.

"Hi, Willie! It's Margie. Can you please tell your friendly front desk person to let me come up?"

"Of course," she said. "Hand me over to him."

It was a brief conversation. He gave me a sour look and waved me to the elevator as he handed my phone back.

"Thanks!" I said, and sauntered over, resisting the urge to stick my tongue out at him. He gave me a moue of distaste.

I knocked at Willhelmina's door a few minutes later. "You're here!" she said, pulling me into a hug when she answered the door. "How's your hubby's boyfriend?"

"He's okay," I said. "No major organs hit. It'll be a while until he's back onstage, but he's supposed to make a full recovery."

"Thank goodness," she said as I followed her into the apartment. The space was enormous and decorated in all kinds of rather unappealing African hunting trophies from her late husband's overseas trips.

"Now, sweetheart. Can I get you some tea? Or something stronger?" She peered at my face. "You still look kind of swollen."

"Thanks, but I'm good," I said.

"So," she said, gesturing at a zebra-print couch and settling into a massive chair across from it. "What brings you here?"

"Two things, actually," I said. "First . . . How are things going with Elwood?"

"Oh, just great," she said. "He's so cute . . . I'm smitten. I don't know what I saw in that guy down on the second floor. Elwood is just so much more fun!"

"I can imagine," I said. "Has he mentioned anything about . . . tattoos?"

"Oh, I don't care about things like that. In fact, I think it's kind of sexy!"

"So he hasn't said anything about . . . well, about his hobbies?"

She shook her head. "What are you so worried about? He's a nice, normal man who thinks I'm sexy. I'm a happy woman!"

I bit my lip. I'd promised Elwood I'd give him a week, but things seemed to be progressing awfully fast. "Willie," I said. "There's something I have to tell you about Elwood."

"Oh no," she said, wincing. "He's not gay, is he?"

"No," I said. "That's my husband. Not Elwood."

"Right. Thank goodness. Not that I mean—" Her cheeks turned pink. "Oh my. I'm so sorry."

"Elwood's not gay," I said, "but I solved the case of the Shamrock Streaker."

She clapped her hands together. "I knew you'd do it! Who is it?"

"Umm . . ." I took a deep breath. "It's Elwood."

Willie blinked at me. "Elwood? He . . . He's the one with the sock?"

"I gave him a week to tell you, but since you two are already seeing each other, I thought I needed to tell you earlier."

"Well," she said, sitting back. "That's . . . not what I expected."

"You'd figure it out soon enough," I said. "Not that many people have rainbows tattooed on their stomachs."

"How did you find out?" she asked.

"I was on an undercover assignment at a waxing salon," I said.

"So . . . You waxed him?"

"No," I said. Thank God.

"Why did he do it?" she asked.

"Because he was too chicken to ask you out on a date," I told her.

"Oh, that's so sweet! And romantic, don't you think?"

I didn't know what to say, so I just nodded.

"Well, on the plus side, the garden club president can stop carrying nitroglycerin to meetings," she said. "And he's pretty well endowed."

"Actually, that was kind of enhanced," I told her.

"How do you know?"

"He had a Hickory Farms sausage in the sock," I told her. "I thought you saw it! Twinkles—my daughter's pig—grabbed it and took off with it."

"How did I miss that?" she asked. "Did you ever find Twinkles?"

"No," I said. "She's still missing."

"Surely someone's seen her. I'll ask the garden club to keep an eye out. I mean, how many pigs can there be running around Austin?"

"You'd think, wouldn't you?" I said. "I put signs up everywhere, but nobody's called. Anyway . . . I'm sorry I had to tell you that about Elwood."

"No," she said. "I'd rather know than not." She sat quietly for a moment. "I'm not sure it changes anything, though. I mean, it's not often a woman my age has such an enthusiastic suitor. Besides, he's a lot of fun; and Lord knows I like to show a little skin sometimes, too."

"True," I said, thinking of the micromini I'd seen her in a few months ago.

"And anyway," she told me. "What do I have to lose? I don't know how long I'm going to be here; why not have a little fun?"

"Go for it," I said. "I just thought you needed to know!"

"Thanks, Margie," she said, reaching out and squeezing my hands. "What do I owe you?"

"Not much. I'll send a bill," I said.

"I should pay you double," she said. "If you hadn't . . . unmasked him, so to speak, he might never have asked me out, and I wouldn't be going to Blues on the Green next week!" She sat back. "How's your dating life going, by the way?"

"Not as well as yours, I'm afraid. I've got another question for you while I'm here," I told her.

"Shoot," she said, rubbing her hands together. "Does it involve another cat?"

"No," I said. "It's a new resident in your building; or a former new resident, really. Tristan Prescott."

"Oh, I know him," she said. "Or knew him. He had a great butt."

"Well, someone killed him, and I'm trying to figure out who."

"So you want to get into his apartment," she said.

"Umm . . . Yes," I said. Willie always knew.

"You're in luck. I'm friends with the lady across the hall from him. We can go down and ask if she's got a key."

"Really?"

"Honey, I know everyone in this building," she told me. "Let's head down to the sixth floor, shall we?"

"You're amazing, Willie. You should be sending me a bill!"

She waved the idea away as I followed her out the door.

• • •

Willie did know everyone in the building. Within twenty minutes, we were standing in Tristan's apartment, on the pretext of me being a long-lost cousin.

"The police were in here just the other day—so sad! And it was so awful seeing the crime-scene tape," Willie's neighbor Rhoda said. "I'm glad they got rid of it; I think enough people complained about it that they had to take it down." She looked pensive. "I wonder who the new neighbor will be?"

There was a pretty high mortality rate in the building, I thought. This was the second murder victim in the past year; in fact, I'd met Willie in the process of investigating the first one. Maybe they should start giving discounts on rent.

"Anyway, just give me the key back when you're done," Rhoda—a member of Willie's bridge club, it turned out—told us. "I'm so sorry about your cousin," she told me, touching my arm.

"Thanks," I said, shooting Willie a grateful glance—she'd made up the story on the fly.

"So," Willie said when Rhoda had exited. "What are we looking for?"

"Financial records, for starters," I said. I wanted to find proof that Frances had given money to LifeBoost so I could talk them into giving it back. "This place looks expensive."

"It is," she said. "Five thousand a month."

"Wow," I said, surveying the sleek leather couches and massive flat-screen television. "When did he move in?"

"A few months ago," she said. Geneen at the gym had told me he'd only gotten funding from the venture capitalist recently, I thought. Had he been using some of his "investments" to fund his lifestyle?

"Where do we start?" she asked, surveying the room, which looked like it had been purchased and delivered from a designer modern-furniture store, right down to the modern art on the gray walls.

"I'm looking for a desk or a filing cabinet," I said. "I'm guessing any computers were taken as evidence."

"Think they'll find anything?"

Unless I was wrong, I was guessing they'd find incriminating messages between Pansy and Tristan . . . making it all the more crucial that I find out who really had done him in.

"It's in here!" Willie called from the bedroom. "And look what I found!"

"What is it?"

"Bank statements," she said, holding up a file.

"It's a good start," I said.

We spent the next thirty minutes combing through Tristan's files, and came up with a few interesting facts. First, he'd received several cash inflows of three to five thousand dollars . . . and only some of them had gone into the LifeBoost accounts.

"I know someone gave him twenty grand," I said, "but I don't see it here."

"Big deposits get tagged," she told me. "He probably broke it up so it wouldn't trigger a report to the government."

"And because it's cash, there's no record of where it came from," I said.

"No paper trail," she said. "Smart. Where do you think it came from?"

"I know where some of it was from," I said. "He was sleeping with at least two married women."

"And he talked them into investing, didn't he?"

"He did," I said.

"Looks like he got a big vote of confidence not too long ago, though," she said, picking up a statement from the LifeBoost account. "A million dollars."

"Not too shabby," I said, looking at the account statement. There were checks written to East Austin Bottling Company, a few advertising venues, an ad agency, and something called Pharma Plus.

"Ever heard of Pharma Plus?"

She shook her head, and I pulled out my phone. Nothing turned up on Google. "I think it may be time to ask Peaches about this," I said. I took photos of all of the bank statements with my phone as Willie continued to go through the drawers.

"This is fun!" she said. "I feel like Nancy Drew." She looked up at me. "This isn't illegal, is it?"

"Well, technically we didn't break in," I told her.

"Good enough for me," she said. "Hey . . . If you ever think of hiring, keep me in mind."

"The pay isn't terrific."

"You think I care about the pay?" she asked, eyes twinkling. "This is the most fun I've had since Elwood did the Mashed Potato in the street after that fundraiser."

I grinned as she dug into the next drawer. I moved to the short stack of books on the night table: they all had titles like *Making the Cut*, *Bulletproofing Your Diet*, and *Staying Hot After Thirty*. As I picked up *Staying Hot After Thirty*, something fell out of it. I reached down and picked it up; it was a note scrawled on a piece of paper. There was a logo at the top: *AMD*.

John's out of town until Tuesday, it read. *Let's meet tomorrow morning at the usual spot. I have something for you.*

No signature.

I showed it to Willie. "What do you think of this?" I asked.

"Sounds like another assignation," she said.

Tristan, it seemed, was a very busy man. I took a picture and tucked it back into the book.

• • •

"Can you look something up for me?" I asked Peaches once I'd said good-bye to Willie and headed back down to the lobby. I nodded at the man at the front desk as I walked by him; he gave me a tight smile.

I had pictures of the bank statements and the note, but we hadn't found anything else in Tristan's apartment.

"Sure," she said.

"I'll text you some photos," I said. "If you could find out what Pharma Plus is, that would be great."

"I'll do what I can," she said. "What are you up to now?"

"I'm going to visit Pansy," I said.

"She still out of jail?"

"For now," I said.

"Good luck with that," she said. As I stepped outside, a siren sounded, and there was a scream off to the right.

"That thing stole my hot dog!"

"Ma'am, animal control is on the way . . ."

As I watched, a turkey-size object squirted out from between the legs of a woman in skinny jeans, a hot dog dangling from its mouth.

It was Twinkles.

"Somebody stop that pig!" someone shouted, but I was already in motion.

I shoved the phone into my purse with Peaches still talking and hurtled down the sidewalk toward Twinkles, who had galloped about ten yards with her prize before hunkering down behind a scooter to devour the hot dog. I slowed down and waved the crowd off.

"I've got her," I said, hoping I wasn't lying, and dug in my purse for some string cheese. She perked up at the sound of the wrapper crinkling.

"That's it," I crooned. "You know me. Come here, Twinkles!"

She wolfed down the rest of the hot dog and then took a few tentative steps toward me. "That's right," I said in an encouraging voice, and dangled the cheese. "See? Dessert!"

Twinkles eyed me warily, but she must not have eaten so well since escaping in Zilker Park, because she kept walking forward, as if drawn by some power greater than herself.

"Good girl," I said as she edged closer and closer. Finally, when she was just out of reach, she stretched her snout forward and attempted to liberate the cheese. I gave her a little bit, and then pulled it closer. She took one tentative step, and she was in range.

I was just about to grab her when she darted forward, grabbed the cheese, and turned tail.

"Twinkles!" I yelled, launching myself after her. She squealed as my hand closed around her back hoof, and both of us hit the ground. I scrabbled forward until my arms were around her; we were lying on the sidewalk, Twinkles squealing and wriggling as I held her in a bear hug. Or pig hug.

"I got her!" I crowed.

"Margie? Is that you?"

I looked up to see Michael and Salima standing over me, both looking like fashion models in dark suits and shiny shoes.

"Oh," I said, trying to sit up without letting go of Twinkles. "Michael. Salima. Hi."

"Good to see you again," Salima said. "I'd shake your hand, but . . ." She nodded her delicate chin toward Twinkles.

"Got it," I said, lurching to my feet with the squealing pig.

"Ma'am? Is that pig registered?" the policeman asked.

"And are you going to reimburse me for my hot dog?" demanded the woman whose lunch had disappeared down Twinkles's gullet.

"Michael, we're going to be late," Salima said, glancing at her watch.

"Margie, are you going to be okay?" Michael asked.

"I might die of embarrassment, but other than that, I'm just swell." He grinned, but Salima tugged at his elbow. "Come on."

"I am late for a meeting, but if you need help—"

"They'll be waiting for us," Salima said, her voice tight.

"I'm fine. Really," I said.

"Well, if you're sure . . ."

"I've got it," I told him. "Thanks so much, though."

"Right. Okay. Well, then, catch you later," Michael said, and disappeared down the street with Salima in his wake, leaving me with a policeman, a squealing pig, and an angry fifty-year-old hot dog connoisseur.

On the plus side, I told myself, at least he didn't see me drive off in the Bananamobile.

CHAPTER THIRTY-FOUR

Much to Rufus's dismay, I dropped Twinkles off in the laundry room at home. I never thought I'd be so happy to have a pig in the house; maybe Elsie would perk up now that Twinkles was around to steal tortillas from her. As soon as she was secured, I got back into the Bananamobile and headed to Pansy's house.

Pansy answered the door on the second knock, looking like she hadn't slept in weeks. Isabella was clinging to her leg; I was guessing her mother's jail time had really upset her.

"She's not at school?" I asked.

"She was too anxious this morning. Thanks for coming over," she said as we walked to the kitchen, Pansy moving like a woman in a three-legged race, with Isabella stuck to her leg like a cute barnacle.

"I wanted to show you something," I said, and pulled up the picture of the note on my phone. "Look familiar?"

She squinted at it, then frowned. "That dirty rat," she said.

"What?"

"Look!" She walked over to the island, still dragging Isabella, and pulled the note card off a gift basket.

The handwriting matched.

"What's this?" I asked.

"A basket Phyllis gave me last week," she said. "Some 'thanks for being PTA president' thing; even though she wants the job herself. I know that note was from her; her hubby's name is John, and he works at AMD."

"What was in it?" I asked.

"Oh, some low-carb muffins, some vanilla protein shake stuff, and some fruit."

"Wait. Vanilla protein shake?"

"Yeah," she said. Then her eyes widened. "Oh my God. Do you think that is what did it?"

"Is it open?" I asked.

She picked up the can and popped the plastic lid. "It is. And some of it's gone."

"Did you or anyone else drink any of it?"

She shook her head. "Mark wouldn't touch it with a ten-foot pole, and Isabella wouldn't know how to make it." She turned to Isabella. "Honey, did you have any of this?"

Isabella shook her head.

"Well don't, okay? It may be poisonous."

Isabella nodded solemnly.

"Some of it's gone, but I haven't had any of it." She sat down on the stool. "If she delivered poisoned drink mix to my house, I'm going to kill her." She looked down at Isabella. "If you're right, and my daughter drank any . . ." She paled and reached down to touch her daughter's head.

"I don't think Isabella was the target," I said.

"You mean . . . me? But why?"

"Can we talk alone for a moment?" I asked, glancing down at Pansy's daughter.

"Oh. Right. Of course," she said, and spent a few minutes getting Isabella settled in front of the television. It took at least three minutes to pry Isabella off her mother's leg and attach her to a worn teddy bear instead. I felt a pang thinking of Elsie's fry phone and Twinkles . . . As if Frances were psychic, my phone buzzed. It was another picture of the fry phone—only this time tied to what looked like a railroad track.

"I think Phyllis may have been trying to kill you, not Tristan," I said.

"What? Why?"

"She was really upset when she found out he died, for starters. She was obviously meeting with Tristan . . . I'm guessing they were having an affair."

"Why would Tristan sleep with someone like Phyllis?" she asked, looking puzzled.

"I'm guessing he was having affairs with a good number of the PTA moms," I said, thinking of Frances. "That's how he was funding LifeBoost . . . and his downtown apartment."

"I gave him money, too," she said. "That rat bastard. I never thought I'd say it, but I'm kind of happy he's dead."

"I get it," I said.

"But I still don't understand why Phyllis would want to kill me."

"I suspect she was in love with Tristan," I said. "And jealous of you."

"What? Really?"

I nodded. "The thing is, how do we prove it?"

"Well, we have this," she said, pointing to the basket.

"Yeah, but you got rid of the glass he was drinking from. Plus no one knows he died here . . . or that you and Tristan were seeing each other."

"I see your point," she said.

"Maybe if we record her while we're talking to her?" I asked.

"You think she'll confess?"

"It's worth a shot," I said. "When's the next PTA get-together?"

"I can call her and meet her at the school," she said. "Tell her I want to go over the PTA finances."

"That should get her," I said. "What should we do with Isabella?"

"We'll take her with us. She can always play Minecraft on her iPad." As I watched, she texted Phyllis. A moment later, her phone buzzed.

"She'll be there in an hour," she said. "You have the receipts?"

"Peaches picked them up for me," I said. I'd given Peaches copies of the register and the bank statements, and she'd rounded up copies of the receipts from the stores listed in the register while I was investigating the LifeBoost bottling company. It was no surprise that the receipts didn't match the written records.

"I assume she didn't spend nine hundred dollars on helium balloons and party favors?" she said.

"More like fifty-three dollars," I said, "at least according to the receipt the store gave Peaches."

"Why do you think she needs the money?"

I thought about Frances. "Something tells me she was investing in Tristan's new company," I said.

"I know I did," Pansy said. "But not that much. Only a few thousand. I knew Mark would never miss it."

I swallowed. Obviously Pansy and I were in very different tax brackets. "Another mom contacted me about some missing money, too."

"Frances, right?"

"What makes you say that?"

"She was totally in love with Tristan," she said. "I didn't know he was sleeping with her, though. What a cad."

"Seems like it," I said. "Meet you there?" I asked as we walked to the front door with Isabella in tow.

"Do we need a gun?" she asked.

"I don't really think she'll be armed, do you?" I asked.

"You never know," she said.

"I don't actually have a gun."

"Me neither. What's she going to do in the PTA workroom, anyway?" Pansy asked. "Staple us to death?"

I wished I shared her optimism.

• • •

I pulled into the Austin Heights Elementary School parking lot with Pansy and Isabella in my wake. As I got out and slammed the door, every banana on the station wagon quivered.

"What in the name of God is that thing?" Pansy asked as she and Isabella got out of their Suburban.

"It's a Bananamobile," Isabella said, as if it were obvious.

"It's a loaner," I said. "Someone rammed into me until my minivan blew up the other day."

"Your minivan blew up?"

"It's been a rough week," I said as we walked to the front door together.

As we passed a giant white Suburban parked near the front of the parking lot, Pansy said, "She's here."

"Wait," I said, stopping. "This is her SUV?"

"I recognize it by the ballet sticker," she said, pointing to the back window.

"Hang on a moment." I walked around to the front of the car. The front bumper was dented, and there were flecks of familiar paint on it.

"She's the one who blew up my car," I said.

And she was also likely the one who shot at Frank, I realized.

"Pansy," I said. "Where were you during the performance at the event the other night?"

"Near the front of the stage," she said. "I'm lucky I didn't get hit; a bullet pinged off a flowerpot only a foot or two away from me. Thankfully, Mark made me get behind him. He does have his good moments."

255

My stomach turned. Frank hadn't been the intended target; Pansy had. He had slid across the stage just as the shots rang out . . . and accidentally right into the line of fire. And Phyllis's Suburban was the SUV I'd seen peeling out.

"She may have a gun," I said.

"She's not going to use it in the school," Pansy scoffed. "And we need that confession."

"Okay," I said. "But be careful."

"I will," she said, and marched into the school holding Isabella's hand.

Once we were in, she took her daughter to the library to read and play on the iPad. "We'll be in the workroom by the teachers' lounge, honey, but we'll come get you soon. Okay?"

The little girl nodded and sank into a beanbag chair, intent on her iPad.

"Ready?" I asked Pansy as we exited the library and turned left.

"I am," she said. "Are you recording, or am I?"

"I think we both should," I said. "Just in case. Are you sure you want to be here? You're paying me, after all."

"No," she said. "I want to be there to confront that bitch face-to-face. Besides, I want to take care of it before it's time to pick up the kids."

"All right, then," I said. "Let's go."

When we arrived, Phyllis was sitting at the end of the table in the PTA workroom, looking tense.

"Phyllis," Pansy said smoothly. "Thanks for coming. I wanted to talk to you about the finances."

Phyllis's eyes darted to me. "What is she doing here?"

Pansy gave her a tight smile. "She's helping me. Now, about the finances."

Phyllis blinked. "What about them?"

"Oh, I just wanted to go through them with you. Thanks again for the basket, by the way. I really enjoyed the vanilla shake."

Phyllis's eyebrows shot up. "Really?"

"Oh yes," Pansy said. "It's delicious. So thoughtful of you. Anyway . . ." She sat down and spread out the sheaf of papers. "We have a few inconsistencies here I want to discuss. Like this receipt from Party Pig," she said, pulling out the copy of the receipt Peaches had gotten for me.

"What about it?"

"Well, it's only for fifty dollars, but in the ledger here, you—it wasn't Janelle, because I recognize your handwriting—put nine hundred. And someone seems to have gotten rid of the copies of the checks."

"What do you mean?" Phyllis said, her eyes darting around nervously.

"You needed the money to cover the cash you gave Tristan, didn't you?" I asked.

"I don't know what you're talking about," Phyllis said.

"Oh no?" Pansy said. "What about the note you wrote him, asking to meet at your regular spot? On the AMD notepaper. Doesn't your husband work for AMD?"

She blanched. "You're making all of this up."

"I'm not. And you know it," Pansy said.

Phyllis's face contorted suddenly. The sour-faced woman was gone, her mild features replaced by a mask of barely contained rage. Her voice when she spoke was a rough hiss. "You always get everything, don't you? The PTA presidency. The big fancy house. And Tristan."

"From what I can tell, you were the one sleeping with Tristan," Pansy pushed, seemingly unaware of the transformation that made me want to find the nearest desk and hide under it. "And you tried to kill me with that vanilla powder, only you killed the man of your dreams, instead."

She paled.

"You could have killed my daughter with that stuff!" Pansy told her.

"It was meant for you!" Phyllis spat, then realized what she'd said.

My instincts had been right. "And you tried to kill Pansy at the event the other night, too . . . only Frank slid in front of you just as you shot."

"Who's Frank?"

"Madonna," I supplied, trying to buy time as I figured out how to get us out of here. Thank goodness the school had a no-gun policy; at least she wasn't armed. "And then you tried to get rid of me because you knew I was a private investigator and you were worried I saw you drive off. So you rammed my minivan and tried to make me crash."

"You were supposed to be in it when it blew up," she said. "I should have shot you instead of Pansy. Good thing I brought my gun."

She pulled a gun out of her purse. I felt my gut wrench; this was the second time this year I'd been held up in an elementary school. I'd survived the first time. With luck, I'd figure this time out, too.

"I knew we should have brought a gun," I told Pansy.

CHAPTER THIRTY-FIVE

We didn't have one. And we were going to be late," Pansy said. "Shut up," Phyllis said, putting her free hand to her temple. She looked like she was having a migraine. "Shut up, shut up, shut up. Let me think."

"I'm not sure I want to let you think," Pansy told her.

She swung the gun and said, "You've got the key to the supply closet. Give it to me."

"Why?"

"Stop asking questions. Just do it."

Pansy fished in her purse and handed it over. "There's no room for anyone in there, much less three of us," she said.

"There are only going to be two," she said. "Come on. Let's go." She stood close behind Pansy and pressed the gun into her back, and the three of us made our way to the storage closet. Phyllis held the gun in one hand as she unlocked the closet with the other. Several balls erupted from the small room as she pushed us both in and then closed the door behind us.

"Someone's going to see the balls, you know," I pointed out.

"Pick them up," she told us. We opened the door again and carried them into the closet with us. Once you got past the balls, there was more room than I expected. I scanned the room, looking for a weapon, but all I saw was a giant tub of Tickle Me Elmos, several piles of construction paper, a dozen Hula-Hoops, and a giant stuffed polar bear.

"What's with the Tickle Me Elmos?"

"We had trouble in the kindergarten a few years back—all the kids wanted them—so some parent pitched in and bought enough for everyone. Of course, then they all lost interest."

"I don't care about Elmo," Phyllis said, looking around the room. "Ah. This will work. Pansy, I need you to duct-tape Margie."

"What?"

"Just do it," she said, handing her a roll of baby-blue duct tape decorated with rubber ducks. "Put your hands behind your back," she ordered me, and supervised as Pansy taped my hands together—and then my ankles. I sat down awkwardly, still trying to figure out how to get out of this—and wondering what exactly Phyllis had in mind.

"Good. Now let's do you," she said, taking the tape back from Pansy. "God, I've wanted to do this for forever." She pulled off a strip of tape and stuck it over Pansy's mouth. "That felt so good," she moaned. "Now hold your hands out."

I'm not sure how she managed it, with a gun in one hand and the tape in the other, but before long, Pansy was trussed up beside me. Phyllis paused and started looking around the crowded room again.

"Ah," she said, reaching for the huge stuffed animal. "Petunia will work."

"Petunia?"

"That's the polar bear's name," she said, and knelt next to Pansy. "The first grade class named it at the Christmas party last year. Say good night, bitch," she hissed at the PTA president, and then pressed Petunia's fluffy tummy to Pansy's face.

She was going to suffocate her.

"How are you going to explain that?" I asked.

"You two got trapped in here and suffocated."

"That's weak," I said.

"You got any better ideas?" she asked as Pansy began to flail.

I looked around wildly, but I couldn't come up with anything to save Pansy. Or me.

And then . . .

I scooched over toward the tub of Elmos. If I could manage to tip it, then maybe . . .

Phyllis looked up. "What are you doing?"

"Just moving," I said. "The tape is really uncomfortable."

"You won't feel it for long," she said, and pressed harder on Pansy's face. Pansy's movements were becoming jerky; I didn't have much time.

I swung my legs out and toppled the tub; all of a sudden, dozens of Tickle Me Elmos started giggling.

"Stop that!" Phyllis said, easing up a bit. I heard Pansy gasp for breath before Phyllis pressed Petunia back down on her face. I rolled myself toward the Elmos and began wriggling around. A moment later, there were a dozen vibrating, giggling Elmos below me.

"I said stop that!" Phyllis ordered. But I kept moving, smashing Elmos until the room was filled with giggles. "That's it," Phyllis said, pulling the bear away from Pansy's face. The PTA president sucked in air through her nose with a whistle as Phyllis advanced on me.

"Say good night," she said, and pushed Petunia down on my face.

I flailed harder—partially to keep the Elmos giggling, but mostly to get out from under Petunia. Phyllis was strong, though, and with my wrists and ankles duct taped, there wasn't much I could do.

I heaved my body up toward her; she lost her grip long enough for me to get another bit of air, but then the white fur closed in on me again. Little flashes of light started appearing in my vision, and my lungs burned; I couldn't hear the Elmos anymore, but I could feel them. Would they be enough?

"Phyllis!" I heard in the distance. "What are you doing?"

I felt myself floating, my arms and legs limp. *Nick, Elsie. I'm sorry.* I was just starting to drift away when the darkness was replaced by a bright-white light.

"Margie?" came the voice. "Breathe! Margie!"

As if jolted awake, I sucked in air, feeling dizzy and nauseated.

The room came into focus. It was Mrs. Wilson, standing over me, with an entire kindergarten class standing at the doorway.

"What was she doing with Petunia?" a little girl's voice asked.

"It's not my fault!" Phyllis was screeching. "They made me do it! They made me! They made me!"

The last thing I wondered was if my phone was still recording before I passed out.

CHAPTER THIRTY-SIX

I t was about an hour before Detective Bunsen let us go home.
When I finished telling him what had happened, he summed things
up. "So she killed him—and you've got a confession."

Fortunately, my phone had recorded the whole thing. When the
door opened, the kindergarten teacher had called 911; faced with
twenty five-year-olds, Phyllis had relinquished the gun.

"Plus she tried to murder us," I said, "and I think you'll find she's
the one who shot Frank the other day. Plus, it was her Suburban that
smashed into my minivan the other day. I saw the paint on her front
bumper."

"This still doesn't explain the location of the body," he said.

Pansy and I looked at each other and shrugged. "That's a mystery,"
she said.

"And he drank the vanilla shake at your house," he said.

"He did come over for a . . . workout," Pansy said. "And he drank
the shake while he was there—I was afraid to say anything about it—
but he must have wandered over to the club once he left."

"On foot? Leaving his car by your house?"

"I've heard poison does strange things," I said. "What was it, by
the way?"

"Classified," he said. "But it's nasty. It's a good thing your daughter didn't get into it."

Pansy shivered.

"At least now I know why his phone was at your house," he said. "What kind of workout?"

"Just a normal one," Pansy said. "For some reason, Phyllis thought we were . . . having an affair."

"You weren't?"

"Of course not!" she said. "I'm a married woman."

"Of course not," he said. "Well, we're dropping the charges—for murder," he said. "Are you sure you didn't move any bodies?"

Pansy smiled her most beguiling smile. "You've got the murderer. Do you really need to go looking for anything else? Besides," she said, "I kind of enjoyed going down to the station and meeting everyone. I might stop by with donuts more often."

"Krispy Kremes?" he asked.

"My favorite," she said, although I was pretty sure a donut hadn't passed her lips in the last fifteen years. Maybe longer.

"Well, I really should—"

"We'll talk tomorrow," she said. "You're on in the morning?"

"I'll be in the office at nine," he said.

"Perfect. I'll stop by after I drop off the kids." It was all I could do not to roll my eyes as she put a hand on his arm. "Thank you so much for coming to our rescue today," she said. "It was terrifying; I thought she was going to kill us with that polar bear."

"I never thought I'd say this, but thank God for Tickle Me Elmo," I said. As I spoke, my iPhone buzzed again. It was Frances. *Running out of time.* Attached was a picture of Elsie's fry phone dangling over a sewer drain.

I texted her back. *Don't do it!*

Almost immediately after that, a text came in from Peaches. *Got results. Chinese herbs are Adderall.*

Well, that explained why Brianna almost had a cardiac arrest the other day. Her father was force-feeding her amphetamines. "I'm glad you're here, Detective Bunsen," I said. "I think it might be time to look into LifeBoost; I just got a chemical analysis of the 'herbs' they're putting into the drinks. They're straight Adderall."

"What? How do you know this?"

"I was investigating Tristan Prescott's death for a client, and I had some of it analyzed."

"How?"

"I'm an investigator, remember? I thought his death might have something to do with his company. I hear the investor—Steven Maxwell—is in financial trouble, too. His house is on the market." I wondered if Maxwell knew what was in the drinks he was peddling— and hoped that Dr. Flynn would be taken out of circulation immediately, before anybody died from a Ritalin-induced heart attack. "You might want to look into Maxwell and a Dr. Flynn," I said, telling him what I'd found at the bottling plant.

"So the magic supplement is an ADHD drug?"

I nodded. "I think it sent a little girl to the hospital the other day. It needs to come off the market ASAP—before something else happens."

"You've been busy," he said, sounding almost . . . impressed.

As Pansy and I walked out to the parking lot a few minutes later, my phone buzzed again.

"That was just amazing," Pansy said. "Thank you. I owe you big time. If there's anything I can do for you and Elsie, just let me know."

"Actually," I said, looking down at the picture of Elsie's fry phone. "Maybe there is."

• • •

"What are you doing here?"

Pansy and I stood on Frances's immaculate doorstep, staring at Frances. I was trying to ignore the poodle, who seemed to recognize me and didn't have fond memories of our last encounter—despite the brie.

"Where's Margie's fry phone?" Pansy asked.

"What?"

"Can I see your phone?" Pansy asked me. I handed it over, and she showed Frances the picture of the fry phone dangling over a sewer drain.

"I don't know what you're talking about."

"I know your number, Frances. Now let us in and give Margie the fry phone, or I'll tell your husband all about what's been going on with Tristan."

Frances said nothing.

"Seriously?" Pansy asked, and pushed past her with me in her wake. "Where is it?" she asked, striding into the living room, which was strewn with toys.

Frances darted past her to the kitchen. The fry phone was sitting on top of her Dooney & Bourke tote bag.

"There it is!" I said. Pansy sprang into action, but Frances was too quick for her.

Frances grabbed it and ran around to the other side of the island. In the meantime, the poodle was squaring off with me as if it had a score to settle.

"Good boy," I said.

"He doesn't like you," Frances said. "Were you the one who broke in the other day?"

"What do you mean?"

"The housekeeper saw someone. And whatever you fed him gave him the runs."

Excellent, I thought to myself, but limited myself to saying, "I don't know what you're talking about."

"That was ten-dollar brie," she said. "I almost had to take Winston to the vet because of the wrapper."

That I felt sorry about, even though Winston was looking at me as if he'd like to remove a limb. I positioned a bar stool between the poodle and me and kept one eye on him and one on Pansy.

"I know all about you," Pansy said to Frances. "And I know your husband. All it would take would be one little word."

"And what about you?" Frances asked. "I'm sure your hubby would love to know all about you and Tristan."

Pansy shrugged. "I can live with it."

"All I want is my money back," Frances said.

"So he fleeced you, too?"

"What?"

"How much?" Pansy asked.

"Twenty thousand," Frances said.

Pansy looked at me. "How much is that fry phone worth to you?"

"Unfortunately, it's the only one left on the planet, as far as I can tell," I said, edging around the bar stool.

She looked at Frances. "I'll give you five thousand for it."

Frances narrowed her eyes at her. "Eight."

Pansy shook her head. "Six. And that's my final offer."

Frances hesitated, then looked at me. "No documents?"

"Not a thing," I said. "And I looked everywhere."

"Crap," she said, then turned to Pansy. "I guess it's a deal." She moved to hand it to me, then withdrew her hand, still clutching the fry phone. "How do I know you're good for it?"

Pansy gave her a look. "Really, Frances?" Frances didn't say anything, so Pansy pulled out her wallet, pulled out five hundreds, and handed them over. "I'll get you the rest of the cash this afternoon," Pansy said. "But we never talk about any of this again. Got it?"

"Got it," I said, and Frances nodded. After a moment's reluctance, she relinquished the fry phone.

"And could you call off your dog?" I asked.

She gave me a withering glance, then walked over to grab his collar. I let out my breath for the first time since we walked into the house.

Pansy turned to me. "Ready to go pick up your kids?"

"Yes," I said, clutching the fry phone. "Thank you so much."

"It's the least I could do," she said. "You got me out of jail."

"And you got me out of the doghouse," I said. "Well, not literally."

"All's well that ends well, then. Except for Tristan."

"Except for Tristan," I agreed.

• • •

Pansy stared at the station wagon when I parked it next to her at the school at pickup time. The bananas were waving gently in the wind; the effect was almost spellbinding. "Maybe I should have given the cash to you, instead. You're not really going to drive that thing all year, are you?"

"I hope not," I said as we walked over to the line of waiting children.

Elsie was sitting with her arms wrapped around her knees, away from the other kids, rocking. Pansy looked at me. "Did you get her checked out?"

"I did. We're going to do antidepressants as a first line of attack, then see if that helps. There's been a lot of upheaval at our house lately."

"If you need any help, let me know," she said.

"Thanks." I smiled at her, and then walked over to Elsie. "Hi, sweetie! I've got good news!"

No answer.

"Missing this?" I asked, taking the fry phone out of my pocket.

Her face lit up. "You found it!"

"And Twinkles is home in the laundry room," I told her.

"Really?"

"Really."

"Mom, you're the best!" She threw her arms around me. "Can we go see her now?"

"Absolutely," I said. And for the first time that week, I didn't even care that I was driving around with five hundred plastic bananas stuck to my car.

• • •

Soccer that night was a family affair. My mother, Twinkles, and Nick accompanied us to the field; to my surprise, Blake was already there, with Frank in tow. After the shooting, we'd told the kids that Frank was a special friend of Daddy's. We hadn't told them how special, but it was a step in that direction.

"I'm so glad you're up and around!" I told him.

"Thanks," he said. His arm was in a sling, and he was no longer wearing a cone-studded bustier, but he still looked dapper in a dark button-down shirt and khaki shorts. "And thanks for finding out I wasn't the target. I was a little afraid it might be your father-in-law, to be honest," he said, sliding a sideways glance at Blake.

"Nope," I said. "Just a crazed PTA mom."

As he finished speaking, I heard my name from behind me. "Margie!"

It was Michael, with Zoe in tow. I blinked, and then took a mental inventory of my outfit. The torn polo shirt and shorts weren't one of my best, unfortunately.

"Michael!" I said. "What are you doing here?"

"I, uh, was hoping to talk to you," he said to me, glancing at Blake.

"Hi, Michael. Good to see you . . . Go right ahead," he said.

Michael gave him an uneasy look, then drew me over to one side.

"Thanks for getting me the job at the bottling plant," I told him. "It was a huge help."

"I'm glad," he said. "It looks like the soccer guy's lawsuit against LifeBoost—they think that's what caused his kid to have palpitations on the soccer field—has some heft behind it. Maxwell skipped town when the coach wouldn't take the payoff."

"That's what he was talking about!" I said, remembering the conversation in his office. "He wanted someone to take care of something . . . It must have been paying off Trey!"

"Good thing he didn't accept," Michael said. "He's going to make a fortune, assuming there's anything left in the company to sue for. His kid was so hyped up on amphetamines her heart rate was through the roof. Becky told me she was already on Ritalin; the compound effect almost gave her a heart attack."

"I'm glad she's okay," I said.

"So am I," he said. "But I wanted to ask you about something else."

"Oh?" I asked, feeling apprehensive.

"Are you . . . You know, this is awkward, particularly with your husband standing there . . . but . . . are you free for dinner next Friday?"

I blinked at him. "Dinner? You mean . . . like a dinner date?"

"Yeah," he said, pushing at the dirt with the toe of his shoe.

"What about Salima?"

"We, uh, broke up."

"I'm sorry," I lied.

"It's okay. We weren't really a good match."

"Oh." I couldn't say I disagreed. "Well. Yes. I'd love to."

His face broke into a smile. "Great," he said. "I'll pick you up at six?"

"Terrific," I said. "Just . . . no sock puppets, okay?"

"Sock puppets?"

"A date that went wrong . . . and ended up taking off my back bumper a couple of days later. Before the minivan blew up, that is. It's a long story. I'll explain it next Friday," I said as I spied Blake's parents.

I still hadn't heard back from the insurance company, but right now, that was not my top worry. "Uh-oh."

"What?"

"This should be interesting," I said.

I watched as Prudence led Phil across the field toward us. He was walking stiffly; I got the feeling he wasn't there voluntarily.

Prue gave my husband a quick hug, then reached out to shake Frank's uninjured hand. "I'm so glad to see you up and around," she said. "My husband wants to apologize for his treatment of you." She turned to Blake's father. "Right, Philip?"

He cleared his throat and gave a sharp nod. "Glad you're doing better," he said. Then he gave Blake an awkward clap on the back. "Son."

"And Connie . . . ," Prue continued, turning to my mother. "I'm so sorry about the other day. I know things have been . . . tense between us, but I'd like to try to make it better."

"Oh . . . That's so sweet," my mother said, and pulled her into a hug. "Maybe we can go to Casa de Luz for lunch someday. They make a great—"

"Mom!"

It was Elsie, tugging at Twinkles's leash. One of her teammates was sitting on the grass, eating a ham sandwich, and Elsie's pet had caught a whiff of it.

"Don't let her get it!" I warned.

"I can't hold her. Mom!" As she spoke, Twinkles gave a mighty yank and broke loose.

Again.

"Catch her!" I yelled, and my entire family leaped into motion at once.

All of us surged toward Twinkles, but we were too late; she'd grabbed the sandwich and was streaking across the field toward Trey, who had turned and bolted for the parking lot, his chicken legs pumping so fast they were almost a blur.

In short, it was just another day with the Petersons.

ACKNOWLEDGMENTS

Thank you as always to Eric, Abby, and Ian, my experimental subjects, for inadvertently providing research material for this (and every) book. Thank you to Carol and Dave Swartz, Dorothy and Ed MacInerney, and Marian Quinton and Nora Bestwick for cheering me on from the sidelines. And deepest gratitude goes to the Thomas & Mercer team for doing such a great job of getting Margie out into the world—and for helping bring her to life. Special thanks to JoVon Sotak, for shepherding things through (and being patient when I realized that my original plot wasn't working); Jessica Tribble, whose comments were invaluable in the development of the manuscript (and who is tremendous fun to drink hurricanes with); and the incomparable Charlotte Herscher, whose keen eye and insightful comments I rely on more than she knows. (Sarah Shaw and Gabrielle Guarnero are pretty awesome, too.) Thank you to my wonderful writing community for supporting me throughout the writing of this book, particularly Jason Brenizer and Kate Baray. Thank you to Chloe Shepard, Stephen, and all the other lovely folks at Trianon Coffee for greeting me with a smile, a kind word, and a cup of good coffee when I straggle in with my laptop. I am endlessly thankful to Ellen Helwig for suggesting a murder victim, and to both Ellen and my friend Peggy Pletcher for taking the time to sit in a coffee shop with a bunch of giant Post-it notes and helping me figure out "whodunit." And thank you to all of my wonderful readers, particularly those I'm connected with on Facebook, and especially the MacInerney Mystery Mavens. None of this would be possible without you. I am beyond grateful.

ABOUT THE AUTHOR

Photo © 2008 Kenneth Gall

Karen MacInerney is the housework-impaired author of fourteen books, including the Gray Whale Inn series, the Urban Werewolf trilogy, the Dewberry Farm Mysteries, and the Margie Peterson Mysteries. She lives in Austin, Texas, with two children, her husband, and a menagerie of animals. For more on Karen and her work, visit www.karenmacinerney.com.